The Queen sends for Mrs Chadwick

DAVID
SANDERS

The Queen sends
for
Mrs Chadwick

CENTAUR PRESS

First published 1979 by
Centaur Press Ltd., Fontwell, Sussex

Copyright © 1979 by David Sanders

ISBN 0900000 88 0

Printed in Great Britain by
Villiers Publications Ltd.,
London NW5

AUTHOR'S NOTE

Near the end of this book is a trial scene.
Some readers may think that the issues raised
bear some resemblance to court proceedings
which attracted public attention in Britain
in the second half of 1978. I cannot stress
too strongly that this book is not an attempt
to fictionalise actual events. It was drafted
many months before anyone had any idea that
the proceedings I have mentioned would be launched.

IT WAS ten days since the President had returned from Washington after his State visit to London. Now he was due for a Press conference and was not looking forward to it; not at all. They would try to nail him down over the Chadwick woman. Well, he damn well wouldn't let them nail him down. What was that idiotic cricket phrase he'd heard some stuffed shirt use at the State dinner? Something about playing down the line. That was it. Keep your eye on the ball and play down the line. That's what he'd do. Play down the line.

Reporter: Mr President, have you any observations to make on the case of Mrs Chadwick?

The President: I think that is a matter for the British to deal with. It would be presumptuous of me to express any opinion. If you can imagine the case in reverse, I am sure you would agree that any suggestion of interference from London would be deeply resented on this side of the Atlantic.

Reporter: Mr President, during your discussions with Mrs Chadwick in Washington and London, did you have any clue, any inkling whatsoever as to the way things were developing?

The President lied, and lied convincingly.

The President: I did not. All I can say at this stage, all that it would be proper for me to say is that I found Mrs Chadwick a most charming lady, who showed great vigour and ability in representing the interests of her country. But in view of what has happened, I must ask you not to press me further.

She moved into the outer lane of the motorway, and took a long, careful look into her driving mirror. Nothing in sight but a couple of family saloons and a Mother's Pride bread van. She eased her foot down; just perceptibly, the purr of the 4000 cc Jaguar assumed a more purposeful, pleasurable rhythm, like that of an already contented cat acknowledging a tickle under the chin. The needle moved from seventy to eighty, to eighty-five, to a shade over ninety.

He said: "You do like playing with your new toy."

She said: "Does it good to give it a breather now and again."

7

The slip road they had just passed did not show in the mirror. Not all of it. But the crew of the police car which was just joining the motorway saw the silver-grey shape flash past. The sergeant in the passenger seat pressed the button which illuminated the "Police" sign on the roof.

"Get 'em," he told the driver.

She was still doing ninety when she saw the police car. She eased up. He sensed what had happened, and looked over his shoulder.

"Christ. We could have done without this."

She said: "Leave it to me."

"I'll do just that. It's all yours."

Both cars pulled over to the hard shoulder. He remained in the Jaguar. She went to meet the two officers.

"Good morning, sergeant. Lovely day, isn't it? So nice to feel some warmth in the sun. How's your rheumatism?"

"Much better, thank you. Tell me, madam, where's the fire?"

"I was pushing on a bit? That's the trouble with this sort of car. You don't notice if you go just a tiny bit above the limit."

"You were doing ninety."

"You call *that* speeding? You should have seen me coming along here last week."

"I'd better see the licence, madam. And the insurance certificate, if you have it with you."

She returned to the Jaguar to rummage in the glove box, leaning over to do so. The two officers surveyed the scene with interest. They had already had a front view of this tall, blonde woman in her mid-thirties. Now they saw the other aspect. It was handsomely displayed in lime-green trousers.

She handed the licence to the sergeant and he began to write: "Mrs Helen Mary Chadwick, 19 Pargate Mansions, Westminster." The licence already bore two speeding endorsements. One more would mean suspension.

Then he stopped writing. It was, as she had said, a lovely day. In that sort of car, as she had said, seventy was a dawdle. She hadn't whined, as so many do when they are two down and one to play. And there had been nothing dangerous about her driving. She could handle the car; he was sure of that. He judged her to be that sort of person.

"Suppose we let it go this time . . ."

"I leave it up to you, officer. You must do your duty as you see fit."

Cheeky bitch. But he let it go.

"Good morning, sergeant," she said. "I'm so glad about the rheumatism."

The police car eased back onto the motorway. The driver, who came from Norfolk, said: "That's a right 'un, that is. And I tell 'e wun thing. She only had tiny littl'uns."

"Little what?"

"Thingummy bobs. Get those green'uns down, sarge, and you'd be right in."

Life had been pretty good to Helen Chadwick. Whenever the gossip columnists mentioned her, which they did from time to time, they described her either as a millionairess (which was not true) or as the "boot and shoe heiress", which she was. This description was truncated in headlines to "The Boot Queen".

The money had come from her father. He had built up the Midland Footwear Company from scratch, and had lived to see its products, made in the factory at Midhampton, go on sale in every High Street in the land. He had kept a tight personal control over the company, and when he died (his wife having predeceased him by ten years) he left the lot to his only child.

He had done so in the sure knowledge that his régime of benevolent authoritarianism would endure. He had moulded Helen for this task. He had let her win a place at a local grammar school rather than send her to an expensive fee-paying establishment. He had brought her, at the age of seventeen, into the company as a secretary. He had put her through the various departments of the business: design, buying, marketing, management. When she was twenty-five, he made her a director.

It was true that when he died, she became chairman because she had the controlling shareholding. It was also true that she had more drive than any of her fellow directors.

She had money. She had Nordic features and figure. She used them all to get what she wanted. She was seldom thwarted.

Only in one respect had life gone wrong for Helen Chadwick: marriage.

Bernard Chadwick was a civil servant, a senior one in the higher echelons of the Home Office. When Bernard's colleagues discussed the state of play in the bar of the Garrick or the Travellers, they were agreed that in the fulness of time he would undoubtedly get his C.B.E. Some thought he would get his K.

"Only one thing can stop him," said one. "That's if he does what old Smithy did."

Old Smithy, on the brink of appearing in the New Year's Honours, had put his hand up a girl secretary's skirt.

"Not much chance of that with Bernard."

In fact, there was no chance at all. Helen would gladly have sacrificed the prospect of becoming Lady Chadwick for such a cause. It might have presaged a revival of their own relationship. The spark, on Bernard's side, always feeble, had for eight years been extinct.

She had asked him to seek medical advice; not from their own doctor – she knew that he would never bring himself to speak of that problem to their extrovert G.P. who told risqué jokes when he dropped in for sherry – but from some remote, Harley Street consultant. Bernard's pride would not let him do it.

Bernard was suave, kind, gentle, amusing. They kept up the pretence of the marriage to save Bernard's face when the Minister invited his senior staff and their wives to cocktails. But that was all.

When, for the second and obviously final time, he refused to seek help, she told him: "I'm not a nun, you know."

He said: "I do know that, my dear. I shall understand."

He had understood when her name began to appear on the chit-chat pages of the newspapers; about her being seen at a point-to-point with a captain of the Welsh Guards; about her prolonged stay at Lech where, said the gossip writers, the racing driver Freddie Chambers was also enjoying the skiing; about her escorts at Ascot and Wimbledon.

The gossip merchants had not yet got around to Keith Shalton, Tory Member of Parliament for the Surrey suburban constituency of Helford which, with a majority of 19,021 at the last count, was just about the safest Tory seat in the country. Nor, if he could prevent it, would they.

That was why he had been displeased when Helen was stopped for speeding. Supposing there had been some sort of dispute and he had had to give evidence as a witness? It was all right for Helen. She did not give a damn about her name appearing in the papers, or in what context. With a career to think about, and a wife, he had to be rather more circumspect.

Everyone said that Labour would go out next time. If that should happen, Keith was not without hope of preferment. In fact, there had been a hint that this was in the wind. Over a late-night drink at the last Party conference, the leader, Christopher Marlowe, had drawn him aside and said: "If you're not too busy with your constituency, I'd like you to keep an eye on home affairs. Immigration, police matters, demos, that sort of thing. We're a bit weak in that territory. Might come in useful later . . ."

Marlowe had not officially nominated Keith as Shadow spokesman on Home Affairs. Keith suspected, rightly, that the wily Marlowe had said much the same thing to at least one other aspirant, and was waiting to see how they shaped. But it was a chance, a definite chance, and Keith had taken it. He had made a couple of speeches in the House that had attracted some small attention, one calling for heavier penalties for football thugs, the other inquiring if the immigration quotas were being adhered to.

He'd be thirty-five at the next election. Just the right age to get a toe in the door. He was Winchester and New College. Five or ten years ago, that might have been a bit of a handicap. Now it was not at all a bad thing. He suspected that the Party was ending its flirtation with the grammar school ethos, and was returning to a more Patrician style. Marlowe was Eton and Balliol.

Marlowe was also a High Church man. There would be no place in a Marlowe administration for philanderers. Then there was Cynthia. True, he and Cynthia had been getting a bit tetchy with each other lately. But on the surface she was still the supportive wife, doing the right things, wearing the right things, even having the right children. Rupert and Samantha could have appeared with credit in any colour mag. advert for the upper suburban way of life. The time might come to do something specific about his marriage; but not yet. He needed Cynthia. Helen was a highly desirable optical extra. He saw no reason why, with good staff work (a phrase of his father's, who had been a brigadier), he should not have both.

As they rejoined the motorway, and progressed at a sedate sixty-five, he wondered what Helen really thought of him. It was difficult to tell, with her alternations of laconic detachment and total involvement.

In fact, she was wondering why he was wearing his M.C.C. tie. They were not going to a cricket match. Perhaps all members of the M.C.C. wore the dark blue "town" tie on their assignations with women. It could be some sort of secret sign, understood only by members of the Lords mafia.

She was not sure about Keith. Of his virility there was no doubt. On that score, he had astonished her. But she had never had any previous acquaintance with a politician, and she sensed that he belonged to a world that she did not understand. She herself had been a right-wing Tory all her life, without thinking about it. It was an attitude she had inherited from her father. Now, for the first time, she was getting a glimpse of politics as seen from the inside, the in-fighting and manoeuvring that went on at Westminster and the Party conference. His little in-stories from the smokeroom and bars of the House of Commons amused her. He was a charming tutor.

Charm. That had been the thing about him that first commended him to her. Their initial meeting had not been in happy circumstances.

Midland Footwear had won a design award, and the President of the examining panel, the eighth Earl of Fallerton, was to come to the factory to present it. Helen had gone to a lot of trouble. She had personally ensured that every worker to be presented, man or woman, had a brand new set of overalls bearing the company's emblem. She had organised a lunch in the boardroom. Then on the morning of the ceremony, there had been a phone call. His lordship had a most urgent engagement which had just come up (Helen suspected that it was a game of golf) but a perfectly splendid chap, a member of the panel, would be coming instead. Would that be all right?

Helen slammed the phone down in a rage. "They're sending the bloody office boy," she told her manager.

She had intended to be openly rude to this nonentity of a stand-in. But his genuine embarrassment at the situation, the dazzling smile he produced for an old lady who had spent forty years at the work-bench, these things disarmed her.

The next day there had been a dozen red roses for "my charming hostess". Things had progressed from there. Dinners at an Italian restaurant in Soho. Love-making, twice at an hotel in Brighton, once in the flat at Pargate Mansions. This was at lunchtime, with the radio on and a cricket commentator lamenting on the collapse of the English batsmen against the Australians.

"I'm a middle-order batsman myself," he told her. "Quite often they send me in just before lunch to hold the fort."

"What about after lunch?" she asked. "Are you still on form then?"

"One's concentration tends to diminish."

"Then you'd better get cracking now."

Afterwards, he said modestly: "Not one of my classic innings, but adequate, I hope."

It had been more than adequate.

Tonight would be the fourth time. He had it all organised, at a place just off the motorway (good staff work). But first there was work to do. For both of them.

He was to address a meeting of Tory agents in the Midlands. He had written a paper for Central Office on constituency organisation, and as a result he had been roped in to attend this assembly. He was shrewd enough to realise that the engagement had undoubtedly been declined by at least three more senior members of the Party who regarded it as an insufferable bore. He had taken it to show he was keen. Marlowe liked keen people.

The meeting was at three o'clock. It would be over by six. Helen would pick him up at half-past, at a pub well away from the Conservative Club in Wellingham where it was being held (he wanted no gossip among the agents), and they would drive down the motorway and be in the hideout in time for dinner at eight.

"What time is *your* little confrontation?" he asked her.

"It will start as soon as I get there. It has no fixed agenda."

"Don't you pay a management chap? Do you need to get involved personally?"

"I've left it to the management chap for ten days, and damn-all has happened. I'm going to give a few people a piece of my mind. My precious manager Hibbert, and that bloody agitator, Cowper or Cooper, or whatever his name is."

For the first time in its forty-five years of existence, the factory of the Midland Footwear Company at Midhampton had been stopped by a strike. It was to do with piece rates for operating recently installed machinery. The new machines had cost the company, that was Helen, £150,000. She thought she ought to get her money back through the increased output of which the machines were capable.

Bert Cooper had a different view: if output were to be increased by twenty per cent, then piece earnings should also go up by twenty per cent, even if operating the new machines required less skill and effort than working the old ones. At first, it had looked as if the strike he had called at a thinly attended meeting of militants might fizzle out. But there had been enough people willing to take an extra fiver, if he could get it for them, to keep it going. He had hit the factory where it hurt. He had organised picket lines across the works entrance to stop lorries bringing in supplies, or taking out the finished product. The Midland Footwear factory had been brought to a halt.

"I am going to put a boot up Hibbert's arse. And another one up Cooper's," she said savagely.

"My dear girl, where do you get these quaint expressions from?"

"From my father. That's what he would have said. That's what he would have done. That's what I'm going to do."

She dropped Keith at Midhampton station, where he caught a train for the short journey to Wellingham. Then she drove to the factory on the southern outskirts of the town. It was a long, white, two-storeyed building, with a bit of grass and some flower beds around it. If not a workers' paradise, it was

14

certainly no dark Satanic mill.

"Well," she asked Hibbert, "anything to report?"

"Not since I phoned you yesterday."

"Two lorries waiting to go, and nothing coming into the factory?"

"Nothing except canteen supplies."

"What do we need canteen supplies for if people are on strike?"

"There's the maintenance men. They're still working. And . . ."

Hibbert, facing her in her austere office, was clearly uncomfortable.

"And?"

"Well, the pickets take it in turn to man the gates, and go into the canteen for their breaks."

"You let people who are trying to bankrupt this company go on using the canteen?"

"It's a tricky situation . . ."

"It's a damn silly situation. Ring the canteen. Now. Find out if they are still there. And if they are, tell the canteen manageress to shut the place down."

Reluctantly Hibbert obeyed, adding "It's Mrs Chadwick's orders . . ."

"Why Mrs Chadwick's orders? I pay you to give orders. Now about the lorries. The drivers are not members of the shoe union. So why aren't the vehicles getting out?"

"One of the drivers did try. The pickets wouldn't let him."

"Was he beaten up?"

"Shoved around a bit."

"And what were you doing while all this was going on?"

"I tried to remonstrate with Cooper."

"You tried . . ." The phone rang. She snatched it up, listened for a moment, then said: "I'm coming down – now."

She turned back to Hibbert. "Would you be so kind as to escort me to the canteen? It appears that a little local difficulty has arisen."

She strode purposefully out of the office. Hibbert followed, two paces behind.

The canteen could seat about two hundred. There were

15

around twenty men and two women there when Helen entered, with Hibbert still tagging behind. They gazed at her in silence as she walked across to the corner where they were seated.

She had never spoken to Bert Cooper before, but she knew him by sight. He was a thick-set man, almost bald, but with bushy side-burns. She stopped in front of his table. He sat there and waited for her to speak.

"Mr Cooper?"

He flicked some ash off his cigarette before replying. "Correct."

"Would you mind standing up?"

Cooper sensed that to comply would mean losing face with his acolytes.

"I can hear you sitting down."

"If you are determined to behave like a boor . . ."

Cooper shoved back his chair and was on his feet.

"Don't you start lecturing me about manners."

She had needled him, as she had meant to do.

He ground out his cigarette. "And don't start coming the high and mighty with me. It won't work. People in this country have a right to go on strike. It's not a Fascist state – yet. If you want to talk about the strike . . ."

She cut in.

"There's another matter to settle first. What are you doing in this canteen?"

"The strike committee is holding a meeting. And I don't recall that you were invited."

"Then hold your meeting somewhere else. Somewhere where your committee or your union pay the bill. This is a subsidised canteen. I don't see why I should subsidise people who are trying to put this company out of business. So get your committee out of here. Now."

Cooper was aware that every eye was on him. He leaned across the table, his jowly jaw thrust forward. "I said I don't want any high and mighty stuff. So don't try it on. This is our canteen. We've a right to be here."

With icy calm, Helen told him: "This is not your canteen. It is *my* canteen. You do not have any right to be here at all. Every person who comes into this canteen does so as my guest.

16

I restrict my guests to people who work for the company. You are not at this moment working for the company. So you can get out. All of you."

The man next to Cooper said: "Don't stand for that, Bert."

"I'm *not* bloody well standing for it. We're here and we'll bloody stay here until we're ready to go. So stick that up your jumper."

Helen turned to the woman behind the counter. "Mrs Harris. It is Mrs Harris, isn't it? Mrs Harris, put the shutters down."

"Don't you touch them shutters," shouted Cooper. The woman did not know what to do.

Helen walked towards the counter. Her intention was obvious. But Cooper moved quickly and blocked her path.

"No you don't, fancy pants. Your old man may have made you a nice little present when he copped out, but we're the people who made his money for him. And don't you forget it." He turned to his mates. "Madam needs a little lesson in industrial democracy, and by God, she's going to get it."

Helen said: "Would you please stand out of my way?"

He stared at her malevolently. She moved slightly to the right. He matched her movement.

"Tell me, Mr Cooper, do you intend to use physical force to stop me doing what I choose with my own property?"

"You ain't shutting this canteen. I can tell you that."

"All right, Mr Cooper. Now listen to me carefully. Listen to me all of you. It costs money to keep this canteen open. Money for rates, light, power. Money for staff. Money for food. And the prices you pay don't cover half of it. I don't know exactly how much it comes to, but I do know it runs into hundreds of pounds a week. If you keep this canteen open against my orders, then you will get the bill. I will have it worked out by the accountant. And it will come to you, personally, Mr Cooper. And it would be no use tearing it up and throwing it away because I would sue you in the County Court. And I will get my money if it's the last thing I do."

She walked out. Hibbert, who had said not a word, followed her.

Had she looked back, she would have seen that some of the swagger had left Bert Cooper. The strike was not official. There

17

was no union money behind it. He did not know whether Mrs Chadwick could make her threat stick. He knew that she would have a damn good try.

"The bitch," he said. But the bitch had won the first round.

Twenty minutes after Helen had stalked out, Mrs Harris locked up the by then empty canteen, and left the keys in Hibbert's office.

That was at half-past eleven. By half-past twelve, Bert Cooper was rallying his troops. He was in a car with a loud-hailer, driving round the streets near the factory, where many of the employees lived. His blaring voice proclaimed there was to be a mass meeting at the factory gates at three o'clock. "Defend the liberty of the workers. Rally round your leaders. Be at the factory gates at three o'clock . . ."

The sound penetrated Helen's office. "Have *we* got one of those loudspeaker things?" she asked Hibbert.

"We've never needed one."

"Well get one, quick."

"I'm not quite sure . . ."

"You're never quite sure about anything. Try the football club. Dammit, we give them five hundred quids worth of free boots every year. Send a car for it."

Well before three o'clock, people began assembling at the factory gates. It was not just Cooper's loudspeaker tour which had attracted them. News had got around that two television camera crews were outside the factory. This was a rare honour for Midhampton. Normally the TV people came for a couple of third division football matches every season, and nothing else. But on this otherwise slack day for news, both the B.B.C. and the commercial television's Roving Eye team had decided to look at the strike situation in Midhampton.

From her window overlooking the factory forecourt, Helen watched the crowd gather, and the TV crews establish them-selves at vantage points. She picked up the loud-hailer which Hibbert had obtained from the football club, and went down to her car parked in front of the factory. Already there was a sizable crowd. Bert Cooper was in the middle of the throng. She was pretty sure he made a vulgar gesture. There was a burst of laughter from his mates.

18

At three o'clock precisely, Bert Cooper went into action. He stood on a box, his stocky figure raised above the throng. "Brothers and sisters," he began.

This caused an ironical cheer; more than half the Midland Footwear workers were women, but there was something ludicrous about Bert Cooper claiming as sisters the pert teenagers who took home pay packets of forty pounds a week.

"Brothers and sisters," Cooper persisted, his voice booming over the heads of the crowd. "Your committee has instructed me to call this mass meeting to inform you that the woman over there" – he pointed to where Helen was sitting in her car – "has taken a diabolical liberty with the constitutional rights of the workers in this factory. I have to inform you that when your democratically elected committee was holding a meeting in the canteen this morning to discuss the legitimate grievances of the workforce of this factory we were accosted by the proprietor and ordered to leave the premises.

"Brothers and sisters, I have been your properly elected representative for ten years, and never have I been subjected to such insulting behaviour. And mark you, it was not just me she was insulting. By insulting me, she insults every one of you. This is a blow in the face of industrial democracy. It's treating the workers with contempt. Are you going to stand for it? I ask you, brothers and sisters, are you going to stand for it?"

He paused. There were some cries of "No" perhaps not as vociferous as Cooper had hoped for. Most came from the inner group around his rostrum.

"Your committee thank you for your unstinted show of confidence. But I tell you, brothers and sisters, words are not enough. We must back our words with deeds. We must show this rich woman, who's never done a day's work in her life, not as you and I understand it, that she cannot treat British working men and women like slaves on a plantation, much as she would like to.

"Your committee has decided there is only one way to bring this female Hitler to her senses. Brothers and sisters, your representatives have been ordered out of the factory. But we

19

are going back. I tell you we are going back, and we are going to stay.

"Your committee has decided that until our just claims are met, the workers of this factory shall take over these premises and remain in them until such time as we choose to leave. I hope the representatives of the capitalist media will tell the whole country of the fight for democratic freedom made by the workers of this factory."

"We will, chum, we will," said the director of the B.B.C. crew to his nearest assistant.

Bert Cooper fumbled in his pocket and pulled out a piece of paper. Laboriously he began to read.

"On behalf of your committee I now put the formal resolution to the meeting: That the workers of the Midland Footwear Factory refuse to be intimidated by the reactionary management and hereby resolve to continue their fight for their just claims until victory is won. And further, that in view of the attitude of the management to the elected representatives of the workers, this meeting formally resolves that the workers take over the premises of the Midland Footwear Company as from tomorrow, the fifteenth, until further notice.

"Fellow workers, I now put this resolution to the meeting. All those in favour, signify in the usual way."

Up shot some arms near Bert Cooper. Other hands went up, more slowly, in other parts of the crowd. Probably about half of Cooper's audience had voted in favour.

"All those against."

A smaller number of hands went up, some rather hesitantly.

"The motion is carried by an overwhelming majority," boomed Cooper. "Brothers and sisters, thank you for your loyalty to the cause of freedom. The meeting is over."

Helen picked up the loudhailer which had been lying on the seat of the car, got out, and hoisted herself onto the bonnet of the Jaguar. Most of the crowd still had their eyes on Cooper. They were startled to hear a new voice.

"This is the slave-driver speaking." Helen's voice reached the crowd, loud and clear. "Mr Cooper has had his say. Now I'm going to have mine. Firstly, I tell you this. If there are any slaves here, they can liberate themeselves this very afternoon.

They can cast off their shackles for ever. All they have to do is to go and collect their cards."

Both television teams had latched on to this new development. Their cameras homed in on Helen.

Bert Cooper snatched up his loud-hailer again. "This meeting is for union members only," he shouted. For a few moments there was noisy conflict between the two amplified voices fighting for supremacy. But Helen's instrument was far the more powerful. Her voice won through to the crowd.

"Bert Cooper's meeting was declared closed a few minutes ago," she shouted. "Now *I'm* holding a meeting. Do you want to hear what I have to say?"

There were a few cries of "No" but most of the crowd were intrigued by their employer's intervention. She stood with her legs braced apart, the breeze ruffling her blonde hair. The men, at least, found her an interesting sight. Already, most of Cooper's audience were moving towards her. When the crowd had reformed, Helen began again.

"Well, all you slaves, what about it? Who wants to be liberated? The offer's still open."

There was silence.

"Right. Now since you have decided to stay in captivity, let me tell you what *I* think about what has been going on in this factory. Firstly, although the whole idea of the new stitching machines is to increase output, I know and you know that it doesn't mean that anybody is going to be asked to do any extra work.

"The new machines are easier to work and much quieter than the old ones. We shall be able to reach our targets by running them for fewer hours. That will mean that on some days, on Fridays, we shall shut the line down earlier. That means that you will get home earlier. I explained this to the union people when we ordered the machines. But has Mr Cooper explained that to *you*? I don't suppose he's capable of saying a single good thing about the management of this factory. It might make you forget that you are poor downtrodden slaves. *Did* he tell you that? I don't know. You tell me."

Somebody shouted to Cooper, who was now in the fringe of the crowd: "What about it, Bert? Did she say that?"

"All piss and wind!" shouted Cooper. "Ask her if it's in writing. Ask her that."

"It will be in writing," said Helen. "It will be, as soon as we have had a chance to see just how the new machines work out. So what have you gone on strike about? Some people go on strike to get a shorter working week. You've gone on strike because you've been offered that. That's what you've let Mr Cooper do on your behalf."

The crowd were completely silent now. The long-legged woman standing on the car had their full attention. She spoke for ten minutes. She told them about a company pension scheme that was being drawn up. And she told them about Jack Barnett.

Jack Barnett had worked for Midland Footwear for thirty years. A solid, reliable, popular fellow, in the darts team, in the bowls team, in all the social club affairs; a man never slow to stand his round of drinks.

Jack Barnett had been killed in a road accident.

"I wasn't going to tell you this," said Helen, "not until I started hearing about slaves on plantations. But when Jack Barnett was killed, the mortgage on his house had eight years to run. I can tell you that arrangements have been made so that Jack Barnett's widow will never have to pay another penny to a building society. And when Jack's son goes to university in the autumn, he will have a few extra quid to top up his grant to see him through. If you don't believe me, ask Harry Barnett here." Harry, an under-foreman at the factory, was Jack Barnett's brother. Heads turned towards him. He nodded.

"Great stuff," said the head of the Roving Eye team.

"Now," continued Helen, "the thing is: Do you want this firm to go bust or not? Because if you do, you're going the right way about it."

She pointed across the forecourt to where the two captive lorries were still standing. "You see those lorries? They're loaded with the stuff you made. Sixty thousand pounds worth of it in each lorry. That's your pension money standing there. I want those lorries out of this factory, and I want them out today. So who's in favour of getting them where they ought to be – on the road?"

Bert Cooper could not let that pass. He still had his loud-hailer with him. He used it. "Those lorries stay where they are. Don't nobody touch those lorries."

Helen's speaker was again too strong for him.

"Any drivers here?"

Two men edged forward.

"Well, what about it?"

"I'm willing," said one. "We're not on strike. It's the pickets, they won't let us through. They keep the gates shut."

Cooper thrust himself forward. "And the pickets will damn well see that the gates remain shut."

"What about you?" Helen asked the other driver.

"O.K.," said the man. "So long as there's no rough stuff."

Helen addressed the crowd again. "There are two drivers here willing to take the lorries out. One says so long as there's no rough stuff. I say those lorries are going out whether there's any rough stuff or not. And I'm going with them."

"Whacko," said the B.B.C. cameraman.

Helen athletically vaulted down from her perch. Instantly her way was barred by the bulky shape of Bert Cooper. "No you don't," said Cooper.

"Yes, she does." The voice was that of Harry Barnett. Harry had done a bit of boxing in his time. Amateur stuff. But quite useful. Middleweight.

"Out of my way, Cooper," said Helen.

"You and whose army?"

It was then the fighting began.

Barnett eased himself in front of Helen to try to clear a way for her. One of Cooper's mates, a husky bearded type, blocked their way. "Don't let the Fascists get away with it," he shouted.

"Who the hell are you calling Fascists?"

"Bloody Fascist traitors!" That, in itself, would probably have been enough to spark a conflagration, but at that moment somebody shoved Barnett in the back and he lurched towards the bearded man. Barnett might just have controlled himself, but the bearded man struck first. It was a mistake. Barnett's fist landed on the bearded man's face. Hard.

"Christ! You've asked for it," yelled Cooper. He squared up in front of Barnett. The little bastard's got guts, thought

23

Helen, as the mêleé swirled around her. She thought Barnett would flatten Cooper. Then somebody jumped on Barnett from behind. Barnett's supporters, and it was clear he had quite a few, tried to drag the man off. Within seconds, the fight had embroiled about forty men, all cursing and lashing out viciously. The television crews were having a field day.

Soon another, separate affray was going on near one of the parked lorries. One of the drivers had quietly moved towards the vehicle and had climbed into the cab. But when he started the engine, he was at once surrounded by a mob of strikers. One heaved himself into the cab and started grappling with the driver. "Have him out. Get him down here," shouted a man in the crowd. Another striker got into the cab, and together they grabbed the driver and forced him onto his back, and started to tip him out of the cab, head-first. The man was terrified. He thought his head was going to be dropped on to the tarmac. But finally, though he was yanked out with brutal force, someone caught his shoulders before he hit the ground. He lay there with his assailants' boots inches from his face.

"You got the message, mate?" He'd got the message all right.

Around Helen the main battle was still being fought with fury. She was being jostled violently. Struggling men crashed into her, nearly knocking her over.

Suddenly a voice behind her shouted: "Give us that," and a hand snatched at the loudhailer that she was still carrying. Whoever grabbed it, and Helen never knew whether he was friend or foe, did not have speechmaking in mind. He was going to use it as a flail. But as his arm swept upwards with his weapon, its rim banged viciously against Helen's right cheek-bone. She felt a searing pain. She knew at once that her flesh had been cut. When she put her hand to her cheek, it came away red and sticky.

It was one of the strikers who first realised what had happened.

"Christ, look at her!"

Abruptly, the commotion died down. On both sides, men were shocked at the consequences of the brawl. "Must be bloody proud of yourself," said Barnett, addressing the strikers in general, and Bert Cooper in particular.

"Never touched her," screamed Cooper. "Never touched her. Anyway, serves her damn right. She started it. Her and you."

The blood was now streaming down Helen's cheek. "Where's there a first aid box?" demanded Barnett. "There's one in the lorry," said the driver, the timid one who had stayed on the fringe.

"Let her through," ordered Barnett. The mob stood aside. Helen, holding a handkerchief to staunch the flow of blood, followed him across the tarmac. The men who had been involved in the scuffle around the truck were still there, including the driver who had been ejected from his cab. Barnett assumed control. "Get the first aid box," he ordered. The driver obeyed. Helen leaned against the side of the vehicle. "Wish that big bloke would move out of the way," said the Roving Eye cameraman. "It's blood we want. Let the British public see blood, damn it!"

Barnett said: "You'll need stitches. Better put something on it straight away, then we'll get you to hospital. Sit down and I'll fix it."

She did not argue with this man who obviously knew what he was doing. But she spoke to the driver, who was fussing around, achieving nothing. "You had a go at getting out?"

"They was too quick for me. Eight to one, it was."

Barnett was deftly applying sticking plaster. Helen was still speaking to the driver. "Did they get the keys?"

"No. The keys is still in the ignition."

Barnett told somebody to go and ring for an ambulance.

"I'm all right" she said. "I can drive."

"You're not driving anywhere."

She straightened up. "I am. Just watch."

Before anybody could do anything about it, she had put her foot in the step in the side of the lorry and heaved herself into the cab. She switched on. The starter whirred, then the engine fired at the second attempt. Barnett leaped into the cab beside her. "Don't be bloody daft," he shouted above the noise of the engine.

She gave him a grin which was made grotesque by the blood

drying on her face. She shouted back: "Coming along for the ride?"

She fumbled with the unfamiliar gear lever, and found a gear, but not the right one. The lorry jerked forwards, scattering men in all directions. In fits and starts, she headed the vehicle towards the gates, which had been left open for the meeting. Bert Cooper ran into the lorry's path, waving his hands. Again she thought: He's got guts.

To Barnett she shouted: "Where's the horn?" She fumbled for it, but could not find it. Cooper was still there. She wrenched at the wheel, thinking it would need great strength to change the vehicle's course. She was astonished at its vivid reaction. It swerved violently, missing Cooper, but making others jump for their lives. She got it back on course, but hadn't mastered the accelerator pressure. The big van progressed in a series of sickening spurts and abrupt slowdowns. She drove it through the gates. And on for another fifty yards. Then she switched off.

A dozen men had chased after the lorry. The first to arrive was the driver. Helen looked down at him from the cab. "Do you think you can manage now, or do you want me to drive the bloody thing all the way to London?"

The television cameraman arrived just in time to film Barnett helping her down from the cab.

"I SEE," said Bernard, "that you've been breaking the law, my dear."

They were in the living room of the flat in Pargate Mansions. Bernard was pouring sherry. Bernard's sherry had been bottled for the Common Room of his Oxford college, but a few bottles were available for people who kept in touch.

Helen's head was bandaged, and the wound was still throbbing.

26

"I got copped on the motorway for speeding. But they let me off."

"I was thinking of your subsequent exploit. Driving a heavy goods vehicle without a licence."

"God! I never thought of that. Will that be another endorsement?"

"I shouldn't think that any little busybody would wish to spoil your hour of glory."

Was he sneering? It *was* her hour of glory. Millions had sat enthralled by their television screens, following every detail of the previous day's events at the factory. All the morning newspapers had given it the big treatment. BOOT QUEEN BATTLES WITH STRIKERS, said one headline. Another, wrapped round a picture of her bloodstained face, read BLOODY BUT UNBOWED. *The Times* reported more soberly: Woman director in fracas.

The Battle of Midhampton, as one paper called it, had caught the nation's imagination. It was real blood the people saw on their colour screens, not tomato ketchup. Overnight, Helen had become a heroine, a national celebrity.

At the Midhampton General Hospital, where she had spent the previous night, the telegrams of praise and congratulation started arriving for her within an hour of the first showing of the films. A brigadier, retired, wired from East Grinstead in Sussex: "You have made me proud to be British again." The hospital staff had had great trouble in keeping the Press out of the ward. When she did appear at the hospital entrance, a tribe of reporters and photographers were waiting for her.

She had revelled in the instant fame. But for the moment, she had had enough "And what sort of day have you had?" she inquired. Despite the sexual emptiness of their marriage, they maintained the civilities.

"Pretty routine. My master is tetchy." Bernard's master was the Rt. Hon Rupert Lilley, Secretary of State for Home Affairs.

"What's agitating the little man?"

"Some Opposition M.P. is breathing down his neck about immigration figures. So I've had to chase the Registrar General to find out whether more black babies were born here in the first six months of this year than there were last year. What

27

possible use that information could be to anybody I cannot imagine. It's such an appalling bore. There are so many more useful things to be done." He gave a wry smile. 'I suppose Mr Shalton, like God, moves in a mysterious way his wonders to perform."

"Shalton?"

"He's the fellow who's stirring it up. M.P. for some place in Surrey."

For some reason, Helen's pulse began to beat a little faster. She had never boasted of her conquests to Bernard, and never made any great effort to conceal them. She assumed that he always heard about them eventually. But they had never discussed her lovers. It was the first time he had mentioned one by name.

"I shall have to keep an eye on Master Shalton," said Bernard. "He's obviously making a play for the Department if the Tories get back. He could well be my next master."

She said: "I've met him, you know." She described how Keith had been press-ganged into going to the factory.

"What do you think of him?"

"He seemed brighter than most."

"Does he crop up in your social whirl?"

"We've bumped into each other occasionally."

"Then I might be asking you to put in a good word for me one of these days. How's your head?"

"Aching a bit."

"You must keep the bandage on for a day or two. Your public will expect it."

Again, was he sneering? Again, she was not sure. Nor was she quite sure that his interest in Keith was as casual as it seemed

As always, they went to their separate rooms. In the morning, as always, he was up first and brought her tea on a tray. The perfect husband. Except for one thing.

With the tea, he brought a batch of morning papers. The products of the photographers' activities were again on show. "If this goes on," he said, "I shall have to sell my story to the Sunday papers. My life with the Battling Boot Queen." He stooped and gently kissed her cheek.

Bernard left at nine o'clock. By ten the phone was ringing.

People she knew, people she had never heard of. Invitations to appear on a television panel, and to give an in-depth interview for a Sunday newspaper. The general callers all said more or less the same thing. About time somebody did something about the strikes that were sending the country to the dogs. One retired naval captain made an expensive call from Inverness to tell her he was going to propose her health at a British Legion dinner. The post brought an avalanche of "Get well" cards. Flowers started to arrive.

Then there was a call from the factory. The strike, she learned, was over. This was through the initiative of Harry Barnett. He had called a meeting and taken a vote. Bert Cooper had protested, no doubt correctly, that this was unconstitutional, that Barnett had no right to go over the heads of the strike committee. But the strike was over, and there was nothing Bert Cooper could do about it.

Helen appeared on a TV programme, and gave one long newspaper interview. These caused a new flurry of phone calls, telegrams and letters. Then things began to simmer down. There was no shortage of news, all of it bad. The country was in a pretty rackety state. Inflation was roaring on. There was a railway strike, and a docks strike in the offing. The stock market was sliding. There was much talk of how long the Labour Government, headed by Percy Bainbridge, could last, and speculation about a general election.

In the midst of these happenings, there were two items which attracted relatively minor attention.

George Robertson, the sixty-five-year-old Labour M.P. for Midhampton, was found unconscious by his wife on the lawn of their garden. He had had a stroke while pruning the rose trees. Two days later, he died in Midhampton General Hospital.

The other item was not mentioned in the national press, though it was covered in the Midhampton Argus, the town's local evening paper. Harry Barnett, Helen's champion in the "Battle of Midhampton", and the man who had ended the strike, was also in the General Hospital.

On a Friday night, with two weeks' holiday money in his hip pocket, he had spent a cheerful evening in a pub. Then, walking home, along an alley, possibly a little hazy, but certainly not drunk, he had been mugged.

It seemed that his assailants must have known that he had his extra pay on him. That pointed to involvement by someone at the factory. Another, quite different factor, also pointed that way. Were the mugging and robbery in revenge for the role he had played? Police were making inquiries at the factory, and being non-committal. Meanwhile, Harry Barnett lay in a coma in an intensive-care ward, his brain possibly damaged beyond repair.

THE Leader of Her Majesty's Loyal Opposition, the Right Honourable Christopher Marlowe, invited Keith Shalton to lunch at the Salisbury Club. He quite liked Keith, and thought he might do well in a middle-grade post. He had almost, but not quite, decided to make him Shadow Home Secretary. The chap had ideas. That was clear from the way he had tackled his so far limited brief. And now Marlowe sensed that Keith had another idea he was itching to unload. He gazed into his brandy and waited. Here it came.

"This Midhampton by-election," began Keith. "should be quite a good one for us. The polls put us up eight points overall. I should think we might well do better than at Midhampton. It's important we put up a good show."

"Don't see why we shouldn't," said Marlowe. "What about going up there and giving a hand? Get the local people to slot you in for a speech on the Saturday before the poll. Then you'd get a good show in the Sundays. Do you know the place?"

"I've been there once or twice. It's one of those in-and-out places. We had it twice before last time. Labour had it before that."

"Could be a bit tricky," said Marlowe. "I don't pay too much attention to the polls. A lot could depend on the candidate. I don't think it's a place for a high flier. Wouldn't go down well there. I'd sooner see a sound local chap given a go."

Keith said: "I've been thinking about the candidate problem . . ."

Marlowe cut in sharply. "Not Willerby. Not the right place for him. That wouldn't work at all."

Willerby was the one slightly black mark on Keith's otherwise unspotted book. Willerby was a squash-playing friend. Keith had put his name up to the leader as a possible candidate, and Marlowe had casually passed it on to the local selection committee of a South London committee. Understandably overawed by the leader's interest in their affairs, they had opted for Willerby. But Willerby had not done well. Nobody was very pleased over the Willerby incident, least of all Marlowe, who thought he had been put in the position of backing a dud.

"I wasn't thinking of Willerby," said Keith. "But I know someone who *would* suit the place."

"For instance?"

"Mrs Chadwick. Mrs Helen Chadwick."

Marlowe sipped his brandy pensively. Keith said: "She's the woman who was in that uproar at the factory just over a month ago."

"I read the newspapers."

"I'm sorry. What I'm trying to say is that she's just right for that one. If anyone could get the Tory vote out at Midhampton, I reckon it would be her. They'd love her. She's local. At least, she's got roots there. Owns a factory. And she was the nation's darling after that rumpus."

"Do you know her?"

"I've met her once or twice. I went to a presentation thing at the factory."

"Is she one of us?"

"Her heart's in the right place."

"You might have something there; I say *might*. Do you think you could sound her out? Do you know her well enough for that?"

"I think so."

"Of course, even if she's eager for the fray, the locals have got to accept her. There must be no suggestion that she is being imposed from on high. Local committees are touchy about that sort of thing."

"They've got the last word. But surely there wouldn't be any problem in getting her on the short list? I know the local chairman. Had some drinks with him at the last conference. How would you feel about my dropping a word in a few ears? Providing, of course, that she's willing to have a go."

"I leave it to you. Leave me out of it."

Marlowe could hardly tell this eager and relatively inexperienced activist that he, Marlowe, was appalled at the prospect of taking on the Government of the country in its present state, and that the best thing for the Tory Party would be to stay on the sidelines for at least another three years while things got worse before they could hope to get better; or that there was little that the Tories could do which had not already been tried by Bainbridge's Labour Government.

The game had to go on.

"I give you just two words of advice," said Marlowe. "Remember Agag."

"Agag?"

"He trod delicately.'

When Patrick Brendan Maloney first moved into the White House, he found many things he did not like. For instance, the President did not like the English butler. In fact, he did not like butlers at all. He thought they were snooty bastards who had been invented by the English to ensure that anyone who had made a fairly quick ten million bucks, as Patrick Maloney had done, should be kept in permanent awareness of the fact that the best people just do not do that sort of thing; if they needed money, they inherited it.

Of the entire butler species, it was the English variety that irritated Maloney most. They were urbane. He had no urbanity himself. What he felt came to the surface, quick. His craggy, deeply lined face, which was topped with wiry, iron-grey hair, could produce a scowl so black that senior White House aides could feel the sweat running down their spines; or it could crinkle into a huge, ugly-beautiful grin which would make them feel good for the rest of the day.

But neither scowl nor grin had the slightest effect on Gilbert Parkinson. Maloney did not like people who did not react. They damn well should react. For all those reasons, the President would have dearly loved to tell Gilbert Parkinson to get his ass out of the White House and take it back to Kensington, or wherever he came from in the first place.

His wife would not let him.

Martha Maloney was a Flynn from Boston. Her family had once had money — the right kind, the inherited kind — but Martha's grandfather had drunk and gambled most of it away. Thus Martha had had a deprived childhood. No butler. But the first thing she had done when she and Patrick had moved into the White House had been to contact a prestigious London employment agency on the subject of butlers. They had come up with Gilbert Parkinson.

Patrick Maloney knew his limitations. He could issue the order that would send clusters of nuclear bombs to annihilate twenty-seven pre-selected Russian cities. But he could not fire a butler.

Another thing Patrick did not like about the White House was that there were too many creeps around the place. He had thinned them out, but there were some who could not easily be replaced. Pete Mansell, for instance. Assistant Press secretary, but doing the number one job because the top man, Willie Hodge, had unreasonably developed haemorrhoids and was in hospital recovering from an operation. If someone had programmed a computer to produce the authentic White House smoothie, it would have come up with Pete Mansell. Harvard. Three years *Washington Post*. Knowledgeable about wine and

33

colonial period furniture; charcoal grey suits; always just the faintest whiff of one of those executive man perfumes advertised in the glossies.

Yet another thing the President did not like about the White House was the working breakfast. Godammit, a man ought to be able to have his breakfast in peace and read the sports pages if he wanted to. But President Maloney found that so much paper flowed through his office that unless he made a start with it at breakfast, he could not cope for the rest of the day. So he had directed that the FP file should be put on his breakfast table. FP stood for foreign press. The file was a folder of cuttings from foreign, mainly European, papers – those things that, in the opinion of Pete Mansell, should be brought to the attention of the President of the United States.

Mansell had been somewhat puzzled to receive a direction from Maloney to "put more British crap in the file". What Mansell did not know, because Maloney had kept it mighty close to his chest, was that the first delicate negotiations were in progress for a State visit to Britain by the President of the United States, with all the trimmings: the drive along the Mall with the jingling escort of Household Cavalry, the State banquet at the Guildhall, the lot. America had never had a more down-to-earth President, or one who was outwardly more scornful of the rituals of monarchy; but in fact, the idea of a State drive with the Queen at his side activated Maloney's considerable sense of vanity; and Martha could hardly wait to set foot in Buckingham Palace.

Furthermore, the visit might have practical value. The few senior advisers whom the President had taken into his confidence were cautiously in favour of the project. Negotiations were in progress for a big new American concession in North Sea oil, and in this one field Britain was in the position of granting favours. The State Department view was that the visit might help to soften up the Brits.

The Brits, of course, wanted something in return. They wanted a whacking loan to tide them over their immediate problems. The talking would be tough.

Mansell, though in the dark about all this, did as ordered and provided the President with an ample selection of cuttings from

34

British newspapers. The only trouble was that when it came to judging what was interesting or important, he was just not on the same wavelength as the President. The President was utterly bored by the cuttings of long speeches by British politicians that Mansell provided for his perusal. But Mansell's efforts were not entirely wasted. What the President did was to turn the marked cutting over and see what was on the other side. By this process, he found snippets which gave him insights into the British scene that were far more interesting than the interminable orations of members of Her Majesty's government. For instance, the President learned about the price of potatoes in Britain; and about the sexual attitudes of the British, as disclosed in the reports of divorce and rape cases. He observed the British obsessions with cricket, even when the nation was lurching towards bankruptcy. He learned about football pools, and the Plymouth Brethren.

Picking up the latest FP file, the President was not surprised to find that the first item was a four-column report of a speech by Christopher Marlowe exhorting the nation to show the Dunkirk spirit.

Maloney grunted and flicked it over.

There, on the back, was a picture of a tall, blonde woman standing on the bonnet of a car. Around her was a seething mob. The woman's name, he found, was Helen Chadwick.

He liked the look of Helen Chadwick. He liked what he read about her in the report which accompanied the picture.

It struck Maloney that Mrs Chadwick was quite a woman.

"THE THING is," said Keith, "my master wants to know if you are eager for the fray."

They had finally achieved their assignation in the hotel off the M1, and had disrobed.

"I usually am eager at this stage. But I don't like being kept waiting."

"I don't think you are giving this matter the full and deep consideration my master expects."

"Are all M.P.s as pompous as you?"

"Most are more so."

"Then include me out."

"Think of the rich rewards, my girl. A seat in the mother of Parliaments. Membership of the best club in the world. And somewhere to park your car in London. We spent three million quid of the taxpayers' money fixing ourselves up with a car park at Westminster."

"Now you're talking."

"Free travel to and from Midhampton. First class, of course. Buckshee trips to Hawaii to study democracy in grass skirts."

"More your sort of thing than mine."

"Every word you utter, in the House that is, recorded for posterity in the imperishable columns of Hansard. And if you want to call someone a cretinous oaf, you can do so, provided that you do it in the House. Parliamentary privilege."

"At this moment, I am beginning to feel somewhat under-privileged."

"I shall endeavour to remedy that."

When he had done so, she said: "I suppose it's having to keep it bottled up for all those years that makes you Winchester chaps so randy in later life."

"It's the mix," he said. "Team spirit, corporal punishment, and the Anglican religion. Get the mix right, and there's nothing like it for bringing a chap on."

"I will say one thing. It was damn decent of you to take off your M.C.C. tie. I do appreciate that."

He smacked her rump.

"Cut it out," she said. "I'm not one of your Central Office playthings."

"Well, what about it? Do I start dropping words in ears?"

"Not content with raping me, you want me for voting fodder too. I suppose you put this up to Marlowe, not the other way round?"

36

"I mentioned it *en passant*."

"You're using me not only to satisfy your animal passions, but to further your career."

"You're a fine one to talk about animal passions."

"You are a swine. A well-bred, Winchester, Tory, M.C.C. swine."

"I know. But what about it?"

"Don't rush me. Let me get dressed. Fix me a drink."

He raided the drinks cabinet the management had provided, emptied two miniatures of Scotch, and added water and ice.

"Now . . ."

"I am just not going to discuss the representation of the people in this condition."

"Then get your knickers on. I never realised that you were such a prude." But he could see that she would not be shifted. He waited until they were dressed and were settled down with their drinks. Then he explained to her what she would be letting herself in for: late-night sittings, committee work, sessions with constituents, weekend speeches.

"Of course," he said, "it does not follow that you will get the nomination. I can't promise you that. Nor can Marlowe. Nobody can. It's up to the local committee. They choose whom they like."

"Come off it. If some little local bigwig who's the chairman of the committee gets a nod and a wink from God, surely that fixes it."

"Probably. But not for sure. There will be other people after it. Probably a local chap. And one or two ex-M.P.s who got tipped out from other places last time. But my guess is, and it can be no more than a guess, that with a nudge from the right quarter, and all your local fame, you'd be home and dry."

"Even if I get the nomination, it doesn't follow I'd be elected."

"That's one thing I can promise you. In the present state of play who ever gets the Tory nomination for Midhampton will walk it."

She had practically made up her mind. Just one or two doubts.

"All that committee work. It sounds appallingly boring. I'm

not a committee person. I like to do things on my own."

"Well, everybody has to do their stint to start with."

"What do you mean, to start with?"

"You must understand that what I say now is entirely my own hunch. It doesn't come from Marlowe or anyone else. It's just my own hunch of how things might work out."

"I'm listening."

"If you stand for this election, you will win it. Then you will, of course, stand again at the general election, which must come in about a year, perhaps sooner. The Tories are going to win that election. Now, have you any idea how many Ministers there are in a Government?"

"About twenty-five. Something like that."

"Wrong. That's just the people in the Cabinet. For each senior minister there is at least one and sometimes two or three junior ministers. Around eighty altogether."

She was suddenly alert. "You mean I might become a minister of something. Or an under-minister?"

"Probably not in the first dish-out. Marlowe has quite a few hangers-on he's got to find jobs for. But there will be changes half-way through the Government's run of office. Perhaps sooner. I'd lay an even tenner that something would eventually come your way."

"Eventually?"

"Dear God, girl, you don't think that people who've been standing in the queue for five years or more are suddenly going to stand aside and let you go to the top?"

"An even tenner, you said."

"I did."

"You're on."

On just one count, Helen's decision to offer herself as the Tory candidate for Midhampton caused her some slight unease. She would have to tell Bernard.

There was almost an element of guilt about it, though why this should be so, she could not explain to herself. She wondered if he would sneer. He would not do so openly, but he might regard her new venture as a short-term, childish fad. She had had other enthusiasms, some of which had been short-lived. Once she had been part-owner of a racehorse. It had proved expensive, and she had abandoned it after a season. Bernard had been gently tolerant, making occasional inquiries about the animal's performance, and tactfully ceasing to do so when it became clear that the venture was a flop. He had never said to her: "It's your money, and if you want to make a damn fool of yourself, don't let me stop you." Sometimes she wished he *would* say something like that, instead of cloaking his thoughts, whatever they might be, in skilfully feigned casual interest.

If he did feel any derision about her political adventure, he kept it totally hidden. "My dear," he said, "how marvellous! I wish you all the luck in the world. You will be an ornament to the House."

"I don't want to be particularly ornamental. I want to get mixed up in things, and to know what's going on."

"I am sure you will."

He poured out sherry to drink to her success. "If it all works out, I ask just one thing."

"Yes?"

"Do promise me that when you are elected you won't get up in the House and ask the Home Secretary if he has any information about the number of Ugandan immigrants with ingrowing toenails and no means of support who have arrived here in the last six months. Mr Shalton is already keeping me fully employed in that field. One is enough."

He raised his glass. "To the new lady member for Midhampton."

She said nothing. Was it just coincidence that he had brought Keith into it? He was eyeing her quizzically. She could not be sure. It was so difficult to be sure about anything with Bernard. The Civil Service mask hid all.

KEITH briefed her for her appearance before the selection committe.

"You must remember," he said, "that there will be some women on the committee. So don't put their backs up. Don't flaunt yourself. Let the men see just enough to arouse a flicker in their ancient loins, but don't overdo it."

She must make it clear that though she had never been actively involved in politics, she had always been a firm supporter of the Tory approach on the economic situation, on defence, and foreign policy.

"What about law and order?" she asked.

"You're in favour of law and order."

"What about sex? Am I in favour of sex?"

"I think one can say in general terms that the Conservative and Unionist Party is in favour of sex. Though I should hardly think that that would crop up at your induction meeting."

In that, Keith Shalton was to be proved to be utterly wrong.

BRIGADIER Pennington-Smythe, M.C., T.D., cleared his throat, settled his bulk in his chair, and addressed the members of the selection committee in a private room at the Midhampton Constitutional Club.

"Ladies and gentlemen," he said, "having disposed of the routine business, we now come to item four, which is the selection of a candidate to stand at the by-election. I think you will agree that the short list is an exceptionally strong one, which represents all the main strands to be found in our party."

He waffled on for a few moments. Then: "Unless anyone has

any objections, I propose that we take the candidates in alphabetical order. Miss Price, would you be so kind as to ask Mrs Chadwick to join us?"

Following Miss Price along the corridor and up the stairs, Helen wondered what she would find waiting for her. What she found was a group of thirteen men and three women, all middle-aged, seated at tables which had been arranged in a U-shape. In the centre of the U was a solitary chair.

The chairman, a military gent, made a token effort to rise, and so did some of the other men. It was clear that her place was on the penitent's stool. She took up her position, crossing her legs carefully and smoothing the skirt of her discreet fawn outfit, so that all that should be seen was on view, and nothing else.

The military gent made some welcoming noises. Her fame had preceded her, he said. Damn good show. That's what the party needed, people with spirit, people ready to stand up for their convictions. However, standing for Parliament was a serious business, not quite so easy as kyboshing a few strikers, as she surely realised. He finally ran out of words, and the members of the committee got into the act. It seemed that everybody, to justify their presence, had to ask at least one question. In fact, most of the information sought was already set out in the questionnaire which Helen had filled in.

No, she did not live in Midhampton, but would establish a residence there if elected. No, she had not previously been active in politics. Yes, she had always voted firmly Tory.

Had she had any experience of public speaking?

"I did a bit of public speaking at the factory six weeks ago."

That went down well. Then came the time for her personal declaration of faith. As Keith had advised, she kept it low key. She was for incentives, both for employees and the employer; she was not an anti-unionist, but her experience had taught her how easily the sheep could be led by the wrong people. She believed this country could still show the Germans and the Japs a thing or two if it was possible, just occasionally, for an employer to sack an idle or insubordinate employee and not start a strike. She was aware that she was not putting up a brilliant performance, but Keith had warned her against brilliance. They either won't recognise it, he had said, or if they do, they won't like it. She ended rather lamely by saying: "Is there anything else that any member of the committee would like to know?"

It was then that everything went wrong.

"I have a point."

"Certainly, Mrs Harper," said the chairman.

Helen had been studying the faces of the committee and wondering what sort of people got themselves elected to this kind of jury. She had been particularly interested in the three women. Miss Price, the bespectacled woman who had escorted her from the waiting room, looked pretty harmless and witless. Probably she was in the party to look for a husband. The two other women were different. Both in their fifties. Both the successful business-woman type. Both pretty hard and shrewd, she guessed. She hadn't liked the look of either of them. The one she liked less was the one now identified as Mrs Harper, a bosomy woman with a blue-rinse and too much jewellery.

"There is one matter," said Mrs Harper, "on which we might have a little more information. In answer to Item Three on the questionnaire, that is the one dealing with marital status, you just say 'married'."

"Doesn't that answer the question?"

"Isn't it – well – just a little uninformative? Could you tell us something about your husband?"

The chairman intervened. "I'm not quite sure that this is entirely relevant—"

But Mrs Harper cut in again, rudely. "*You* may not be sure, but I am. In the case of male candidates, it is accepted as absolutely right and proper that the committee should have some background information about the candidate's marital status, and know something about the candidate's wife. About whether she, too, is committed to the Party, and to what extent she is prepared to help her husband. I see no reason why the corresponding questions should not be put to a woman candidate about her husband."

"I am sure Mrs Chadwick . . ."

Mrs Harper again overrode him. "I say it is both our right and our duty to know something of the background of the candidate we present to the voters. I see no reason why an exception should be made because a candidate is a woman."

Helen had been feeling her pulses beating a little faster, but she willed herself to remain icy calm.

"I have no wish to be an exception," she said with studied politeness. "I am quite prepared to meet this lady's point. My husband is a civil servant. Rather a senior one. In the Home Office. Does that answer your question?"

"Up to a point."

The chairman wanted to wind it up, but once again, Mrs Harper was too quick for him. "I think we still need a little more. Mrs Chadwick, do you have any children?"

"No. Should I?" If this bitch wanted a fight, she could have one.

"The question of whether you have children does not directly affect your fitness for this vacancy, but . . ."

"Then why ask it?"

Mrs Harper, despite her interruptions of the chairman, did not take kindly to being interrupted herself. "Because we are entitled to the complete picture, Mrs Chadwick. I repeat. The *complete* picture." There was something infinitely sinister in the woman's emphasis, thought Helen.

She waited to see just what was on this Harper woman's mind.

"Is your husband a supporter of this party, Mrs Chadwick?"

"I've never asked him."

"That's a rather strange thing for a candidate to say."

"Why? Do you tell your husband how to vote?"

"I regard that remark as rather impertinent."

"I regard your whole attitude as impertinent."

She knew, as soon as she had said it, that she had blown it.

The chairman was making a token attempt to assert his authority. "Mrs Chadwick has told us that her husband is a Civil Servant, and that means, of course, that he cannot take part in any political activity. So I think we might leave this subject unless any other member . . ."

Mrs Harper said: "Just one more question. Or perhaps two. For the good of the party." She's slimy as well as tough, thought Helen.

43

"All right. But briefly, please."

"Mrs Chadwick, would you say that your marriage is a *good* marriage?"

"What do you mean by that?"

"You know perfectly well what I mean. Let me put it like this: Is it a stable marriage?"

"We have been married for fourteen years."

"That was not what I asked. I asked if yours was a *stable* marriage."

Somebody's put her up to this, thought Helen. She's not doing it off her own bat. Harper had her in a corner. One solution would be just to get up and walk away. But she hated the idea of leaving the bitch triumphant.

"There has never been any talk of divorce in my marriage."

It was absolutely true. Perhaps she still had a faint chance. There could be a backlash against the Harper woman. After all, there were twelve men to three women. And Miss Price looked a nice gentle person and could be on her side. She decided to take the initiative.

"I hope, Mr Chairman, that the committee is now fully satisfied on the points that have been raised."

Harper struck again. This time it was a deadly blow.

"Your husband," she said, "must indeed be an understanding person."

Helen accepted the challenge. She could do nothing else.

"Just what do you mean by that?"

"I mean this. Your name appeared prominently in the newspapers about six weeks ago. But that was not the first time you had attracted the notice of the Press, was it? The other occasions were less recent, and may have been forgotten. Just little items tucked away at the bottom of the page. But in my view, those items have a direct bearing on your fitness to represent this borough in Parliament; and furthermore, I think they indicate that you have been less than frank with this committee."

From underneath the pile of papers in front of her, she produced a single sheet.

"Mr Chairman, I wish to submit this document to the committee. I think they will find it interesting, and that it has some

44

relevance to the fitness of this candidate."

She passed the sheet to the chairman. While he fumbled for his spectacles, it lay on his table. Helen, looking at it obliquely, could not read the details, but she recognised its contents at once. Photocopied on to the one sheet were reproductions of a number of newspaper paragraphs – paragraphs she had seen before. They formed the complete file on her activities as reported sporadically by the gossip columnists over the last half dozen years or so: the ski instructor, the racing driver, a picture of her at Wimbledon with her Welsh Guards captain; and several others including one which was completely untrue but which she had never bothered to deny because it was so absurd. It said that when she had visited Biarritz, her arrival and departure times had coincided with those of a playboy brewery heir. It was sheer chance that they had stayed in the same hotel. Their contacts had not extended beyond a casual greeting in the lift.

All those paragraphs were years old. There had been nothing, absolutely nothing, for the last two years. How had a complete set of them suddenly come into the possession of this Harper woman, who could not have foreseen that she would ever have any possible use for them? Somebody must have been keeping them, saving them up, waiting to use them when the time was right. Waiting for seven years or so. It was that long ago that the first of the stories had appeared.

In God's name, *who?* Then she knew. Cooper. Bert Cooper. He was cunning enough, shrewd enough to keep a file on his employer. And spiteful enough to use it in this manner. Cooper. It *must* be Cooper.

The chairman had now pulled himself together. "This document which Mrs Harper has handed to me," he told the committee, "appears to contain some reproductions of newspaper items about Mrs Chadwick."

"What sort of items?" came from a voice down the table.

Helen was on her feet. She was in complete control of herself.

"Mr Chairman, it seems that one member of your committee has developed an inordinate interest in my personal life. Why this should be so, I cannot imagine. I can only assume that the lady has had some unfortunate frustrations and disappointments in her own life. In these circumstances. I am sure you will understand if I withdraw my application for this vacancy."

She turned and walked to the door with her head high. Miss Price, whose duty it was to escort candidates in and out, sat riveted to her seat.

They finally chose a bull-necked barrister.

KEITH was furious. But not for the same reason as her. "It was a put-up job," she stormed. "That woman never did that on her own. Somebody's been keeping a bloody file on me."

"There are cutting agencies where you can buy that sort of thing."

"I'd bet it was Cooper, the cunning little swine."

Suddenly it dawned on her that Keith was not particularly interested in who was responsible. His anger was directed against *her*.

"You told that woman that she was jealous of you because she could not get a man of her own?"

"Words to that effect."

"You bloody fool."

It was then she realised that he was concerned not about her but about himself. It was blindingly clear. Her candidature had been *his* project. If it had come off, *he* would have got the kudos, the pat on the head from his master. But it had not come off. It had gone disastrously wrong. And he would have to carry the can when word of the happenings in the committee room got back to Marlowe. He had blotted his copybook; or rather, she had blotted it for him. It was not the stifling of her political career at birth which was agitating him; it was the effect which the affair would have on the career of Keith Shalton. Her assessment was precisely correct. "Christ!" he thought to himself. "Willerby. Now this."

"It appears," she said, "that I rather let the side down."

"You didn't play it according to the rules."

"Dear God, don't talk to me about rules. What about that horse-faced bitch? Did *she* stick to your precious rules?"

"The committee is entitled to gather information about candidates."

"You're taking *her* side against me?"

"I'm just telling you how it is."

"You might damn well have told me how it is before you let me in for it."

"How the hell could I know that it would work out like that?"

"You might have used your political prescience and judgment."

"And you might have played it differently."

"Kept a low profile? That's the jargon, isn't it?"

"It's also commonsense."

"Are you telling me that that woman was entitled to call me a tart?"

"If she thought you were a tart – yes."

She slapped his face.

THREE days later she drove up the M1 alone. She had business at the factory. The terms of the strike settlement had to be formalised. She presided at a meeting with the union people in the boardroom. Bert Cooper was there, of course. She looked at him long and hard. There was no sign of triumph in his putty-coloured face. He fought doggedly over the piece-rate figures. Just a dour, sullen man sticking to his brief. But a sly one, too.

The meeting lasted most of the morning. Then Helen had another appointment – at Midhampton General Hospital. Harry Barnett was still there, in the intensive-care unit. There had been no improvement in his condition; in fact it was gradually worsening. Day after day, he lay on his back, staring with eyes that registered nothing at the ceiling. He had not spoken a word. No one knew whether he understood what was said to him. When Helen arrived, Mrs Edna Barnett was at the bedside, listlessly holding her husband's hand. She had almost given up hope; but not quite.

"It's four weeks, now," she said. Then in desperation: "Sometimes, when they're like this, they do get better, don't they? You read about it in the newspapers."

"I am sure it does happen," said Helen. She was lying. Mrs Barnett knew she was lying. Helen looked at the shell of the powerful man who had shouldered a way through the throng for her. He had become a cabbage.

She drove Mrs Barnett home, to a council flat on the outskirts of the town. In the car, Mrs Barnett said: "Why do you think they did it? Was it just the money they were after, or was it because of what happened at the factory?"

"I honestly don't know. Have the police said anything to you?"

"They don't say much. They've been asking all sorts of questions at the factory. I do know that. But they haven't got anyone. I don't suppose they ever will now."

"No," said Helen, "I don't suppose they will."

She was deeply depressed when she got back to the factory. She hated being beaten on anything, and Cooper had beaten her on a couple of little things at the meeting. The candidate business still rankled. The break with Keith had left her feeling oddly adrift. And the hospital visit had been disturbing.

At half-past twelve she was ready to drive back to London when her secretary told her that Mr Henderson was on the phone. She knew no Henderson. What did he want? A pause. Then the secretary said: "Mr Henderson says he's in the downstairs bar at the George, and would be greatly honoured if you would join him for a drink. He wouldn't say any more."

It had been a miserable morning, and somebody she had

never met would be honoured to buy her a drink. "Tell him I'll be there in twenty minutes."

The George was the main hotel in the town centre, used by the Rotary Club and other worthy organisations for their meetings. The downstairs bar, she found, was a rather masculine place, dark wood and leather, and beer from the barrel. But the men there, most of whom looked like well-heeled sales reps, were drinking spirits; doubles. It was obviously a sort of men's lunch-time club.

A few eyes flickered as she sat on the leather couch which ran along the wall. She was the only woman in the room, apart from the busty barmaid. She wondered what sort of man it was who had chosen this place to meet a woman. She knew there was a brighter lounge, more of a ladies' place, on the ground floor.

The drinkers were in hearty groups. But there was just one man at the bar alone. A tall man, a rather saturnine type, with an untidy mop of black hair above a face that was almost hawk-like. She judged him to be somewhere between fifty-five and sixty. This was evidently her man. He detached himself from the bar and came towards her. He did not hurry. One reason why he did not do so was that he walked awkwardly, with the aid of a heavy stick.

"I'm Henderson," he said. "What can I get you?"

"A gin and tonic."

He limped to the bar and limped back with the drinks. His own was a large, neat Scotch. He put his stick on the couch, and stretched out his stiff leg. She had a vague idea that she had seen that rather forbidding face before, but could not think where.

"Well?" she asked.

"I congratulate you. You put up a good show. I thought you won on points against Harper."

Then she knew. He had been on the committee, right at the end of one of the tables. He had taken no part in the proceedings.

"I could have done with some support. I didn't hear you acting as counsel for the defence."

"Wouldn't have done any good. I know that lot. I've been

49

on that dreary committee for eight years." He took an envelope from his inside pocket and tossed it on to the table. "That is my resignation from the Midhampton Conservative and Unionist Association."

"What am I supposed to do? Cheer?"

"Not unless you feel so inclined."

"Then why have I been lured into this dungeon?"

"I am going to proposition you. But before I do so, I had better tell you something about myself. The name is Robert Henderson. I am an insurance broker. I suppose my business is the biggest of its kind in this town, which is not saying much, as there are only three others. But it ticks over. I have lived in this town most of my life. I am fairly well known in these parts. Perhaps too well known. I have made a few speeches from time to time, as a result of which some people think I am some kind of Fascist or Nazi."

"Are you?"

"I do not delude myself. If I had been born in Germany, I think I would have been a Nazi. In the early days, anyway, when the thing started up. And probably for most of the war. But I was not born in Germany, and I am not a Nazi. One reason I am not a Nazi is that I went into Belsen on the first day the British troops got there, before the place had been cleaned up, so I saw what had been going on. I saw the bodies. I saw people crawling about in the dust because they were too far gone to stand up. And I know the Nazis did that. So anyone who says I'm a Nazi is a bloody liar."

"What are you?"

"I suppose I am what is called an authoritarian. And I feel faintly sick when I hear and read of the pap turned out these days by politicians and television know-alls and judges."

"You're not the only one."

"Let me be more specific. I'm a hanger and a flogger. I would bring back conscription, if only to make the kids get their hair cut. I would abolish half the universities in this country and tell the kids to earn a living. I do not see why citizens from our beloved Commonwealth should be pampered with three-star hotel accommodation at the tax-payers' expense when they dump themselves on us without making any

50

arrangements on their own behalf. I feel that having sustained a somewhat painful injury in the service of my country, I am entitled to protest when I find half my earnings being taken away in taxation to support layabouts who can't even be bothered to stand up when the anthem is played. Tell me, *am* I a Fascist beast?"

"Possibly."

"What about you?"

She took a long, thoughtful sip of her drink. Then she said: "I agree with pretty well everything you've said. I've never really thought about it deeply, not even when I let my name go in for that candidate thing. What you've done is to take all the snippet thoughts I've had at various times, and put them together in one piece."

He emptied his glass, unhurriedly placed it on the table, and looked at her squarely.

"In that case, I am now ready to proposition you. How would you like to stand as a Parliamentary candidate for this borough?"

She felt let down. "I did have that idea. That cow Harper kyboshed it."

"It could still happen."

"I'm not with you."

"There are, you know, such things as independent candidates."

"They never get anywhere."

"They *seldom* get anywhere because they are cranks, they are hopelessly out of touch with the mood of the country, and they have no organisation and no idea of how to go about it."

"Most of that would apply to me."

So far, he had been speaking in a rather detached way, almost like a tutor addressing a pupil. Now he leaned forward, suddenly intense.

"None of it applies to you. You are *not* a crank. Neither am I. We are patriots. I know that's a quaint, old-fashioned word, seldom heard these days. But the idea is not the least quaint or old-fashioned. I believe there's a devil of a lot of people in this country who think exactly as we do. But they're afraid to get up and say it, in case someone slaps the Fascist thing on them.

51

But they're waiting, *aching* for someone to give them a lead.

"I reckon that about eighty per cent of the people who vote Tory really want *our* brand of Toryism, but there's one thing for sure, they won't get it from Marlowe and the lot who are now running this party. Nor from the other side. The way things are, it doesn't matter much which party is in power. They've all gone trendy. Must be polite to the workers. Must never tell a so-called worker to get off his backside and do some work. Mustn't hang a lout who's clubbed some old woman to death. It might strain his neck. Mustn't tan a young thug's backside. It might do him some terrible psychological injury.

"No politician ever admits hankering after the 'bad old days', not in those terms. But if one of them ever did come out with it, I reckon he'd be astonished to find how many people agree with him.

"Then why don't *you* get up and say it?"

"I have done so, once or twice, locally. But I've the wrong image for putting it over with any success. I'm known in these parts as a disgruntled old reactionary. I'm the wrong age. Possibly the wrong sex. I don't see the public falling over themselves to get me personally into Westminster. But what I've been saying *could* be put over by a new voice, a new face, a new personality. And I think *you* could do it. Look what happened after that affair at the factory. You really sparked something off.

"And you could spark something off in this by-election. That is, if you really believe in the things I've been saying. Of course, if you've got any doubts, any doubts at all, then I've been wasting your time."

She scrutinised this strange, intense man. He had fire in his belly. What a difference between his declaration of faith and the casual, flippant briefing Keith Shalton had given her. And a long time ago, she had heard much of what Henderson had been saying from the lips of the one man who had imposed his authority on her.

"You know," she said, "you and my father would have got on pretty well."

"Well, what do you say?"

"This independent candidate business. Would it work? The

big parties have got offices and hordes of people working for them. Is it possible to make any kind of a show without that sort of set-up?"

"The accommodation thing is no problem. I'm in the process of moving my business. The old place has not yet been re-let. I own the leasehold. Three rooms. Just right for a headquarters. Near the centre of the town."

"What about canvassers, stamp-lickers, that sort of thing?"

"You don't need a big team. Too many people would be a liability. You need a small team, every single worker who knows exactly what he's got to do. I reckon twenty would be enough. I could get ten this very day, people I've mulled things over with. And once you put the the flag up, you'd have hordes of volunteers."

"But would people really vote for an independent? Wouldn't they stick with the party they'd always voted for?"

"You'd split the Tory vote, because what I've been saying is the sort of Toryism a lot of people want. But you'd do more than that. You'd take quite a few off Labour too."

"I can't see that happening."

"I can. Very clearly. Take the ordinary Labour chap in his snug little council house. He does a good day's work, he digs his garden, he has his pint, and he sends his daughter to a teachers' training college. That chap, I tell you, is really the most conservative person in the land, in the true sense, because he's got something to conserve. Not something he inherited, but something he himself worked damned hard for, and he doesn't want to see the whole lot chucked into the ditch by a gang of Trotskyites, and he doesn't want to see it just slide into the ditch because the people he's sent to Parliament to stand up for him are too scared or idle to do so. And he's scared stiff that that is just what will happen the way things are going now. So I reckon if you stood up in the market-place and spoke your mind, quite a few horny-handed sons of toil, the genuine ones, not the layabouts, would say: That's the one for me."

She sipped her drink and pondered this. It could just be true. "You really think we could make it work?"

"*You* could. Particularly if you went on parade dressed like you were for that affair at the factory. You'd get the bum-

53

watchers' vote."

"You mean my feminine charm would be an electoral asset?"

"I mean you'd get the bum-watchers' vote. Well, what about it?"

"There is one thing we have not considered."

"Which is?"

"Harper may have a stroke."

"I am prepared to risk that."

"I am, too."

AGAIN, she felt an unaccountable embarrassment when the time came to tell Bernard. She had not told him of the details of her rejection by the Tories, and nothing about her confrontation with the Harper woman had leaked out. On that occasion, Bernard had been sympathetic. "A great pity," he said. "You would have made an admirable member."

When she told him of her new venture, his enthusiasm seemed qualified. He pointed out a factor which had been at the back of her mind, but with which she had not yet fully come to terms.

"For some reason," he said, "the Tories turned you down. Now you will be standing against a Tory and probably doing him a lot of damage. Won't some people say you are acting out of pique or for revenge?"

That, she knew, was part of the truth. Not the whole of it, but a definite part of it. But she did not want to admit this to Bernard. She tried to explain the philosophy which Henderson had expounded, but under her husband's cool, detached gaze, she could not put the words together as convincingly as she would have wished. Some husbands might have told her that she was making a bloody fool of herself, and that if she wanted

54

to behave like a tarted-up Fascist, she could pack her bags and get out. If Bernard had said that, or anything like that, there would have been a flaming row, and just possibly she might have changed her mind. But there was no chance, no chance whatsoever, of Bernard saying anything like that. It was impossible to have a flaming row with Bernard.

He said quietly: "If that's really how you feel, my dear, that's what you must do."

She made a couple of trips to Midhampton. The first was for a session on tactics with Henderson in his office. The second meeting was at the hotel off the motorway where she had finally had her assignation with Keith Shalton. The unexpected choice of this venue by Henderson jolted her into thinking briefly about Keith. She realised he was in for a shock. She wondered whether it would be the civil, decent thing to give him some hint of what was to come. But Henderson insisted on secrecy for the moment. That was why, for this assembly of his chosen aides to meet the prospective candidate, he had picked this place out of town, away from the local gossips.

It was a conspiratorial affair. The men, about a dozen of them, arrived by cars, in twos and threes. They drifted into the bar where Helen and Henderson were having a drink, but gave no sign of recognition. Then, with ostentatious casualness, they left the bar in small groups and sauntered along the corridor to Conference Room Number Two. According to the board in the hotel foyer, Conference Room Number Two had been booked for "Insurance meeting".

When they had all left, Henderson said: "Right. Come and meet the company commanders." He led her into the small conference room. The men turned towards her expectantly, looking her over, undressing her.

"Gentlemen," said Henderson, "allow me to present to you the lady who is the prospective independent candidate for this borough in the forthcoming by-election. If you will be seated, we can get down to business." The men arranged themeslves round an oblong table, leaving two central places for Henderson and Helen.

Henderson spoke first: "We in this room," he said, "are of like minds. I think each one of us would call himself a patriot.

Alas, there is not all that much patriotism around these days, at least, not as we understand it. Our brand of patriotism is one that implies an honest, hard-working, orderly, disciplined way of life. Discipline. That's another dirty word these days, but I do not apologise for using it. Only by discipline, self-discipline preferably, but imposed discipline if need be, can this country once again become successful at home and respected abroad.

"We look for patriotism, our brand of patriotism, in high places, in Parliament, on the judge's bench, in the higher councils of the Church. We do not find it. Clearly, if we want to be represented at Westminster by someone who feels and speaks as we feel and speak, it is no use looking to any of the established parties.

"What we want, gentlemen, is a candidate who believes fiercely in the things we believe in, and will speak the truth as we understand it, and to hell with the wishy-washy apologists for everything that once made this country great, and a good place to live in.

"Gentlemen, I believe we have such a candidate in Mrs Helen Chadwick."

While Henderson was speaking, Helen had been intensely studying the faces of the men around the table. They were in the main a beefy, muscular crew. Golf-club types. Rugger-club types. At least one elderly Flying Officer Kite with an enormous moustache and side whiskers. Obviously all were fairly prosperous businessmen. The White Settlers of Midhampton.

She surveyed this assembly and just for a moment wondered what she had let herself in for. Just what sort of society would these people impose on the country if by some incredible quirk they found power in their hands? Then came a comforting thought. Her father, had he lived, would not have been out of place in this group. Her involvement with Keith's lot had been scratching the surface. This, for her, was the real thing.

Henderson had finished. Now he was asking for questions. The R.A.F. type was the first in the field.

"What about the blacks?"

The crudity of the question shocked her. Her instincts told her that unless she was going to become a puppet of this junta, she had to make a stand, and that this was the time to do it. "In my factory," she said, "there are, I think, five coloured women and three coloured men. I'm not absolutely sure about the figures, because I don't keep statistics of that kind. I do know that one is an under forewoman. Is it to be a condition of my standing for this vacancy that I fire these people, or don't take on any more coloured staff in the future? Because if that is so, we can all go home."

Grumpily, the ex-flying officer said: "I didn't mean that. Good chaps, some of them. I've got a black feller who does my garden. Works a damn sight better than the previous chap did."

"Then just what did you mean?"

I've overdone it, she thought. I've put my foot in it again. But the man had been put off balance, and was retreating.

"What I meant was, do you think we've got too many of 'em here, and would you stop them coming in?"

Helen pondered this carefully. She'd got to get it right. And by taking a bit of time over it, she was showing them that they just couldn't press buttons and get any result they wanted. Finally she said: "I think we've got about enough to be going on with, but there can be special cases. But in the main I don't think that black people have the right to come here and start drawing handouts and having babies on the health service the moment they step off the plane. Mind you, I don't think that white people have the right to do that either."

There were murmurs of approval. She sensed that a small crisis was past.

The other questions were more warily phrased. How did she feel about comprehensive and grammar schools?

"I won a place to a grammar school. It was a damn good school, and with luck will remain so. It's going independent to avoid being taken over. They've started a fund to do this. My name is on the list."

How about capital punishment? She was in favour of it for people who went around carrying guns. How about social security for strikers? What about Commies in the unions? What about the number of foreign students in this country? What about the police and demos? Her answers on these points were accepted without demur.

There was just one sticky moment. A middle-row rugger forward said: "What about all these ruddy queers that infest the place these days?"

Helen had never given much thought to the problem of homosexuality. She had never had any personal contacts with homosexuals – unless Bernard was one. She had sometimes wondered about that. She was sure he was not a practising deviationist. His enormous sense of rectitude, which was the pattern of his whole life, would never have permitted it. But it could just be that he was a repressed homosexual. That would explain a lot. The faint thought had been at the back of her mind, but she had never spoken a word of it, to Bernard or to anyone else. If that *was* the cause of his inadequacy in their relationship, she felt neither anger nor contempt towards him; just deep pity.

She deliberately paused, to let them know that they were not going to get a pre-packaged answer. Then she said: "I am not sure that being a homosexual is in itself such a terrible crime, or even a crime at all. I think it's a bit like being left-handed. If you're born like that, it's difficult to change, just to conform with the majority. I know. I was born left-handed, they tried to make me change. But I won in the end. Of course, there's one thing. Children have got to be protected. Anyone who mucks around with children has got to be taken out of circulation. But what adult people do in their own homes, providing there's no form of compulsion, and providing they don't annoy other people, is their own business."

It was not quite what they had expected. There were some non-committal grunts.

Henderson decided it was time to wrap it up. "Well, gentlemen, what do you say? I believe we have in this room enough organisational ability to mount an election campaign. Further, I believe we have a candidate who has a good chance of winning. She will need your support, in terms of time and effort, and to a certain extent in the matter of money, too. I think we can do it. That is, I think Mrs Chadwick can do it, given your full support. What do you say? Do we have a go?"

There was nothing so formal as a show of hands or a count

of votes. It was not needed. The unanimous decision was: *We have a go.*

They departed, as they had arrived, as conspirators. When she and Henderson were left alone, he lit his pipe and said: "You can leave most of the details to us. But there's one thing which the candidate alone can decide."

"Which is?"

"What label are you going to stand under? What are you going to call yourself?"

"I thought I was going to stand as an independent."

"You are. But that's not a particularly good label. It's an umbrella for all sorts of nut cases. I think we want something more specific. Something a bit closer to what we shall be trying to put over. I have a suggestion."

"Tell me the word."

"The word is Patriot. It sums up what we believe in. And I think it suits you."

"Patriot." She savoured the word. "It's got an old-fashioned ring about it."

"That's part of its merit. It evokes nostalgia for the days when there really were such people as patriots. When everybody was a patriot."

"I'd have it on my banners and labels and things – Patriot candidate?"

"That's it."

"But there isn't any such party."

"There can be as from this moment. You don't need a Royal charter to create a new party. You just announce it."

"Patriot Party . . . the Patriot candidate . . . I like it."

"I thought you might. And it has one further advantage which may commend it to you. The Tories have always claimed a monopoly on patriotism. It will make them livid."

"That's absolutely fine."

RESENTFULLY, the President watched Gilbert Parkinson clear away the breakfast things, and wondered, as he had done many times before, just what went on behind that inscrutable face. Resentfully, he picked up the Foreign Press file to see what Pete Mansell had selected for his scrutiny. What he read confirmed his view that Britain was going down the drain. The Labour Government was clearly tottering towards its death-bed. The unions had abandoned any pretence of co-operation with the Government over wage restraint. The ports of Hull, Southampton and Bristol were shut by strikes. Exports were flagging. There were sit-ins in universities and race troubles in the midlands. The whole country, it seemed to the President, needed to get off its butt. There was just one item of cheerful news. The East Anglian sugar-beet industry was doing well. Sugar-beet, it seemed, was impervious to the weather, economic chaos, and Australian fast bowling. It just grew.

But the President found sugar beet uninspiring. He flicked the cutting over to see what was on the back. There was the blonde woman again. The woman who had been in the shindig at the factory. What was her name? Helen something. Helen Chadwick.

Mrs Helen Chadwick, the President read, was standing for Parliament.

Good luck to her, thought the President. He liked her style.

HELEN'S first meeting was in the Corn Exchange, the town's main assembly room on the Market Square. It held five hundred, and it was packed. Henderson presided. Some of his junta supported him on the platform, others were deployed around the hall. The stewards had been selected for their muscle.

The first thing Helen noticed when she took her place on the platform was the presence of Bert Cooper and a squad of his mates in the second and third rows. They had clearly worked out their tactics and were well drilled. While Henderson was speaking, making his brief introduction of the candidate, there was some stamping and booing, but not enough to prevent his being heard. It was when he said: "I now call on the candidate to address the meeting" that the Cooper faction really went into action.

"Fascists out! Fascists out!" they chanted in rehearsed union.

Helen stood there facing them. The chanting went on for a full minute. Then other people in the hall began to get restive. There were shouts of "Shut up", "Let her speak". It looked as if the meeting were going to start with a punch up. Henderson signalled to Paddy Milligan, an Irish Rugby international, whose label euphemistically proclaimed him to be chief steward. Milligan in turn signalled to other beefy individuals stationed around the hall. They started to move in slowly towards the Cooper group. Then the chanting stopped. Cooper had evidently decided not to precipitate an immediate showdown.

Helen spoke for about twenty minutes. What Britain needed, she said, was discipline, and since all attempts to establish effective self-discipline had been wrecked by irresponsible or evil groups, the time had come for discipline from above to be strengthened. That way, she said, a few extremists might have their activities curtailed, but the great mass of people would be liberated from the dictatorship of minorities who had little loyalty to Britain or the British way of life as most people understood it.

She found that her voice carried well. She gained confidence with each minute. It was quite an exhilarating experience to address this throng. She made her points with warmth and vigour. When she sat down, there were some jeers and catcalls, but they were overwhelmed by the cheers and applause.

Then she asked for questions. They were predictable. Should students on sit-ins have their grants stopped? Should immi-

61

grants be allowed to jump the housing queue? Her answers were equally predictable, but they were delivered with sincerity. Each won applause.

It went on for about half an hour. Then Henderson called it a day. "This meeting," he declared, "has performed a most useful purpose, because it has enabled a large number of people to judge for themselves what sort of candidate the newly-formed Patriot Party has put before the public of this town; in turn, the candidate has learned much about the issues which are of real concern to ordinary people. Thank you for your attendance. I now declare this meeting closed."

Bert Cooper was on his feet.

"Not so fast, Hitler," he shouted. "So far we've heard a lot of cock. Now it's about bloody time we heard some sense."

"The meeting is closed."

"*Your* meeting may be. Mine is just beginning."

Henderson again said: "The meeting is closed. Everybody who had anything to say had a chance to say it." The muscular stewards began to move in towards Cooper.

"Look out, Bert," somebody shouted. "They're coming to get you."

Cooper had already seen the danger. "That's right," he yelled. "Send for your blackshirt bullies."

Scuffles were beginning at the edge of the hall, where the stewards were trying to ease their way towards Cooper, and were being obstructed by his supporters.

"Ladies and gentlemen" – Henderson had to shout to make himself heard above the rising hubbub – "we do not want any disorder at this meeting. I ask you *please* to disperse quietly."

"It's please, now, is it? Isn't it nice when the Blackshirts say please?"

Blows were being exchanged at the end of the row. Cooper knew his time was short. He made the most of it.

"Look at her," he bellowed, pointing at Helen. "What the hell does she know about earning a living like other people have to? She's an absentee landlord. That's what she is. Absentee landlord. Looks in at the factory when she feels like it. Drives a damn great car at the workers' expense. What's she standing for Parliament for? I'll tell you why she's standing. Because her daddy left her a boot factory, and now madam finds it all a bit boring. She's just a spoiled, arrogant bitch."

The stewards were closing in, but before they got to Cooper, a man two rows behind him, a military type with a toothbrush moustache, threw petrol on the fire, "Go home, scum," he shouted.

Cooper rounded on him, and began climbing over chairs to get at him, his thickset frame bursting wtih fury. "Scum, is it, by God? We've got some scum here tonight."

He got in one punch at the military man before the stewards were on him. Within seconds, the whole of the front part of the hall became a whirling mêlée, with oaths and punches being traded, and screaming women trying to disentangle themselves from the mob. Other fights were developing at the back of the hall. The whole place was in uproar. It lasted five minutes. The two police officers who had been on duty in the vestibule could do nothing but separate one or two of the fringe fighters, and speak into their walkie-talkies to call up reinforcements.

The main victors were Henderson's strong-arm squad. When police sirens sounded outside, and a hurried dispersal began, it was seen that among the broken chairs, three people were lying on the floor, two moaning, one ominously still. There were more sirens: police vans and ambulances. Seventeen people, including Bert Cooper and four of Henderson's men, were taken to the police station, but were finally allowed to leave without being charged. The chief constable said the next day it had been impossible to establish who had started the disturbance. He expressed the hope that the rest of the campaign would be conducted in the best traditions of British democracy.

His hope was not to be fulfilled.

MARLOWE put the tips of his fingers together, gazed reflectively at the ornate moulding of the ceiling in the dining room of the Salisbury Club, and said: "It's up to you. But personally I advise against it."

It was Keith's first meeting with the leader since, at that same table a month previously, he had put to Marlowe the idea of sounding out Helen on the question of standing for the Tories.

There had been no eruption of anger from Marlowe, but that was not Marlowe's style. Keith had no doubt that in Marlowe's icy, calculating mind, he, Keith Shalton, was now listed as a hopeless bungler, utterly lacking in judgment, never to be trusted again.

"I feel personal responsibility for the Midhampton shambles," he said.

"A good try that went wrong."

But did Marlowe really mean that, or was he just maintaining the lunchtime civilities? Was it yet too late to redeem himself? He had been asked to appear on a television panel of M.P.s to discuss the by-election issues. The candidates would be there too. How did Marlowe feel about his accepting?

"If you see it as an act of penance, by all means purge yourself. There's just one thing. I think you told me you knew this Chadwick woman. Slightly, I think you said."

"That's correct."

Marlowe was gazing at the ceiling again. "I don't wish to pry. But there wouldn't be any . . . what shall I call it . . . any personal involvement, would there?"

"I just know the woman slightly."

"Well, it's up to you."

It was a risk. And when the show went on the air two days later Keith knew, before the programme was ten minutes old, that he had blundered again. He was not particularly good at off-the-cuff repartee. Helen, it turned out, was. With the encouragement of the panel chairman, she hogged the show. When Keith tried to challenge her points, she cut in ruthlessly, and the chairman let her get away with it. The big applause from the studio audience was always for her. As soon as the show went off the air, he strode from the studio quivering with helpless rage. Marlowe had watched the programme with his chief whip. "Game, set and match to Chadwick," said the Chief Whip.

Helen's last major meeting in Midhampton was honoured by the presence of the TV cameras. The TV men were hoping for a repeat of the punch-up that had started the campaign. In that, they were disappointed. But their expedition proved to have been well justified.

At ten o'clock that morning, Helen had received a phone call from Edna Barnett. "Harry's gone," she said. "Three o'clock this morning. I suppose it's for the best, really."

The meeting that night followed its scheduled course until a square-built man, who looked like an off-duty policeman, rose to put his question: "In view of the increasing number of crimes of violence, and the recent murders of bank cashiers and security guards, is the candidate in favour of the restoration of capital punishment?"

The question was overdue, but Helen had not thought out a detailed reply in advance. Now it had come, emotion rather than logic framed her answer.

"I imagine," she said, "that the questioner has in mind the deaths resulting from the bank raid at Nottingham a few days ago, and the shooting down of a security guard in London which was in yesterday's papers. Those were shocking affairs, but we do not need to go to Nottingham or London to find examples. There has been a death as a result of violence this very day, not two miles from this hall."

The audience was silent, tense.

"You will recall that a few months ago I was involved in a disturbance at the factory of the Midland Footwear Company. During that affray, I was briefly in danger of being injured. In fact, I was injured slightly. But I was saved from further danger by the intervention of one of my employees. His name was Harry Barnett. He was quite an ordinary man, but also a strong man and a brave man. A brave man both physically and morally, because he was not afraid to take a course of action which he knew would be unpopular with some of his workmates. I had deep cause to be grateful to him that day.

"Harry Barnett was not himself injured in the affair at the

factory. But barely a week later, while he was in a dark alley, he was set upon by thugs – the police think there must have been more than one – and was brutally beaten about the head. He was left lying in the gutter unconscious. Since then he has been in the intensive care unit at the General Hospital. This morning he died.

"The police have been making vigorous inquiries, but so far there have been no arrests. The police are not sure why Harry Barnett was attacked. It may have been a simple case of robbery, by someone who knew that he had a considerable sum of money on him. But it could be that there is another and even more sinister explanation: that the attack on Harry Barnett was a form of revenge for the stand he had taken in the dispute at the factory."

Bert Cooper – he was a regular heckler at Helen's meetings – stood up and shouted: "Come off it!"

Helen continued: "I did not say that Harry Barnett was struck down because the line he took offended some of his workmates. All I say is that this is a possibility which cannot be entirely ruled out, that it is being seriously considered by the police. But the plain fact is that without looking to events in London or Nottingham we have, on our own doorstep, a case of a life being ended by violence. The life of a skilled, hard-working craftsman. The life of a good and loving husband and father.

"You may think it is wrong to form a judgment on such a large and important question as capital punishment on the basis of a personal involvement with one case. But I am glad this question has been asked. I am particularly glad it has been asked this night. My answer is this: Yes, I am in favour of restoring capital punishment for the type of crime that has left Harry Barnett's wife a widow, whatever the motive of the crime, be it robbery or something else.

"If I am returned to Parliament, I shall do whatever I can to see that perpetrators of crimes of this nature are removed from society for ever, because men who can do such a thing are not fit to live.

"I do not delude myself that one voice among six hundred or more at Westminster is going to achieve anything very dramatic. But I will try. I give you my solemn oath. I will try."

The applause was thunderous. Nothing she had said at any previous meeting had produced anything like it.

The late-night television news programmes gave it in full. Next day it was on every front page: "HANG EM, SAYS HELEN" . . . "HELEN THE HANGER" . . .

The other candidates read the reports and knew that hundreds, perhaps thousand of their votes had been switched overnight. Keith Shalton read them and felt jealous that one so new to politics should hit such a nail so unerringly.

Bernard read the reports and sighed. It would not go down well in the office. His master regarded judicial hanging as a barbarism. That, too, was the view in the higher staff echelons of the office. It was his own deeply held view. Of course, he could not be held responsible for his wife's views. There would be no official reaction. Just a studied silence. But he knew what they would be saying behind his back. They would say that if Bernard was any sort of a man, he would make damn sure that his wife did not make an exhibition of herself in public. But then, poor old Bernard, they would say, was not up to that. It was clear, they would say, who wore the pants in that marriage. That is, when she was not taking them off for her latest fancy man.

President Maloney read about it two days later. This time, Pete Mansell had actually marked the right cutting, so the President did not have to read what was on the back. There was a picture of Helen, in tight pants, addressing a crowd in the street. The President briefly thought it would be a pleasurable thing to screw her into the carpet on the floor of the Oval office, and then turned his attention to the reports of the Russian missile ship said to be prowling off Newfoundland.

ELECTION day. In the morning, Helen had a feeling of relaxation, almost of anti-climax. There was little left to do. She made a couple of routine loud-hailer tours of the housing estates; then she and Henderson, on the first occasion since the campaign had begun, had time on their hands. And for the first time she found herself really talking to this strange man who, in the space of a month, had assumed so important a role in her life.

They were in the small private room of the campaign offices. Henderson poured out two large Scotches from the whisky bottle he kept for useful callers. He raised his glass and said: "Here's to the new member for Midhampton."

"You really think we've done it?"

"I think *you've* done it. It may be a tight thing. But I'll tell you why I think you've done it. You've shown you've got guts. That's the missing factor in British politics, the thing the people want to see. Guts."

Then, quite abruptly, he asked: "What about your husband? How does he feel about all this?"

"I'm not sure."

"How the hell can you be not sure?"

"He doesn't say very much. I don't think he really approves of having a politician in the family. Not a Patriot Party politician, anyway."

"Then why does he let you do it?"

"I don't ask my husband what I may or may not do."

"I'd take a strap to you."

"I suppose you do that to your own wife?"

It was a shot in the dark. There had never been any sign of a Mrs Henderson. Never once had he mentioned her. She saw at once that she had touched a raw spot. He gazed morosely into his glass before replying.

"I did once. Back in 1945. Right at the end of the war. I'd just had a month in hospital with this leg. Then I went home on leave. She was a land girl. Perhaps you don't remember land girls. They worked on farms instead of being called up. We had a cottage on the farm where she worked. There were some Italian prisoners of war working on the farm. I found that one of them had been teaching her Italian. But that wasn't the half of it."

"So you belted her?"

"I did."

"And what happened?"

"When the Eyetie went back to Italy, she went with him. As far as I know, she's still there. If she's alive."

"Your method of dealing with marital problems doesn't seem to have been a great success."

"What was I supposed to do when I found her with this Wop? Shake his greasy hand? Ask him what sort of a war he had had? I'm not that sort. This husband of yours. He must be a saint or a rabbit. Which?"

"You'll be able to judge for yourself. He's coming up tonight for the declaration of the result."

At six o'clock she drove to the station to meet Bernard. His decision to be at her side when the poll was announced had astonished and touched her. She took him to the George, where Henderson had reserved a room for the party workers. It was crowded, but they got a table to themselves in a corner.

At first it was small talk. Was she very tired? How was he managing on his own?

Then he astonished her.

"I thought," he said, "that Mr Shalton's role was a little discreditable."

"In what way?"

"In opposing you on that television show. Not that it did him much good."

"He was entitled to say his piece."

"I would have thought he could have found another occasion for doing so. Perhaps a less personal occasion."

She felt her cheeks colouring. "Why – less personal?"

"In view of your – what shall we say – your special relationship with him. By the way, my dear, I gather that your assignations with Mr Shalton are now a thing of the past?"

Her cheeks were definitely reddening. He had never had that effect on her before.

"You *knew* – you knew about Keith Shalton and me?"

"Of course, my dear."

"Why of course? How?"

"Some months ago I caused certain inquiries to be made. There are some people, rather despicable people, I feel, who specialise in that sort of thing. They are quite ingenious. Expensive, too. For instance, one of the items on their bill was for the hire of a baker's van for a journey up the motorway."

She groped in the recesses of her memory. God! There *had* been a baker's van on the motorway that day the police had flagged her down when she had been with Keith. It had gone past when she pulled up. The driver had given a rather long, curious look. She had put it down to one driver gloating over another who had been stopped by the police.

"You've been having me watched?"

"Observed is the phrase they use. They're great observers."

"For God's sake, *why?* Were you collecting evidence? You've been wasting your money. If it's a divorce you want, you could have had it. You had plenty of grounds for it, anyway."

"Not for a divorce. In fact, just the opposite."

"I don't follow this at all."

"It's absurdly simple. It so happens, my dear, that in my ineffectual way, I love you. It is therefore a prudent thing to keep myself informed about the opposition. I was getting a bit worried. I knew that Mr Shalton was assuming a rather larger role in your life than some of your previous – er – acquaintances. Then my observers told me you had stopped meeting. I thought it was perhaps just an election tactic, being careful until after the poll. But in view of your rupture with Mr Shalton's party it struck me as improbable that the association would be renewed. It would clearly be imprudent, from Mr Shalton's point of view, to keep it going. He is, I gather, rather an ambitious young man. But I was not sure. Not until you were on that television show together. From that it was quite clear that that chapter in your personal life was over. To use a vulgarism which I heard on another television programme, it seemed to me that Mr Shalton had had his chips. It is the message that matters, more than the manner in which it is delivered. The message is that my wife had a lover, but that

70

she no longer has a lover. That is the basic position, is it not?"

"Yes, but . . ."

"Then I regard that as a matter for celebration. I hope with all my heart my dear, that you will have something else to celebrate before the night is out."

She did.

At twenty minutes past eleven, the mayor of Midhampton, in full civic regalia, stepped on to the balcony of the town hall. The candidates and their aides sorted themselves out behind him. The crowd in the Market Square below, who for some reason had been singing "We will not be moved", fell silent.

Going through the prescribed rigmarole, the Mayor said: "I, Percival Horace Wilkins, being the returning officer for the borough of Midhampton, declare the votes cast in the election to be as follows: Helen Mary Chadwick, 14,245 votes; John Frederick Harrison, 1,818 votes; Peter James Hudson, 9,311 votes; Gerald Tremayne, 12,303 votes."

The mayor doggedly ploughed on with his announcement that he duly declared the said Helen Mary Chadwick to be elected for the Midhampton division, but his voice, even aided by the microphone, was drowned by the sound of cheers and boos.

The cheers predominated.

It had been a sour election, and remained sour to the last. The ritual congratulations offered to Helen by the other candidates were of the most perfunctory kind. In an astonishingly short time the town hall was deserted except for a few people tidying up. Helen had to face the television cameras, but could think of only trite things to say, about the new mood of the country. She realised she had not made the most of her hour of triumph. There was a brief assembly in the room at the George, but Henderson, his job done, departed quickly, and those who stayed seemed intent on getting drunk. So this was victory. She said to Bernard, who had unobtrusively accompanied her on to the town hall balcony and to the George: "Let's get out of here."

Bernard had not booked in at an hotel. There was a train back to London, a night express from Scotland which made its final stop at Midhampton at 1.30 a.m. He intended to catch it.

"I have a busy day at the office tomorrow," he told her.

71

"Couldn't you have taken the day off?"

"It might be thought that I was using my new-found political connection to obtain favours. We couldn't have anyone asking the Home Secretary in the House what special dispensation of leave had been granted to the husband of the new member for Midhampton, could we? I shall indeed have to be above suspicion in future. But anway, we're twenty-five quid to the good."

"How come?"

"Morrison in the office ran a book on the election. At the start he had you down at five to one."

"You backed me – with a fiver?"

"I could hardly have done anything else, my dear, could I?"

"I find that rather sweet."

"I regarded it as a sound investment. And it will give me the greatest pleasure to take it off Morrison."

Morrison, Helen knew, was a hearty gin-swilling womaniser, and Bernard's least favourite colleague.

It was still an hour and a half before the train was due. "You can't go and sit on the station all that time," she told him. "Come up to the flat."

The flat was a two-room *pied-à-terre* which Henderson had organised for her for the duration of the election. It was above a launderette.

"What on earth is this place?" asked Bernard as they mounted the stairs. "A miniature nuclear power station?" His shirts had never seen the inside of a spin-drier. They were beautifully hand-laundered at a Chinese establishment.

She felt faintly conspiratorial as she led him into the functional living room. "I'm afraid I haven't any drink here. Nothing that would appeal to you, anyway. There is some sherry, but it's from a supermarket."

"Coffee would be fine."

Then he did an unexpected thing. He took her hand, raised it to his lips, and kissed it. "I hope, my dear, that you will be immensely happy in your new life. It might be, sometime, that I could help you a little bit. Procedure, background, that sort of thing. If there *is* anything I can do, you must let me know. There is a widely held belief that it's the Civil Service, and not

72

the legislature, that really runs the country. It's not true, though some of my colleagues like to delude themselves that it is. But we can sometimes give a guiding hand, and stop a member making a chump of himself. Our services are available to all. Not that I can imagine you making a chump of yourself."

In the tiny kitchen, a wild idea took shape in her mind. There *was* something Bernard could do. Perhaps.

She was gone for five minutes. Then she brought the two coffee cups and put them on a low table.

"It's that instant stuff, I'm afraid."

"I've become accustomed to the instant stuff while my wife has been pursuing her public career."

He made no comment on the fact that the new member of Parliament for Midhampton was now attired only in brassière and briefs. But he stood up, and very deliberately, very gently put his arms around her.

Her grip on him was fierce. She pressed her lips against his face. She compressed him in her arms. But there was a problem. The buttons of his waistcoat (he invariably wore three-piece suits) were cold.

"Get the damn thing off. The waistcoat. The buttons are tickling me."

He disengaged from her grasp, took off his jacket, and placed it carefully on a chair. He began to unbutton his waistcoat, but he was not quick enough for her. She ripped at them and forced the garment back over his arms.

"Bernard . . . please . . ."

"The executive must always be at the service of the elected representatives of the people."

"Did you bring a strap with you?"

"That is a somewhat curious question, is it not?"

It was no good. The absurdity of the situation flooded over her. He was now adjusting his tie, which had become minutely displaced.

"I'm . . . I'm sorry, my dear. In Parliament you will have to get used to giving notice of your intentions."

"Your coffee's getting cold. Why don't you drink it and catch your bloody train?"

RITUAL had to be complied with. First, there was the presentation of her credentials to the Sergeant at Arms in the House of Commons, who conducted her through seemingly endless corridors to a room which had two desks, two filing cabinets, a green carpet and a settee. There were some flowers in a vase, suggesting it was used by one other woman occupant, now absent.

"I'm afraid we don't have enough rooms for every member to have one of their own," he said. "We've put you in with Miss Alderton. I'm sure you will be very happy here."

Helen wasn't sure at all. Miss Alderton, she vaguely remembered, was a middle-aged Liberal lady of puritanical views from North Yorkshire. She wondered if under the official's grave and impeccably correct exterior there was some bizarre sense of humour at work.

At three o'clock, with some difficulty, she found her way through the maze of corridors to the entrance to the Chamber. She passed various people on the way. Some gave her a quick glance and looked away. Tories? She could hardly expect the glad hand from them, having robbed them of their expected safe victory. Two said "Good afternoon". Journalists, probably. Lobby correspondents.

Finally, in the lobby, she recognised the man she was looking for: Henry Wilberforce Grant. Mr Grant, a burly, genial man, greeted her with a massive handshake and introduced her to an elderly, grizzled, stooping man, Mr Robert Roberts. Mr Grant was Labour member for the north London division of Carlington. Mr Roberts represented a South Wales mining division.

They were to be her sponsors for her formal introduction to the House. Normally, sponsors are provided by the new member's own party, but when the new member has no party, the Government of the day grudgingly nominates two of its own members to perform this task. There had been no rush of volunteers. Although Helen's opposition to her Labour opponent at Midhampton had been less personal than her clashes with the Tories, the basic divide between her and Labour was greater than that between her and the Tories. To associate with Helen for any reason whatsoever could not be good for a Labour M.P.'s image.

But Mr Roberts was no longer worried about his image. He knew that within six months, perhaps three, he would be beyond any expression of party disapproval. He had inoperable cancer. Soon there would be a scramble among Labour hopefuls for his safe constituency.

Nor was Mr Grant troubled by hints or threats from above. He was a man who made up his own mind about everything. A man who was a nuisance to Whips and Ministers, but who had an unbreakable hold on his constituency.

He was quite a man, thought Helen, as the three of them went through the ritual of approaching the Speaker's chair and solemnly bowing three times. He stood six foot two, and weighed around thirteen stone, without an ounce of fat.

Helen had done some checking on him when she was notified that he had agreed to undertake this duty. She had found that he had driven London buses, and was active in the affairs of the Transport Union; that he had been in the forefront of marches and demonstrations on various issues, and had once gone to jail for assaulting a policeman (though on another occasion he had been praised by a court for shielding a policeman who was on the ground and being kicked); and that twenty years ago he had won fame indeed. He had scored 263 runs in a Test match at the Oval. But the country for which those runs were scored was not England, but the West Indies.

Henry Wilberforce Grant was as black as the ace of spades.

It was Henry Wilberforce Grant who took her into Annie's Bar and bought her her first drink at the Commons. She found his conversation had a quaintly Biblical flavour. She was not sure whether he was quoting or ad-libbing.

"Make welcome the stranger in the House."

"Do you do this for all strangers in the House – all new members?"

"No ma'am. Never done it before."

"Then why me?"

"A woman of virtue is more precious than rubies."

"I'm not sure I come into that category."

"Not all virtue is to be found in the marriage bed."

That was a bit of a shocker, coming so soon after her arrival at the House. Presumably stories about her confrontation with the Midhampton Tories had reached the House, and had gone round the bars, though they had not been published in the newspapers. This place must be the biggest gossip-shop in the world.

"Leaving aside the marriage bed, which of my *other* virtues particularly interested you?"

"You got guts." So Henderson's judgment had been right. It was he who had said that guts were the thing.

"I saw you on that little box," continued Grant. "I like what I see. You fixed the Honourable Mr Shalton. You fixed him good and proper, so he stay fixed for quite a time."

"You don't like Keith Shalton very much?"

"I don't like him. Full stop."

"Why not?"

"He can't help being white. He can help being a white bastard. A white racist bastard."

That was another shock. It had never occurred to her that anyone would apply that description to Keith. He was amusing, cynical, self-centred and could be unscrupulous. But a *racist*? Then she remembered that Bernard had said something about Keith pestering the Home Office for figures about immigration. It didn't mean that Keith was a racist, or even particularly interested in racial matters. Even she, new as she was to politics, realised that as far as Keith was concerned, it was not the issue that mattered, but the opportunity it provided of getting himself a little bit of the limelight. Questions about sewage disposal would have done just as well if sewage disposal had been in the news. But perhaps, if you are black, the issue is important.

It did not seem a very profitable matter to pursue. She looked at a group of members at the bar. They were talking not in loud voices, but in voices that carried. They were Tory types. It would hardly have been reasonable, after what had happened at Midhampton, to expect them to fall over themselves to make her welcome. But she felt the Best Club in the World was being a little chilly to its newest member. Just one man, a black man, had behaved in a civilised manner.

"Can I get you a drink?" she asked. "If it's allowed. I wouldn't wish to break the rules on my first day."

"Not only allowed, ma'am. Encouraged."

"For God's sake stop calling me ma'am. I'm not the Queen, and I'm not here to christen a battleship."

"No battleships these days, ma'am."

"What do I call *you?*"

"Just call me Henry."

"What's it going to be – just Henry?"

"A pint of bitter. Wine maketh merry."

She shouldered her way to the bar. The Tories continued their resonant conversation, something to do with boundary revision. But the barman said: "Welcome to the House, madam." So there was one other human being around besides Henry Wilberforce Grant. She came back with his pint, and a Scotch for herself. She was conscious that eyes were boring into her back, that she and this black man were a conspicuous couple. Sod them, she thought. Sod them all.

"The name," she said, "is Helen."

They raised their glasses. "Cheers," she said. "You've been very kind."

He was grinning. What was funny, she asked.

"When people say 'Cheers' to me, it reminds me of something".

"Such as?"

"I used to play cricket. I played at Lords. Several times. There was one time when me and Charlie Bennett hit three hundred in three hours. Against the M.C.C. it was. Do you know what? When we were having a drink afterwards, one of the young white gentlemen who I'd hit over the screen twice, he come up to me with his glass of white wine and said 'Cheers'. Then he said, 'Good knock, Grant, damn good knock.' I don't need any whitey to tell me when I've played a damn good knock, so I look at him and I say to him' Why don't you piss off?' And he did just that."

"I thought cricket was a gentlemanly game. I never thought cricketers spoke to each other like that."

"They do, ma'am. I assure you they do."

She thanked him again. "It would have been a pretty bleak first day here without you."

"Better a dinner of herbs where love is, than a stalled ox and hatred therewith."

Bernard was waiting up for her when she got home.

"How did things go at the new school?" he asked. "Made any little playmates yet?"

"I'm not sure. I think I may have. One."

BERNARD was right. It was like being at a new school, and she behaved like a new girl, watching, noting and learning with meticulous care the trivial rituals of the House. Her place in the Chamber was on the Opposition benches. She was careful not to occupy any of the seats to which venerable Tory members had established squatters' rights. Initially, she was treated with frigid politeness, but after a day or so, it seemed that there was a slight thawing of the temperature. The new girl was at least obeying the rules; and when that became apparent, there were one or two Tory members who were not averse to sitting next to a shapely leg. She began to identify the more shadowy figures of the Shadow Cabinet. Marlowe, of course, she recognised; and Metcalfe, the Chancellor-to-be if the Tories got back; but there were others who needed names putting to faces.

She sat well away from Keith. In the Chamber, she had no contact with him whatever. But sooner or later, she knew there would have to be a confrontation. It came on the Friday of the second week as the member for Midhampton. They met in one of the narrow, green-carpeted, squeaking-board corridors which are a feature of the labyrinthine Palace of Westminster. Briefly, they were alone. She had to say something. She said: "Hello, lover boy." He said: "Hello, long legs."

They stood there awkwardly. Then he said. "We must talk."

"I thought we'd said it all."

"Not quite all. But not here, not in the House. I'm not staying today, anyway. There's nothing on this afternoon except forestry in the Scottish Highlands, and I don't imagine that enthrals you."

"Hardly."

"A lunch, somewhere. Or a drink."

"I'm going up to my constituency this afternoon." She was surprised at herself, at how soon she had slipped into the jargon of the place. She regretted it at once. She had given him the excuse for the most sardonic of smiles.

"Of course," he said. "I would not wish to deprive your constituents of your services. We must all be good constituency M.P.s, especially those of us who have cocked things up so there's no chance of ever being anything else. That's what *The Times* says, you know, when it does the obituary for some old dead-beat and can't think of anything to say. He was a good constituency M.P. I expect they'll say it of me. But it's good to see that you are getting into the swing of things so soon. Leaving that aside, it so happens that I, too, am heading north in about an hour. How would you feel about making an M1 diversion?"

"I thought our motorway diversions were a thing of the past." The creaking floorboards announced the approach of an intruder. She might as well get it done with. "All right. Half-past one."

He was in the bar, sipping a Martini when she arrived. Without asking her what she wanted, he ordered her a double Scotch.

"Well," she said, "You wanted to talk. I'm listening."

"How's Bernard?"

The question was unexpected.

"Bernard is as Bernard always was. I presume at this moment he's ferreting out some utterly irrelevant information about immigrants to enable some minor minister to satisfy your insatiable curiosity on that subject."

"That's what he's paid for."

79

"How's Cynthia?"

"We're busting up."

"I'm sorry."

"So am I. But I'm not losing any sleep over it. It had been going that way for quite some time."

"Will it harm you? At the next election, I mean."

"I think not. In my part of Surrey quite a few people have discovered the joys of wife-swapping. Including one or two of the bigwigs on my committee. I know the chairman's been at it. It's becoming the main participation sport. So they're in no position to start reading me sermons on the sanctity of marriage."

"And, of course, you still play cricket, which shows you're a decent chap really."

"I do. In fact, I'm playing for a House of Commons side against the Press Gallery in a couple of weeks' time."

This was getting nowhere. She said: "Let's have it."

He ordered them fresh drinks, then said: "I've been brooding over things of late. For instance, over my once-brilliant Parliamentary future. It's less brilliant than it was. In fact, there seems to be a fairly general opinion that it doesn't exist any more. They won't tip me out of my seat. They can't do that. But I no longer see myself on Marlowe's list when he forms a Cabinet. That's gone. For ever."

"And that's my fault?"

"I blamed you at first. But I snookered myself really. I cocked up the Midhampton business in a big way. Marlowe thinks I'm a bloody fool."

"If you're a write-off so far as Marlowe's concerned, why not pack it in? Why not go away and make some money?"

"I rather like the place. And despite what that swine in the *Despatch* said about me last week, something about subalterns who fail the initiative test – and to think I bought the bastard a drink at Blackpool – despite what he and others are saying, I do not yet accept that I have finally and so soon come to the end of the road. Didn't old Bainbridge say something the other day about when one door closes, another opens? If he hasn't said it yet, he will. It's bound to be in the Prime Minister's Book of Clichés. But it does happen to come occasionally true in politics."

"I don't get the drift."

He sipped his drink, still cogitating.

"You know," he said, "I thought some of your election speeches were good. I think you talked sense and put it over strong and clear. I've been waiting to make that sort of speech myself for years, but with the milk-and-water lot who run this party these days, it would be the kiss of death for anyone to come out and say it in public, though lots of people say it when they're propping up a bar. When it comes to it, I'm a bit of a Fascist beast, too. And as one Fascist beast to another, indeed as one Patriot to another, I don't think we ought to be cutting each other's throats, do you?"

Helen saw a glimmer of light. "Are you saying that you are thinking of leaving the Tory Party?"

"No such words crossed my lips."

"I see. It was all in the mind."

"Precisely. In the mind. In the hidden depths. But tell me, just in case the matter should arise – I am speaking hypothetically, of course – if it *should* arise, can anyone join the Patriot Party, or does one have to be put up for it, like a club?"

"We're not particular."

"With your influence, you could get me in?"

"It could be arranged."

God, she thought, what a twister. What an urbane, silk-shirted, executive-scented twister. Loses his great future in one party. Instantly thinks of switching to another. Are they all like that? Then she realised that that was precisely what she had done herself.

"Tell me," she said, "this conversion, this blinding light. When did it hit you?"

"It was not a blinding light. More like a dawn creeping up over the horizon."

"How far does it have to creep before the world can be acquainted with this revelation? Can I announce that the strength of the Patriot Party in the House has been increased by one hundred per cent overnight?"

"No, you bloody can't."

"Why not?"

81

"Because the time is not ripe. It may come. But not yet."

"When?"

"Perhaps a year from now. Possibly less. Some time in the next twelve months there's going to be a general election. Everybody says the Tories will romp in. I'm not so sure. Not so many floating voters these days. Attitudes are hardening. People know which side they're on, and they tend to stay there. The two main parties have about equal strength in the country, and in the House. That could be the pattern for quite a few years. And that, I think, presages an interesting possibility."

"Presages! Why can't you speak English?"

"All right. Indicates. Suggests."

"Suggests what?"

"I am thinking in particular of the role of splinter parties, or parties which might be too substantial to be classified as splinter parties, and would have to be regarded as genuine third or fourth parties. I'm not thinking of the Liberals. They've missed the boat for ever. And the Nationalists parties are beginning to look a bit burnt-out to me. I am thinking of possible new parties, new alignments."

"So?"

"Supposing things work out in the way I have presaged, or suggested, and the two main parties are deadlocked, what would Marlowe and Bainbridge have to do? They would have to seek alliances. They would have to turn to whatever splinter party happened to be closest to their own line. They would have to do a deal. And the splinter party wouldn't hold all the trumps. But it would hold quite a few."

"I think I'm beginning to see."

"I doubt if you see quite far enough yet. Now let us consider this Patriot Party of yours. You will get back at Midhampton. There's no doubt about that. And, of course, you will be putting up candidates elsewhere. Some will get in. How many is difficult to say. Could be half a dozen. Or a dozen."

She cut in eagerly: "It would be enough to make Marlowe do some sort of deal?"

"Don't get ideas above your station in life. If all you could offer him was half a dozen votes in the House, even a dozen, I don't think he would be interested. You must remember that he personally is on the other wing of the Party. Rather than do a deal just to be sure of your dozen or half-dozen votes, my bet is that he would go to the country and there would be another election. But there is another possibility."

"Which is?"

"Supposing, immediately after the election, while the dickering was still going on, your Patriot Party were suddenly to acquire another eighteen or twenty M.Ps. Then it really would have some muscle. Marlowe would just have to reckon with it."

"But how could that possibly happen?"

"It could happen this way: If about twenty Tory M.P.s got together and went to Marlowe before he'd had a chance to form a government, and told him they were not satisfied with his brand of Toryism, and they felt the nation needed something more stringent. And that while they were prepared to support him in general terms, on the big issues – but keeping their options open – they intended to resign the Tory whip and join the new alternative Tory Party, that is your Patriot Party. Then the Patriot Party would really be a power in the land. It wouldn't be in the driver's seat, but it would be in the co-driver's. Marlowe would squirm. But he would just have to have those votes, perhaps thirty or so, to be sure of hanging on. In a fifty-fifty situation, thirty votes in the House just cannot be ignored."

"You said it would make Marlowe squirm. I gather that prospect does not distress you."

"It would not entirely displease me."

She looked at him coolly. "You are just about the most un-principled man I have ever met. I presume that while the greater good of the nation is the main motivation behind all this, there are some more mundane matters involved. For instance, the question of office for the people who would be holding a gun at Marlowe's head. And among them would be you."

"I am glad to see that you are beginning to show a grasp of the realities of the political situation."

"And would it be presumptuous to inquire whether I would be included in this distribution?"

"I would think so. At a junior level, of course, in view of

83

your recent emergence into the political scene."

"Of course. I must not get ideas above my station in life."

He had their glasses filled again. "Tell me," she said, "these eighteen or twenty people. Do they exist? Have you done any research?"

"Research is putting it too high. But I have my ear to the ground. There are people who would switch all right. If they were convinced it would work."

"Why not switch now?"

"My dear girl, you are a child in these matters. If we did it now, it would simply play into Marlowe's hands. All the people involved would be ditched by their local party associations and would have to fight the next election as independents and probably not more than a couple would get in. They don't all have your particular charms. But they do all have safe, solid Tory seats."

"You're saying they would stand as official Tory candidates, and then, a couple of days after the election, perhaps one day after it, ditch the party just so that one or two of them could get squalid little jobs as under-secretary of something?"

"And for the future good of this great nation of ours."

Despite the trickery and treachery of the proposition, she found it enticing. At least it would get her into the centre of things, into the in-fighting which was the real stuff of politics. She asked: "You have this all organised?"

"Don't be too eager. And for God's sake, not a word to any-body. Things *might* work out like that. It would depend, of course, on the state of the parties after the poll. If the Tories had a thumping majority, the whole thing's a non-starter. Marlowe could just tell any defectors to get stuffed, or whatever."

"In that case, they'd just lie low and stay in the Tory Party and be good little constituency M.P.s?"

"Precisely."

She emptied her glass. "I say again. You are a despicable bastard. They'll drum you out of the M.C.C."

"I think not. This little plot, if such it can be called, was in fact hatched in the Long Room at Lords on the last day of the Test."

"What do we do now?"

"Nothing. And *say* nothing. Meanwhile, to more immediate matters, it so happens that room number seventeen is vacant. First floor, turn left when you go out of the lift. I thought perhaps that before resuming my public duties I would go up there and relax for a short time. Perhaps have a look at *The Times* crossword. I think they must have a new chap doing it. I'm not quite on his wavelength yet. You're a bit of a crossword addict, aren't you?"

"You don't miss a trick."

"Alas, I've missed several lately."

Half an hour later, when the mission had been accomplished, and it was time to think about returning to base, she said, "I think that long one, number seven across, must be 'subterranean'."

Languidly he pencilled it in. "Clever girl."

"It must have been something I had on my mind. Something about hidden depths."

THE time had come for her to make her maiden speech. She had waited for the right moment. It came during a law-and-order debate on an Opposition motion that the House should set up a Royal Commission to examine measures which might be taken to curb the alarming increase in violent crime. It was, of course, largely a pointless debate. The Government had no intention whatever of setting up a Royal Commission. It had no fewer than seven commissions already sitting, on subjects ranging from disestablishmentarianism to the state of the tin mining industry in Cornwall, and was running out of pensioned-off judges to act as chairmen. However, it would briefly take the minds of the people off the state of the economy, and it would provide an opportunity for second strings of all parties to get their names in the papers.

The debate was opened by a Sussex Tory who said the police were doing a damn good job, but what about the feller who had robbed a bank in Eastbourne and was now reported to be studying for a degree in oriental languages in Parkhurst Prison? The Sussex member opined that the British public would not stand for that sort of thing much longer. A junior minister then spoke on behalf of the Government.

Henry Wilberforce Grant had acquainted her with the drill. She must send the Speaker a little note saying she would like, if possible, to be "called" and that this would most probably happen after an opening speech on each side. The machinery of the Mother of Parliaments went into its ritual dance as Henry Wilberforce Grant had forecast. When the junior minister had had his say, Mr Speaker, dashing the hopes of several members who were trying to catch his eye, said: "I call the Honourable Member for Midhampton."

She was not at all nervous. She had made notes, but knew it was considered bad form to make too much use of them, and that, above all, there must be no suggestion that she was reading from a script. In fact, she hardly used the notes at all, because she had it all marshalled in her mind.

She looked around the House, which was two-thirds full.

"Mr Speaker, this is the first time I have had the honour of addressing this House. Therefore, if, in my ignorance, I should in any way depart from the accepted procedures of this Chamber I trust that you, Sir, and Honourable members will be indulgent."

My God, thought Keith Shalton, she's a quick learner.

"I have chosen this debate in which to make my first address to this House because the motion before the House does, I think, give me an opportunity to fulfil a pledge I made to my constituents during my election campaign. It may be that the events of that campaign will still be fresh in the minds of some Honourable members."

There were one or two subdued chortles. They quickly died away.

"During that campaign a very sad thing happened. A gentleman known to me personally died in Midhampton General Hospital. He was aged about forty-five. He was greatly respected at his place of employment, and I personally, on one occasion, had a special reason to be grateful to him. He was a married man, the head and provider of a good, solid home.

"He died at that comparatively early age, not through any self-indulgence nor through contact with some lethal disease. He died because, late at night, he was savagely attacked, probably by two or three assailants, in a dark alleyway; he was robbed and left lying in the gutter unconscious. It is not clear whether robbery was the main motive behind this cruel, cowardly attack, or whether there was an even more sinister factor.

"Whatever the reason for the attack, its consequences were calamitous. This man lay in a hospital bed for four weeks without fully regaining consciousness. He was visited daily by his wife, but was unable to communicate with her. This man had kissed her goodbye that morning and had gone to work a happy man. Four weeks later he died without being able to speak another word to her."

The House of Commons is always civil to a member making a maiden speech. This time it was more than civil. It was deeply attentive.

"During my campaign I was asked about my views on the restoration of capital punishment. You will understand that on that very day, I had heard of this man's death, this man whom I had visited in hospital, whose wife I had tried to comfort; and that therefore I was, perhaps, in an emotional state of mind. Be that as it may, at that meeting I made a declaration to those who had come to listen to me. I said that in my view the death penalty was the appropriate, indeed, the only penalty for a crime of that nature. And further, I gave that meeting, and through the medium of the Press a wider audience, a pledge that should I succeed in being elected to this House, I would use whatever small influence I might then have to get the death penalty restored to the law of this land.

"I am well aware that the motion before the House does not directly raise the issue of capital punishment. I know, also, that this issue has been considered at length on previous occasions by the House and that the majority opinion, among members of all parties, is against the return of the rope.

"I do not question the integrity of those who take that view. But I say this: times change, and views change with them. Most of the change, over the last hundred years or so, has been towards leniency. We no longer hang people for sheep stealing. But now times are changing again. In the last five years there has been an enormous increase in the crimes of violence, including murder. So I ask those whose minds are not utterly closed to reason and to the impact of new circumstances to look at this question again, and to consider whether a scale of penalties which has manifestly failed should now be revised again, this time not in the direction of leniency, but towards the one penalty which in the opinion of the majority of people in this country – though not the majority of this House – might abate this evil trend.

"Surely it is the duty of Governments to ensure for their people not merely freedom from want, not merely freedom to worship as they will, but freedom from fear. For ordinary people in this country, freedom from fear means freedom to walk along a dark street at night without a feeling of panic at the sound of an approaching footfall. I suggest that the law, as it now stands, falls far short of ensuring that freedom.

"I gave my constituents a pledge. I have made a first, and I fear not very adequate, attempt to fulfil it. I shall return to this subject again as the opportunity presents itself, but for the moment I feel I have trespassed on the time of the House for long enough. Mr Speaker, Honourable members, I thank you for the attention you have given to your most junior member."

It was a success. There could be no doubt about that. The buzz of approval came from all over the Chamber. And the speaker who followed, a Labour member from Lancashire, while dissociating himself from her views, said he could not recall a member's first speech which had held the attention of the House more closely. "I am sure," he said, "Honourable members will join me in congratulating Mrs Chadwick on the vigour, clarity and sincerity with which she put her views, and in saying that we shall look forward to her future contributions to our deliberations." The "hear! hears!" were resonant.

Suddenly, the ice was broken. She was accepted as a member

of the club. It was the speech which had done it. It was a civilised speech, and the House prides itself on being a civilised place. Also, she had shown due deference; and the House expects a little deference from its newer members.

People started buying her drinks. She began to receive luncheon invitations. Even her prim room-mate Miss Alderton unbent sufficiently to suggest that they take tea together on the terrace.

The papers gave the speech a good show, and it helped to be the woman in the news, though she realised that this situation would not last. She realised, too, that members of Parliament have the normal masculine instinct for being adjacent to a well-built, well-dressed woman. One portly member let his hand stray round her waist. When it began to wander downwards, she moved pointedly out of the way.

Among those who always seemed to be on hand to forage through the mob for a drink was Henry Wilberforce Grant. His greeting to her when they met on the evening of her speech was, "The lips of a strange woman drop as an honeycomb, and her mouth is smoother than oil."

"What the hell am I supposed to make of that?"

It was Henry Wilberforce Grant who got her a taxi after a late night sitting. They shared it as far as Camden Town. "This is where the hewers of wood and drawers of water live," he told her, as he departed into the night, presumably to his home.

It was Henry who invited her to go with him to the cricket match between the Commons and the Press Gallery in which he was playing. She accepted. The next day, this caused her a little embarrassment. Keith Shalton asked her: "Care to come along and see me swing a bat?" She told him she had already received an invitation.

"You're a much sought-after girl these days."

There was no point in trying to hide anything. He would know soon enough. "Actually, it's Henry Grant."

"Good for Henry," said Keith. The Winchester mask slipped. Barely perceptibly. But it slipped.

The match turned out to be more of a social occasion than a sporting event. It was played on the sports ground of the Herald Newspaper company in Essex. Henry drove her there in his battered old Hillman. She found there was quite a throng of members, journalists, wives, secretaries and possibly some mistresses. There was a tea tent and a bar, both doing thriving business. There was some cricket, but it was clearly an excuse for a mini social whirl in the sunshine.

Those who did note what was happening on the field of play were puzzled by one episode. Henry Grant was, as expected, the Commons' star batsman. It was fifteen years since he had played the first-class game, but his eye was still good, his timing near-perfect, and there was plenty of power in those bulky shoulders and arms. He opened for the Commons and quickly got going. When the third wicket fell at seventy, he had scored forty-four. He was then joined by Keith Shalton. By half-way through the next over, Keith was on three, with the strike, and Henry Wilberforce Grant was two short of his half-century. Then Keith pushed one slightly wide of mid-off. The fielder, a portly member of *The Times* parliamentary staff, was not exactly nimble, and it seemed to most of the spectators that the run was there for the taking. That was how it seemed to Henry. He was keen to get the bowling and chalk up his half-century. He went charging down the wicket. But Keith remained immovable in his crease. Two-thirds of the way down the pitch, Henry came to a juddering halt, and turned to get back, but had no chance. He was stranded in the middle of the pitch when the wicket was thrown down.

His displeasure as he walked back to the pavilion was plain for all to see. Helen, with her sketchy knowledge of the game, was not quite sure what had happened, but the conversation around her was illuminating.

"By God, if I was Keith Shalton, I'd keep out of the black man's way for a bit."

"A pretty shabby trick. What the hell was Shalton playing at?"

"I hope that fast merchant puts one in Shalton's courting tackle."

One voice took an apparently dissenting view. "It was Keith's call. It was up to him. He didn't call. At least, I didn't hear him. Old Henry jumped the gun. He wanted to hog the bowling."

The Commons won by thirty runs. The match over, the

serious purpose of the occasion, the drinking and socialising, was intensified. Everyone was very jolly. Or nearly everyone. Henry Wilberforce Grant was not jolly at all. He grabbed Helen's arm and said: "Come on. I've had enough of this crap."

On the way back to town, she asked him about the runout. Was it some sort of misunderstanding?

"Misunderstanding, my left buttock!" he said.

There was another misunderstanding about the cricket match. It is accepted that such social occasions involving M.P.s and journalists are private; that there is a confidentiality about what is seen and heard. A Press officer from the Home Office, who had attended as a guest, either didn't know the rule, or more probably maliciously broke it, knowing that Bernard had a thinly veiled contempt for Press officers, and regarded them as parasites on the true Civil Service. The Press officer met Bernard in the lift a couple of days after the match. "Hope your wife got home all right," he said to Bernard. "That old banger looked a bit shaky to me."

"What old banger?"

"Henry Grant's. You know, the black M.P. chap."

In his lunch hour, Bernard went to a public call box and dialled a certain number. A number he had dialled before.

Two by-elections were pending. Then the two became ten, when an airliner bringing home a deputation of M.P.s who had been studying industrial methods and other more interesting subjects in Japan, inexplicably piled itself into the South Downs on its run-in to Gatwick.

Three days later, Helen had a phone call from Henderson. Yes, of course she would be delighted to see him at the House. When he arived, she rather enjoyed playing the hostess and introducing him to people in the members' bar.

He said: "You seem to be settling in."

"Making progress."

"So I gather."

She wondered what exactly he meant by that.

"I hope," she said, "you think it was worthwhile, all the work you put in to get me here. It was your project. I just happened to come along at the right time."

"You're doing fine. And anyway, you may soon be getting reinforcements. These by-elections. Ten of them. I've been getting phone calls from people in some of those places. I think there could be one or two Patriot Party people standing in those elections."

"Would they have any chance?"

"I think one or two might give the opposition a run for their money."

"Then what?"

"Supposing a couple of them got in. Or say three. Then there is a Parliamentary group of the Patriot Party in existence. It would need a leader. I don't need to tell you who that would be. At first, you might be a leader of a party or group of two, though I think we'll do rather better than that. It seems to me there's quite a ground swell building up in our favour. But whatever happens at these by-elections, there's a longer-range situation, though it may not be so far away. That's the general election. We shall have quite a few candidates in the field then. The by-elections could be important to us in putting over the idea that the Patriot Party is not a local thing, and getting people all over the country introduced to the idea of voting for us."

"Can I help?"

"You can go and make speeches for some of these chaps standing at the by-elections."

"I'll do that. Anything else?"

"Nothing in particular. But there is just one thing."

"Yes?"

"This new rôle of yours, or this possible new rôle, as leader of a group . . ." There was untypical hesitancy in his voice.

"Well?"

92

"When it happens . . . if it happens, you will be in the public eye pretty well all the time, much more so than you have been just as one M.P. on your own."

"So?"

"People will be watching you. Some of them will be sniping at you. In fact, there's a bit of sniping going on already. At least, so I gathered from one of your Honourable and gallant colleagues when I lunched at the In and Out today."

"What are you talking about?"

"All I'm trying to say is: you will have to be careful."

"In what way, particularly?"

"For one thing, in the company you choose."

So that was it. Some tale-bearer from the House had been gossiping at his club. Wasn't there something about women's names not being mentioned in the club? Or was that in the mess? She was angry, but remained cool.

"I think I am of an age to choose my own company."

"You are of an age when you need to be damn careful in choosing your company."

PATRIOT Party candidates stood in six of the by-elections. Helen went to speak for three of them. Each time she was the star of the show.

On one trip to Barham, in south Yorkshire, she found that Henry Wilberforce Grant had been speaking for the Labour candidate on the same night. They met on the station while waiting for the night train back to London.

"Hello, white bitch," he greeted her genially.

"Hello, black bastard."

They travelled back in the same compartment, and when the train arrived at Kings Cross at 2.30 a.m. he had his old car near the station. He drove her home, or nearly home. At her request, he stopped the car two streets short of the flat. For ten minutes, they sat in the car, smoking and chatting. He was in his biblical mood: "The wicked flee when no man pursueth; but the righteous are as bold as lions." She walked the rest of the way to the flat. Neither had observed a decrepit builder's van which rumbled past as he gave her a chaste kiss on the pavement.

At eight o'clock next morning Bernard Chadwick made a telephone call. He listened attentively for two minutes, then said: "I see. You will send it to me in writing as usual."

Twenty minutes later he knocked on the door of his wife's room, received a muffled acknowledgement, and placed a tea tray on her bedside table.

"I thought you might be worn out by your exertions in the Northern counties . . ."

That was so like Bernard. If only . . .

"Bernard?"

"Yes, my dear?"

She knew it was hopeless. "Thank you for the tea."

"Think nothing of it. I must be away. The much-maligned Civil Service begins the day's work rather earlier than our political masters."

She lay in bed, brooding over various matters. If only . . .

THE Patriot Party did rather well in what the papers called the mini-election. Four of the six candidates won. But not at Barham. On the train to London, she had bet Henry Wilberforce Grant a fiver that her man would get in. But Labour won that one by 2,000.

She paid up cheerfully. And anyway, he spent it on her. He

94

took her out to dinner. The place he chose was well away from all the normal haunts of politicians. It was an Indian restaurant in Croydon. They went there separately. Although she was still seething over Henderson's strictures on her personal life, her instinct told her there was some sense in what he had said. She was not the least ashamed of being seen with a black man, but she had no desire to provide the gossip columnists with ammunition. Grant understood this too. The little restaurant had alcoves which provided privacy. None except the obliging and smooth-footed waiters could know that a white woman and a black man were dining in the recess at the end of the room.

The curry was good. They drank lager. She was curious about one thing, and her curiosity was increasing daily: What was his married status? She had looked him up in *Who's Who*, and there was no mention there of a wife, but she knew that the information in that tome was provided by the people who appeared in it, and could therefore be selective.

Over the coffee she came out with it: "What time is your wife expecting you home?"

He finished lighting his cigar, taking his time over it, then said: "No wife."

"Was there ever one?"

"There was. Once. It lasted three years. It was all right when I was playing cricket and getting my name in the papers and was a big man. Then I broke my wrist and had to pack it in a season or two earlier than I had intended. White cricketers get jobs as travellers for breweries. Black ones don't. I had to go on the buses. That didn't suit my little Louise. It didn't suit Louise at all. Not enough class. So she found herself a tame black barrister and he took her off to Zambia. He's a big man out there, I'm told."

"Are they still together?"

"Don't know. Don't care. Now I've got a question for you." She knew what was coming. She'd asked for it.

"You got a husband. But we don't see him around much. We don't see him at all."

"He's a Civil Servant."

"Is he doing his job?"

"He's highly thought of, I gather."

"You know what I mean. Is he doing his job?"

She looked down at the table cloth.

"So smarty-pants Shalton has been doing it for him?"

How could he possibly know about Keith and her? He gave her no time to ponder that mystery.

"Only smarty-pants has now retired hurt."

It seemed pointless to challenge these confident assertions.

"Any more questions?"

"Just one. Just this little question. How about you and me? Could you fancy a black man? I'm clean, you know. This colour don't come off."

She had half-expected that something like that would emerge before the evening was out. But now it had happened, she opted out.

"I shall need notice of that question."

He blew a huge cloud of smoke from his cigar.

"All right, white bitch. You got notice. One week."

At half-past ten, in Croydon, it seemed absurd to go through any security ritual. They left together, and walked to where he had left his car. There was a street musician scraping away on a violin, trying to do a bit of business with people who were leaving the pubs. He had collected a few coppers in his greasy hat on the pavement. Henry tossed in a tenpenny piece. "Blessed is he that considereth the poor. The Lord will deliver him in time of trouble."

When they had turned the corner, the fiddler put his instrument in its case, collected his takings, and used the 10p piece to make a phone call from the box on the other side of the road.

SIMULTANEOUS announcements in London and Washington informed the world that early in the spring, President Maloney would be making a State visit to Britain. Pete Mansell now doubled his efforts in the matter of "putting British crap into the file." Among the items he selected for his master's scrutiny was a ponderous piece from *The Times* headed "The swing to the Right". This reported the arrival at the Commons of the four new members of the Patriot Party, to join the one sitting member. There was an analysis of the voting figures at the by-elections, and a projection of what these trends would mean if repeated at a general election. The writer forecast that the Patriot Party could emerge from a general election with around twenty seats, and thus become the biggest minority group in Parliament.

The President read it closely. He had followed Mrs Chadwick's by-election adventures, and he had seen her speech on hanging. Now the President wondered if it was just possible that on his visit to Britain he would meet this tall, blonde woman. The official diary for the visit, which was already being sketched out, provided for informal meetings with the leaders of all parties. By the time he arrived, he wondered, would this woman in the tight pants rank as a "political leader"? He sincerely hoped so.

Meanwhile, the visit was posing other problems. He was wondering just how much of the astronomical cost of his wife's wardrobe for the occasion could be borne from public funds, and how much he would have to meet himself. He feared the worst.

In Britain, the announcement had made news for a day, and was then displaced by more sombre events. The economy had taken a sickening lurch when the seamen went on strike, crippling the country's export trade. The dispute was settled after three weeks, but not until contingency plans had been drawn up for petrol rationing, the pound had hit its lowest level for four years, and the dole queue had lengthened to two-and-a-half million. The terms of the seamen's settlement infuriated workers in other industries, and started a chain reaction of claims.

The Labour Government of Percy Bainbridge had been in

power for three-and-a-half years. Clearly it was in its death throes. Every time Bainbridge made a public appearance, he was surrounded by demonstrators shouting "Out! Out! Out!" There was another Budget, the third within fourteen months. Inevitably it increased still further the taxes on tobacco, liquor and betting. The Tories bayed for blood. There were two votes of confidence in the House. On each occasion a few left-wing Labour members abstained, claiming that the Government had abandoned Socialism, but the Tories, even with the support of the Patriot Party's five members, did not quite have the numbers to force the issue.

Oddly, the showdown, when it came, was only indirectly connected with the economy. It was provoked by one of Bainbridge's junior ministers, Harold Spencer, the under-secretary for the Navy. When the Government announced that as part of its spending cuts, it was shelving orders for two planned new destroyers, Spencer resigned. That would not have mattered greatly if the exchange of resignation letters had followed the normal restrained pattern. It did not. Spencer, in his letter which was published in the newspapers, flatly called Bainbridge a liar. Bainbridge had said that the Government had never given a formal commitment to the Defence Chiefs that the two ships would go ahead. Spencer said it had, and that there was a copy of a letter recording this decision in the file in his office.

The Tories pounced for the kill. Bainbridge, who had never been closely personally involved in the ships affair, had not deliberately lied to the House; he had merely, in haste, misread a document which had been put before him. But the damage was done. The pledged word of a British Prime Minister had proved utterly worthless, claimed the Tories. How could he any longer speak for Britain either at home or abroad? The extreme Labour left, which had long been dissatisfied with Bainbridge on numerous counts, decided that this was the time to rat on him.

The vote, on the motion "That this House no longer has any confidence in the ability of Her Majesty's Government to conduct the affairs of this nation" was taken at ten o'clock at night after a six-hour debate.

In the hubbub that followed the closing speech, the Speaker

said: "I think the ayes have it." From the Labour loyalists came a furious roar of "No".

The Speaker said: "Clear the Lobbies."

The division bells sounded throughout the Palace of Westminster and in those nearby establishments linked to the bell system.

The House divided. The vote was: For the motion, 320, against 302.

The Government of Percy Bainbridge had fallen.

The drama in the Commons had one incidental consequence. It blew up on the night that Helen was due to make another visit to Croydon with Henry Wilberforce Grant and give him her answer to his proposition. For the moment, she was spared the need to commit herself.

It was a strange election. In the first week, the theme of all the commentators was the disarray of the Labour Party. There were forecasts that the Tories would have a majority of well over a hundred. But the first opinion polls did not support that view. The voters, it seemed, shared the secret fears of Marlowe (who was coming under some criticism from his own side for not being abrasive enough). They did not see how a change of Government could change the condition of the nation overnight. And there was a bit of sympathy for Bainbridge. Perhaps he *had* got the ships thing muddled up, and the Tories had taken advantage of it and had injured the country by forcing an election at the worst possible moment. The new forecasts, when these feelings began to seep through, were of a Tory majority of around forty. But even so, it seemed to Helen that Keith's plotting between overs at Lords was not going to lead to much. "You should have stuck to the cricket," she said when she met him at Paddington Station when they were both on the point of departing to attend meetings in the West Country.

She had, too, one brief encounter with Henry Grant. That also was at a railway station, at Nottingham. Both were encumbered by supporters, and they had only a few seconds together.

"Hello, white bitch."

"Hello, black bastard."

"Haven't we got some unfinished business?

"Remind me sometime when I'm less busy."

"I'll do that."

It was difficult for Helen to judge the success of her own campaign. A total of seventy-six candidates had come forward to stand for the Patriot Party. Some were obviously no-hopers, and Helen thought the party would have been better off without them. But Henderson, who was organising the campaign with dedicated efficiency, said that the party's great need was nationwide publicity, and that even no-hopers added their quota towards that end.

At the half-way stage, the three leading public-opinion polls gave the Patriot Party twelve, fifteen and eighteen seats respectively. Her own meetings, both in Midhampton and in the ten other constituencies she visited, were packed and noisy, and most of the noise was on the right side. The Patriot Party could certainly get people to turn out to listen to its speakers, but how much of this was curiosity attendance, and how many would actually vote for the party was anybody's guess. There was no precedent for judging a national campaign for that type of party.

She saw Bernard only once or twice a week, and then briefly. He was solicitous but not insistent in his inquiries about the progress of her campaign. By tacit consent they never discussed political issues.

Several mornings, when she slept late after exhausting activities, she woke to find a tea tray on the bedside table, the pot still warm under its cosy. He had left it there before silently departing to the office.

If only . . .

It was bad luck on the Tories that with ten days to go, the

North Midlands Fortress Insurance Company went bust, leaving four hundred thousand people, mainly motorists and house-holders, without cover. For the chairman of the Fortress was a Tory City man, Sir Frederick Garrett, and on the board were no fewer than three other Tory M.Ps. It seemed that £2,000,000 which ought to have been in the company's coffers had vanished. The City editors were hinting as strongly as they dared, in view of the law of libel, that it may have been switched to some of Sir Frederick's other enterprises, which were known to be ailing. The Fraud Squad were investigating. Illogically but inevitably, the spin-off affected the image of the whole Tory position. "All tarred with the same brush, if you ask me," said the man on the top of the bus. No-one had asked him, but no one contradicted him. Candidates for the other parties studiously avoided mentioning the affair. They did not need to. Their silence on this issue was deafening. The scandal made the latest opinion poll forecasts – which were already cutting the estimates of the Tory majority to thirty-five – irrelevant. It occurred to Helen, as she made her tour of Midhampton on the morning of the election, that Keith Shalton's conspiracy, of which not one word had leaked to the press, might not be such an academic thing after all.

Henderson drove her relentlessly, right to the end, until the polling booths closed. Midhampton was, after all, the flagship of the Patriot Party cause, and the campaign there had attracted a good deal of attention. The television teams had made several forays and now, with the declaration of the result only hours away, they were installing themselves at vantage points covering the town hall balcony.

This time, Bernard was not coming to Midhampton for the declaration of the poll. "I approve of democracy," he had told her, "but I find the mechanics of the thing a little wearisome. But I hope everything goes well for you, and that your varied activities at Westminster will not be interrupted by anything so mundane as a general election." She had been a little disappointed. She would have liked him to share the triumph she was pretty sure she was going to have (though the Tory candidate in Midhampton this time was a young local councillor and a better type than the barrister she had beaten at the by-election). What would Bernard be doing now? Presumably reclining in front of the ornately-encased television set at Pargrave Mansions, sipping sherry, and pondering in a detached way on the frailties and shortcomings of politicians of all parties.

It was only when the voting stations had closed and she herself was able to take a leisurely drink at the George before going to the town hall, that the thought suddenly struck her: *"Your varied activities at Westminster"*. In his use of the English language, Bernard was always precise, even to the point of pedantry. Her *varied* activities. It was a slightly odd thing for him to have said. Slightly disturbing, too.

THE first three results to be announced on the television were all Labour victories. That, in itself, meant nothing. They were all from compact boroughs where the votes could be collected quickly, and were bomb-proof Labour seats. The Tory strength lay in the outer suburban areas, and in the country districts. What was significant was that the Labour margins in those first three seats were down by around five per cent. The pundits and the computers at last had something to work on. The great show had begun.

Within twenty minutes, seven more results had come in. Henry Wilberforce Grant was back, as everyone had assumed he would be, but his majority was down by 2,000. It was the eleventh result which provided the first real spark: "Tory gain from Labour". And the nineteenth which caused an eruption at the Patriot Party assembly at the George: "Patriot Party gain from Labour". There were two more Tory gains from Labour. Two Patriot Party candidates were defeated. Then it was time for Helen to go to the town hall.

The wily town clerk had arranged things so that no casual

observer could assess how things were going and leak an un-official forecast of the result. But it was clear from the state of the counting tables that the count was more than half over. There was subdued but intense activity. People hurried from table to table on mysterious missions. Around each candidate there was a group of acolytes. The Labour man was stoking a pipe that was already going like a furnace. It had been a fierce campaign, but a clean one. The young Tory came over to Helen with outstretched hand and said: "A bit like pacing up and down outside the maternity ward waiting for one's first-born to arrive, eh?"

"I can imagine so; though I've never had that experience."

"No. Of course. I was forgetting . . ." He drifted away. She hoped she hadn't snubbed him. He didn't seem a bad sort.

One of Henderson's team had a transistor radio with ear-plugs, and kept her up-to-date with the state of play across the country. "We've gone down at Barham." Helen was not sur-prised. "Barrington's in." Barrington was the Patriot Party man in a Bristol division. "Labour thirty-six, Tories twenty, two to us. One Scot Nat." Then: "Shalton's back. Majority two thousand."

At half-past ten: "Labour sixty-eight, Tories forty-three, us four, Scot Nats two."

The other parties' teams in the town hall had their radio reporters, and the figures caused no jubilation whatsoever in the Labour camp. To have a chance of ultimate victory, it was not just a lead that was needed at that stage, but a thumping one. Otherwise, it would be obliterated when the results came in from the country areas the following day. Labour was not getting that lead. But neither was there much joy among the Tories. They had hoped to close the gap more than they had done. The Tory landslide forecast in the campaign was not materialising.

In the Town Hall, Helen could read the signs. Counting had finished, the counters were lighting cigarettes and drinking cups of tea. On the Town Clerk's master table, the final check was being made. It seemed to take an unnecessary time, as if he was doing the same thing over and over again. Now he was writing something, and checking what he had written, and checking it again. Then, with a slip of paper in his hand, he was moving to the platform where the mayor was bracing himself for his moment of glory on television. The ritual of the by-election was followed. The mayor, the town clerk, the candidates and their privileged aides, formed themselves into a little procession which moved across the crowded hall to the steps which led to the balcony at the other end. The balcony was lit like a stage by television lights, and Helen could see little of the scene in the blackness below. But there was evidently a huge throng down there. The noise surged up to the balcony, and it was a full minute before it had subsided enough for the mayor to approach the microphone.

The drama of the occasion was diminished, to a certain extent, by an unavoidable circumstance. Candidates names are always announced in alphabetical order. Thus a no-hoper may have his name read first, keeping the crowd in suspense for the figures that really matter. Not so on this occasion. The mayor, having tapped the microphone, making it produce alarming barking noises, began to read: "I, Percival Horace Wilkins, being the returning officer for the Midhampton Division, declare the number of votes cast to be as follows: Helen Mary Chadwick, 19,304 . . ."

That was enough. Everyone knew that was a winning total. The eruption from the crowd below swamped the mayor as he ploughed on with the other figures. They did not matter greatly. Helen Chadwick was back with a majority increased by 5,000.

On every television network, the waffle teams applied their mighty intellects to the implications of the Midhampton result. Mr Ray Grimshaw, whose many appearances in the anchor-man rôle gave him an almost proprietorial interest in general elections, made one of the more foolish predictions of the night. He said that the Midhampton result meant that the Patriot Party, still awaiting results in many winable seats, could well have forty members in the new Parliament.

In fact, the Patriot Party had precisely half that number. And it was a photo-finish election.

The Ulster group (mainly Tory, but not to be relied on infallibly to vote Tory in the House on all occasions) had twelve. The Scottish Nationalists had six. The Liberals had five.

That left five hundred and ninety-two seats to be split between the two main parties.

The Tories had done it. But only just. They had two hundred and ninety-nine, the Labour Party two hundred and ninety-three.

It was enough, technically and constitutionally, for Marlowe to form a Government. But could a Government with such a tiny and vulnerable majority govern a nation which some said was near to becoming ungovernable? During the election, the pound had slumped. It fell again when the final figures were known. The election, so far from putting Britain on the Right Road (to use the phrase in the Tory manifesto) had led the country into a dead end. No party had a decisive mandate from the electors. But the Tories did have one advantage, though it was not one which aroused any great enthusiasm, either with Marlowe or his senior cadre of advisers. There were those twenty members returned under the Patriot Party label. Surely they would stand by the Tories in this crisis? After all, what was the Patriot Party but a right-wing adjunct of the Tory party? Gone off the rails a bit. But most of them were made of the right stuff. The Chadwick woman was a silly bitch, but she'd behaved herself since she'd been in the House.

In *The Times* office that night a portentous leading article was being drafted. Its tenor was that the country had clearly not made up its mind what it really wanted; and that the only way for this to be determined would be to hold another general election.

But while the leader writer was still hunched over his typewriter, it became clear that a quite different solution was under consideration at Number 10 Downing Street. Bainbridge's Government, which had been operating on a caretaker basis during the election, was still in office. He was still Prime Minister, and would remain so until the Sovereign, acting on advice received, sent for a successor. For the moment, she had received no sufficiently clear advice as to who that would be. She tickled a Corgi's tummy, and let the politicians get on with sorting themselves out. All evening, there was a series of arrivals and departures at Downing Street, mostly by members of Bainbridge's cabinet.

Then, at 8.30 p.m., the Press Association tape machines chattered out the message which caused *The Times* leader writer to tear up what he had written. It generated frantic activity in newspaper offices, and caused every television network to interrupt its programme for a news flash. It was prefixed by the P.A.'s "urgent attention" code. It said: "Rush. Rush. Mr Marlowe arrived at 10 Downing street at 8.25."

Even the messengers who hurried across the news rooms to hand the message to back-bench executives understood its portent.

Bainbridge and Marlowe were cooking up a coalition deal.

Keith Shalton heard the news at a house in St John's Wood, where there was an assembly of the leading members of the Long Room conspiracy. It had been a cheerful assembly. The election had worked out precisely as they had hoped. They were poised to strike. The one thing momentarily holding them back was the possibility that there would be an early announcement of another election. In that event, there would be no point in their showing their hand. The *coup* would have to wait until the alignment of the parties after the new election was known.

The news from Downing Street changed everything.

Keith phoned Helen, who was still at the flat at Midhampton. "Yes, tonight. We may be too late. It's got to be tonight or never."

It was a fine night, and the speed cops were evidently taking their supper break. She arrived at the address Keith had given her at 10.15. While Keith was effecting brief introductions, he was interrupted by another TV news flash: "The following statement was issued from Number 10 Downing Street five minutes ago. The Prime Minister and Mr Christopher Marlowe tonight had preliminary talks on the possibility of the formation of a Coalition Government to see the country through the present critical period. Both the Prime Minister and Mr Marlowe are to consult their senior colleagues. The discussions will be resumed tomorrow morning." The announcer added that Mr Marlowe had left 10 Downing Street ten minutes ago, after spending an hour and a half with the Prime Minister.

Marlowe lived in an Edwardian house in Putney. "I'll give him a quarter of an hour," said Keith, "then I'll ring him. I rather doubt if he includes me among his senior advisers, but perhaps he may have second views before the night is out."

He completed the introductions. The house belonged to Sir Percy Tilson, an industrialist who had represented a Tory pocket borough in the plushier part of North London for twenty years. Apart from him and Keith, four others were there, all holders of safe Tory seats. Helen knew them all by sight. There was Grayson, who had recently inherited the Grayson book publishing empire; Willets who was something in the City; Johnson who farmed in Lincolnshire and was the Tory spokesman on agricultural matters; and Colonel James Ferguson, who saw himself as an expert on defence matters on the basis of his long army service. He, she thought, was the most likeable of the lot. He had taken his commission from the ranks, and had won an M.C. in Korea. So this was the Long Room mob, or some of them. Not exactly the intellectual *crème de la crème* of the Party, but not lightweights. All people of some standing and considerable service. Keith was the youngest, but obviously he had the quickest, most incisive brain.

At ten-thirty, Keith consulted a little pocket book in which he kept a list of ex-directory numbers, and made his call. "Hello. Is Mr Whittaker there?" Whittaker was Marlowe's parliamentary private secretary. "Hello, Charles? Listen, Charles. Keith Shalton here. I have a most urgent message for your master . . ."

Obviously there was some testy interruption from the other end. Then Keith surprised Helen by his ruthlessness. "Charles, let's get this straight. You are the message boy. Tonight there are things going on which will affect the future of this party for the next twenty years. And unless you want it to be said that the Tory Party fell to bits because the message boy was too stupid to receive and pass on a message, you will listen carefully to what I have to say. The message is this: that there is a substantial number of senior members of this party, for whom I am the spokesman, who are deeply concerned over what appears to be happening, so deeply concerned, in fact, that if things develop as they are now going, these members would have to consider their position in relation to the Party Whip. What? No, I am not going to discuss with you how many or

107

who they are. I will do that with Marlowe; and in fairness to Marlowe, and for the sake of the future of this Party, it is absolutely essential that I see Marlowe before he takes an irretrievable decision. And that means tonight. I should tell you that I have a tape recorder hooked to this phone, so it will all be on record, and there can be no subsequent argument about who said what, or whether I made the position absolutely clear. So will you please now go and tell Marlowe it is imperative that I see him *tonight*. Yes, I'll hang on . . ."

Helen said: "I can't see any tape recorder thing."

"Good Lord!" said Keith, "I must have left it at home."

For three minutes, Keith was kept waiting. Then: "Right. Half-past eleven. I'll be there. And by the way, tell Marlowe that I shall be bringing with me Mrs Helen Chadwick."

Marlowe kept them waiting. When they arrived at his double-fronted mansion, the policeman on duty outside made a great performance of checking their identities. Keith guessed Marlowe had put him up to it, just to put them in their places, just to let them know that they were people of no account. Finally, when they were allowed to enter, a middle-aged female retainer showed them into a drawing room, and said: "The master will be a minute or two. He's got some people with him." In fact, it was ten minutes before Marlowe appeared. He was in his most frigid mood.

"I understand," he said, addressing Keith, "you wish to discuss with me some matter affecting the future of the party. I don't wish to seem discourteous, but in that case, should not this discussion be confined to members of the party?"

Keith said: "Given time, we might have a most interesting discussion about who and what is entitled to be called the Tory Party. Different people have different definitions. But there's no time. You will be seeing Bainbridge again tomorrow."

"If I am, do I need the permission of a junior member of the party who has not always shown judgment of the highest quality?"

"We have come to advise you not to get mixed up in any deal with Bainbridge."

"If I require advice—"

"In any dealings you have with Bainbridge, you will be relying on the support of the group of M.P.s led by Mrs Chadwick. You are assuming that that would make you the senior partner, and would ensure a high Tory element in any Coalition cabinet, and among other things would enable you personally to take over as Prime Minister."

"My personal future is of quite secondary importance. As for the support of Mrs Chadwick's group, in general terms it might be an assistance; in my negotiations, it might be an embarrassment."

"Don't let's play games. The parties are split evenly. You just can't afford to write off a group of twenty M.P.s. Not the way things are."

"Mrs Chadwick is a free agent. And since she is here, though I am by no means clear as to her status in this discussion, is she not capable of speaking for herself?"

Helen said: "The Patriot Party is committed to nobody − yet."

"It seems to me, my dear lady," said Marlowe, "that you are in danger of allowing yourself to be used in an intrigue. That is an unwise thing to do for someone who is, shall we say, a little inexperienced in these matters."

"Don't be so bloody condescending."

"It always distresses me to hear ladies swear. Particularly in this house."

Keith said: "Well, here's something that will distress you a bloody sight more. If you do this deal with Bainbridge, you will not have the support of Mrs Chadwick's members. But that is not the half of it. You will not have the full support of the Tory Party."

Marlowe's face remained impassive. "Do I understand that there has been some kind of plot?"

"Consultations."

"And am I to be informed of the nature of these . . . er . . . consultations?"

"There are some people in this party who feel strongly that in recent years the party has run out of ideas. And run out of guts, too. It's gone soft. And that it no longer speaks or acts as a Tory Party should."

"Indeed?" Marlowe was still inscrutable. "And who are these

people to whom this great truth has been vouchsafed? Apart from yourself, of course."

"People who carry weight. Quite a lot of weight."

"And just how many have had this great revelation?"

"Around twenty. Which is enough."

"Enough to do what?"

"Enough, with Mrs Chadwick's group, to form a viable alternative Tory Party. A party which a good many people in the House and in the country would regard as the true Tory Party. And when it got rolling, I reckon there would be a lot more than twenty who would come over. The party would be split, perhaps not down the middle, but quite possible two to one."

"And what exactly is this true Tory Party going to do? Don't tell me it's going to save the Party's soul. I have a great distrust of savers of souls."

Helen said: "We didn't come here to discuss souls."

"Then what did you come for?"

"To put a practical proposition," said Keith.

"Which is?"

"That the Patriot Party should publicly and formally declare its support for the Tory Party. In fact, to give you twenty solid votes. Which means that you can form a Tory Government which will be safe for at least four years, without any fear of getting bounced by some snap vote of confidence late at night. Which, surely, from your point of view, from the party's and indeed from the country's, is a better prospect than a patched-up thing with Bainbridge?"

"How very kind of Mrs Chadwick. I am deeply touched."

Keith said: "There will be conditions."

"I am not accustomed to being presented with conditions from a relatively junior member of the party."

"Then make an exception in this case. And bear in mind that the future of the Tory Party is being decided, here and now, in this room. The conditions are, firstly, that the leadership of the party should point the way back to the traditional concepts of Toryism. I am sure I don't have to spell that out. And secondly . . ."

"Ah, I thought there would be a secondly."

"Secondly, that any new administration formed by you with

110

the support of Mrs Chadwick's group should not only be committed to those concepts, but should be clearly seen to be so committed. That involves some thought to the structure and composition of the administration."

"I see. Jobs for the boys. And for the lady, of course."

Helen said: "The Patriot Party is offering you a damn sight more than you can give in return."

"And supposing I reject this curious proposition?"

Keith said: "Let us do a bit of gazing into crystal balls. You do a deal with Bainbridge. It won't last. I know that. You know that. It will be a botched-up thing, neither Tory nor Socialist, and it will just bring discredit on everybody who's in it. In addition, you will have to face the opposition of an alternative Tory Party, this is, Mrs Chadwick's group, the people I have been in contact with and who are pledged to withdraw from the Tory party in these circumstances, and the considerable though unknown number of people who would join us once the position was made clear. How long can that possibly last? Six months? Nine months? A year at the outside. Then you will want to disengage. You will want to get out. At least, whether you want it or not, the party will demand it. They won't stand for being saddled indefinitely with the Bainbridge mob. They will want to go it alone. Whether you want to or not, the party will *insist* on getting out. But the Tory Party won't come out in one piece. It will never be the same again. There will be two Tory Parties in the country, and that means that the Tories can kiss goodbye to any hope of winning an election for the next ten years. It took the Socialists longer than that to put the pieces together when *they* split up. And when the Liberals split, they *never* put it together again. And you will be the man who did it. You will be the Ramsay Macdonald of the Tory Party. That's what I see in my crystal ball. What do you see in yours?"

Marlowe said: "Have you ever thought of teaching modern political history? At one of the polytechnics, perhaps."

Helen could not help admiring him. His utter calm and impassivity. Poor Keith, she thought. Marlowe will fix him now. Marlowe will fix him for good.

Marlowe moved towards the massive fireplace and pressed a

bell. It was one of those houses where bells could be pressed and people made to appear. The middle-aged retainer stumped in.

"Mrs Hodgkins, I think we should like some coffee. Could that be arranged?" The woman stumped out.

"Mrs Chadwick," said Marlowe, "I agree your maiden speech was admirable. Quite admirable. Personally, I did not agree with the content, but I thought the argument was well put, and delivered with conviction. I gather you feel strongly on the subject of law and order."

"I do."

"That's interesting. Most interesting. Tell me, Mrs Chadwick, how would you feel about serving in my administration as Home Secretary?"

BERNARD was still up when she arrived at Pargate Mansions. "My word," he said, "you politicians keep late hours."

She said nothing of her rôle in the night's events, or of her pending elevation. Better to wait until it was announced officially. She had just the faintest suspicion that when Marlowe saw Bainbridge in the morning, he might renege.

"I think," Bernard told her, "that I am entitled to some small honorarium from the Patriot Party. One doesn't wish to be too mercenary about it. Shall we say a dozen bottles of sherry? I'll tell them where to get it."

"I don't follow."

"Since your emergence as a Party leader, the phone has been ringing day and night."

"Anything important?"

"How would I know? Press people. Television and radio people. And by the way. Do you take carrot juice? I told them

112

I thought you preferred Scotch."

"Carrot juice?"

"It appears that some ladies' magazine is about to produce a great carrot-juice diet to give the mature woman added zest. They want you to sponsor it. They want to present you as the Carrot-Juice Woman."

"Christ!"

In the morning, they had a rare reversal of rôles. It was she who left tea by his bedside. "Up and out so soon?" he asked. "You politicians do lead hectic lives."

BAINBRIDGE began the day as Prime Minister. He had been deluding himself that he could well retain his office if the Coalition Government plan went through. Those hopes were killed by his ten-minute session with Marlowe. That was at ten o'clock. By eleven the evening newspapers had early editions on the streets announcing the pact between the Conservatives and the Patriot Party. The *Standard*'s lead story said: "The Conservative Party and the Patriot Party today issued a joint statement pledging themselves to work in full co-operation to get the nation back on its feet. This kills last night's speculation about the possibility of a Tory-Labour coalition. Mr Christopher Marlowe will be Prime Minister before the day is out."

And so it was. At noon, Bainbridge went to Buckingham Palace to tender his resignation. At three o'clock, the Queen performed her constitutional rôle in the nation's affairs by "sending for" the Right Honourable Christopher Marlowe, and permitting him to kiss her hand, which he did with delicacy, in token of assuming office as Her Majesty's First Minister of State, more usually known as the Prime Minister.

At five o'clock, Marlowe installed himself in 10 Downing

113

Street. At eight o'clock he issued the first list of ministers who would form his Government.

Named as Secretary of State for Home Affairs was Mrs Helen Chadwick.

Keith Shalton got rather less than he had expected. He was made undersecretary at the Commonwealth Office, with special responsibility for liaising with the former colonies on matters of immigration.

Helen had spent the day at Westminster. She went home tired, but exultant. It was, after all, no small achievment to reach Cabinet rank within eight months of entering Parliament. She wondered if it had ever been done before, or if she would qualify for an entry in *The Guinness Book of Records*.

She had assumed that Bernard, in his restrained way, would share her moment of triumph. But his reaction stunned her.

He said: "Damn you!"

It was the first time in their fifteen years of marriage that he had ever openly displayed anger. She was completely mystified.

"What have I done?"

"I will tell you what you have done. You have destroyed my career. But don't let it worry you. I don't suppose it will."

She was still totally in the dark. Then he made all things clear.

"I have tonight put in for a transfer from the Office. There doesn't seem to be much going at the moment. I shall probably end up in the Forestry Commission."

Then it dawned on her what she had done. With her as the political head of the Home Office, it would be impossible for him to remain there as a senior member of the permanent staff. Civil Service procedure would rule that out. So would Bernard's fastidious sense of the Done Thing.

"God! I never thought of that."

"I believe you. I believe you entirely. I'm sure it would be the last thing you would think of. I fully understand that you must have your little prize for coming to the aid of the party. But there are twenty departments you could have gone to. And you just happen to pick the one that means that I have to abandon work which I happen to enjoy and which I believe to be of some consequence, and into which I've put a dozen years on my life."

"I tell you . . ."

"Don't bother to tell me anything. You've told it me all. What's the Office to you? Just a plaything. You'll play with it for six months, and then drop it. But for me, it happens to be a career. And by the time you've moved on to more exalted things, or got bored with the whole lot and taken up rug-making, it will be too late for me to get back."

"Bernard. I'm sorry. I'm really sorry."

"You must brush aside your tears. Meanwhile, if you will excuse me, I'm going to my club. I've packed a bag and booked a room."

"For God's sake why?"

"The Minister might wish to invite some of her Parliamentary colleagues to discuss high matters of policy. It would be inappropriate for one of my humble station to be present. Incidentally, you will find that that is a most useful word. Inappropriate. It is used in the Office quite extensively to justify courses of action that have no legal or moral basis. I find it inappropriate to remain here in view of your choice of Government office.

"And incidentally, there is one more thing which I find exceedingly inappropriate."

"All right. Let's have it."

"I find it inappropriate that my wife, whatever her political status, should consort with a black man. Good night. Possibly we shall meet in the office tomorrow."

THE new Government got off to a good start. Marlowe astonished both his supporters and his opponents by the vigour with which he proclaimed the Government's intentions to see that the interests of the nation as a whole overrode any

115

sectional interest. Some of his more timid ministers forecast that this would lead to an immediate confrontation with the unions. They were wrong. It seemed that the men who headed the big battalions of workers, although making ritual noises, sensed that their members, as much as anyone else, were fed up with the drift towards disaster, and welcomed a new start. For the moment, at any rate, the country was prepared to accept the smack of firm Government.

For Helen, the first weeks of the Tory-Patriot Party alliance were stimulating. First she had to meet the distinguished permanent under-secretary of her department. He turned out to be a bland, highly civilised man in his middle fifties named Ian Blair. She suspected that beneath the blandness there was a bit of steel, and liked him for it. He displayed a deference which fell short of subservience, and seemed genuinely sorry about Bernard's abrupt and enforced departure. "A great loss to the Department," he said, "but a gain for the Stationery Office." That was where Bernard had been shunted to. Helen thought she would get on all right with this Mr Blair, though she wondered precisely how his degree in mediaeval European history (she had looked him up) qualified him to advise on whether an illegal immigrant who had spent two blameless years in Britain driving trains on the London underground should now be deported.

Then there were the Cabinet meetings. The Cabinet, she found, met round a coffin-shaped table in a long room on the ground floor of Number Ten. Marlowe sat in the centre seat of one side, below the portrait of Walpole, with the Chancellor, Metcalfe, on his right and the Foreign Secretary, Torrington, on his left. She was well down in the pecking order, near the end of the table. More than half of Marlowe's ministers had served in previous governments, and Helen had the new-girl-at-school feeling again. At the meetings in the first week, she listened and said little. In any case, she was not directly concerned in the subject which dominated the meetings, the state of the economy. It was the voice of the ponderous Metcalfe which was heard most often.

It was a bank raid that changed things. Two gunmen, surprised by the brave intervention of a bank messenger,

116

abandoned their enterprise and fled to their getaway car. In panic they fired five shots. When the car screeched away, the messenger was left dying on the floor of the bank. And on the pavement outside was a five-year-old girl who had been walking past the bank with her mother. She had a bullet in her heart. She died in the ambulance.

Public outrage was enormous. The demand for the return of hanging erupted like a volcano. And at the end of the next day's Cabinet meeting, when Marlowe said: "Well, I think that's the lot," Helen spoke up from her lowly seat and said: "Not quite."

Marlowe pointedly looked at his watch.

"You've seen the morning papers?" asked Helen.

"Of course."

"Then you will agree we cannot totally ignore this bank raid in Wimbledon.

"You may have to make a statement in the House. I suggest that you keep it short and noncommittal. Sympathy for the relatives. Police making an all-out effort. That sort of thing."

"I don't think that will quite do. You will recall that I have given a personal undertaking on the subject of capital punishment."

"I am aware of your feelings. But nothing you have said in the House or outside it could possibly commit a government that did not then exist. In any case, there are more urgent matters. The time of the House is fully committed."

"Then, Prime Minister, I suggest that the business of the House be re-arranged."

It was the first clash of wills in the new Cabinet. Most of Marlowe's ministers were content to remain interested spectators, and to wait and see how Marlowe would deal with this uppity female. But Helen found she had some allies. One was Willis, the brisk, incisive Minister for Defence. Another was Curtis, Environment; a third was the Secretary of State for Ireland, Matheson. They all said the same thing. That they had for years either been against capital punishment, or had had open minds, but the recent spate of murders, of which the bank shooting was the most shocking, had reluctantly driven them to the view that all existing penalties had failed. Willis said the mood of the country was ripe for a change.

117

"I have no intention," said Marlowe icily, "of governing this country according to the instincts of the mob."

Willis said: "It's not a question of giving in to the mob. I can foresee situations, if the matters we have been talking about this morning don't work out as we hope and expect, in which this penalty might be needed to keep some of the madder elements of the mob under control."

Helen went further, much further, than she had intended.

"Prime Minister, in view of this latest shooting, and my publicly stated position, I do not see how I could remain a member of this Government unless the House is at least given a chance to discuss this issue."

That brought a chilling silence to the Cabinet room. She was playing for high stakes. But Marlowe, as always, was unruffled.

"A little early", he said, "to start talking about resignations, is it not? I am already late. We will discuss this at a later date."

They came back to it three days later; three days in which every member of Parliament had been bombarded by constituents demanding the return of capital punishment; three days of demonstrations and marches; three days of newspaper agitation. Some in the Cabinet who had previously remained silent now spoke. The groundswell of opinion in the country had at last penetrated the Cabinet room at Number Ten. By a small majority, the Cabinet were in favour of the restoration of hanging; with the exception of Metcalfe, who was Marlowe's man in all things, all were agreed that the matter must be put to the House for debate and vote. Marlowe, a sincere opponent of the rope, just had to yield in the face of this pressure. He agreed that Helen should introduce a capital-punishment bill, but insisted that she do so as a private member, not as a minister speaking on behalf of the Government. The Whips would be off. All, including Cabinet Ministers, would be free to vote according to conscience.

It was a fair deal. Twice in recent years the House had voted against capital punishment. Now it was going to have a chance to say whether, in the light of recent events, it had changed its mind. For Helen, it was a victory. She had pledged herself to try. And no matter how the vote went, she had fulfilled that pledge.

118

Outside Downing Street, life was interesting, too.

For instance, the matter of some unfinished business with Henry Wilberforce Grant. Just how much did Bernard know about that? It had been stupid of her, after he had told her that he had known all along about Keith Shalton, not to realise that he would still have been having her watched. Did it matter? How much did he know? In any case, there wasn't much to know — yet.

She had wondered several times just how much of Bernard's anger derived from the job situation, and how much of it was centered on Henry Wilberforce Grant. Clearly he found her association with Grant a far greater affront than all her previous affairs, including that with Keith Shalton. It was odd, really, that Bernard who, of all people, stood for liberal-minded racial toleration, should feel that way. Or was it? Supposing Bernard had had women, supposing he had been capable of having women, would she specially have objected to his having a black woman? She was damn sure she would. It occurred to her in a wry moment that perhaps she had missed a trick. Perhaps she should have told him that she would go to the Race Discrimination Board: "My husband lets me have it off with white men, but he objects now that I have a black man . . ."

In fact, she had decided, before that scene with Bernard in the flat, that it would be a good thing to disengage from Henry Wilberforce Grant. It was not that she did not find him attractive. He was a fine big animal of a man. But some undefined thing inside her put the brake on. That was how it was until that night. But unwittingly, Bernard had opened up the issue again. For the first time in their marriage, he had openly challenged her. It was too late for challenges. If Bernard wanted to make challenges, he should have done so a long time ago, a damn long time ago, when it all started.

But the whole thing was now mixed up by the circumstances of her new life. She found that it was difficult, almost impossible, for a minister to keep an assignation absolutely private. First, there is the fact that the minister's face is in-

119

stantly recognisable to anyone who reads a newspaper or watches television. Then there was the snooping of the Press, with their informants among hotel and restaurant staff; and there was a far greater handicap than all these: the minister's personal detective.

Because of the danger of terrorist activity, every minister of Cabinet rank has a Special Branch detective assigned to him or her (some have two). The detective shadows the minister from his home to the office, from the office to the House, and to his luncheon and dining places. He lunches, at the public expense, at the same restaurant as the minister, choosing a table from which he can keep an eye on the whole room. He shadows the minister back to the House, and on his evening engagements, and finally to his home. Not until the door shuts behind the minister is the detective's work done for the day; it starts in the morning at whatever time the minister decides to leave his house.

Helen's detective was Sergeant Sidney Gardner, whom she soon got into the habit of calling Sid. Sid was a discreetly dressed young man, who looked more like a junior executive in Woolworths than a member of the Special Branch. Somewhere under his quite elegant suit, presumed Helen, there must be a gun, but there was no bulge to show where. Sid was always unobtrusive, but always vigilant. Sid could become a bit of a problem.

Of course, she still saw Henry at the House. One lunch time they found themselves next to each other in Annie's Bar.

"How's life in Her Majesty's loyal Opposition?" she asked.

"Better a doorkeeper in the house of the Godly than to dwell in the tents of ungodliness."

He steered her towards one of the leather benches at the side of the room. She was aware of one or two curious glances, but was not worried. It was, after all, widely remembered that he had been her sponsor; and furthermore, what more natural for an M.P. with a special interest in immigration problems to have an informal word with the minister whose department handles such matters?

But their talk was not about immigration; nor had she expected it to be.

120

He made his position utterly clear.

"White bitch, I fancy you. I fancy you good. I know what you want. I could give it to you good."

"I don't doubt it."

"So what are we waiting for? Where? When?"

"I have a shadow. He tails me morning, noon and night."

"Lose him."

"How? Tell me that? How?"

"You're chicken. White chicken. Do you want it or don't you?"

She paused for quite a while, and then said: "I'm not sure."

"Not sure? What sort of answer is that?"

"It's the true one."

"Chicken. White chicken."

"Do you realise what this great romance of ours amounts to so far? We've had a few drinks together. We've had a meal. I've been in your car a couple of times. And that's it. And on the strength of that you command me to drop my knickers."

"What do you want me to do? Hold your hand? Write poems? I ain't no good at poems."

"That won't be necessary."

"What, then?"

"You seem to think I'm a quick bash. That's the phrase, isn't it? A quick bash. Well let me tell you, I'm not anyone's quick bash."

"Let's make it a slow bash, then. Slow to start with, anyway. Get you in the mood. That's what you're saying, isn't it?"

"The mood might not come at all."

"Let's find out."

"Where?"

"No problem. You got your flat, and Mr Bernard, he don't live there any more, so I'm told."

"We just drive there from the House, and Sergeant Sid writes it all down for the files?"

"Needn't be like that. Supposin' you were to give me the key and I go on ahead. Sergeant Sid wouldn't know anything about that, would he? He don't come in and tuck you up in bed, does he? Then we could take it from there. We could just sit and wait for the mood."

121

So that was the way it was. Sergeant Sid Gardner knew nothing of Henry Grant's arrival at Pargate Mansions, though it did not go unobserved. He was waiting for her in the living room. He was gentle, with the gentleness of a strong man. He did not rush her. He waited until he was sure. Then he said: "Ma'am, with your permission I am now going to do that thing I came here to do. And I'm going to do it good."

She was ready for him. More than ready. "Come with me, doorkeeper," she said. To get to the bedroom, they had to go into the corridor. It was then they heard the sound of a key in the front door.

Bernard said: "Good evening, Mr Grant. Sorry to intrude. I just dropped by to pick up some papers."

Within fifteen seconds he was gone, without speaking a word to Helen.

With him, went the mood.

THE Bill was simple. It was called the Capital Punishment (Reinstatement) Bill. It created the crime of Category A murder, defining Category A crimes as premeditated killing, the wilful taking of life for gain or revenge, or in an attempt to avoid the consequences of other criminal acts – for instance, killing a policeman or guard while escaping from the scene of a crime. Persons convicted of Category A murder would be liable to the death penalty by hanging. The Home Secretary, as before, would have the power to review death sentences, and recommend the Monarch to grant a reprieve if he thought fit.

It was at three-thirty on a Tuesday afternoon that Helen rose to move the Bill be granted a second reading (the first reading being a formality). The House was already pretty full because Tuesday is the Prime Minister's questions day. When the announcement appeared on the closed circuit television screens in the Palace of Westminster: "3.31 Capital Punishment (Reinstatement) Bill – Mrs Helen Chadwick", those few places in the House still unoccupied were quickly filled. The public gallery was packed, and there was a queue a hundred yards long waiting to occupy seats which might become vacant after the first hour or so.

Helen kept it in low key. The fundamental question, she said, was: Did the present system work? She proclaimed that it did not. She gave statistics showing the shocking rise in the murder rate over the last two years.

"It would be foolish," she told the House, "to prophesy that if this Bill becomes law, there will be an instant and dramatic change in the situation. No one can say with certainty what will happen. What can be said with certainty is that the present system of life imprisonment for murder, which in practice usually means a sentence of ten or twelve years, has had a long and fair trial, and has failed. So unless the House is prepared to accept that situation, and to do nothing about it, what is there left to try, when we are dealing with ruthless, heartless men? There is only one measure which has any likelihood of proving effective – and that is the proposal set out in this Bill. I know that many will regard this Bill as a retrograde step, and that it will trouble many consciences. It has been decided, and rightly so in my judgment, that the vote to be taken tonight shall be free from any pressure from the hierarchy of any party. So each is free to search his conscience and act accordingly.

"It may be said that reason, and not emotion, should be the deciding factor. But when I think of that child lying on the pavement outside the bank, I am not sure where lies the boundary between head and heart.

"It seems to me that in that tragic occurrence, there is the essence of what this debate is about. Do you think the possibility of such a tragedy being repeated will be diminished if this Bill becomes law? If you do, then in my view, your course of action is clear. You should use your vote and your voice to see that it does become law, no matter what repugnance you may hold for the State taking upon itself the role of executioner."

She spoke in all for twenty minutes, and when she sat down,

there was a hum of approval all round the House. Twenty-three speakers took part in the debate. There was passion on both sides; and oratory of distinction. The House knew that the eyes of the nation were on it, and rose to the occasion.

The vote was taken at ten p.m. The figures were: To give the Bill a second reading, 371; against 238; abstentions 16.

Within five weeks of the second reading, the Capital Punishment (Reinstatement) Bill went on to the Statute Book and became the law of the land.

The nation avidly followed every word of the controversy, and once the Bill became law, the newspapers eagerly awaited the first occasion on which it would be put into effect. There is no drama that quite matches an old-fashioned murder trial, with the life of the man in the dock at stake. Two men had been arrested for the bank shoot-out, and were obviously guilty as hell, but to the newspapers' chagrin, it was decided that as they had committed their offence before the Act came into force, it could not be applied retrospectively. They received life imprisonment. The newspapers and their readers had to show a little patience. The day would come.

For Helen, the capital-punishment controversy had consequences which she did not find at all displeasing. It focussed the nation's attention on her. Normally the Home Secretary is not one of the most prominent members of the Cabinet, just one of the team, and not one of the stars involved in the more newsworthy topics. But now that situation was reversed. Helen had done something that millions of people wanted to be done. Her rôle in the hanging controversy was central. It was her face, and not the Prime Minister's or the Chancellor's which was on the front pages and on the television screens.

The political correspondent of *The Times* wrote: "It was fashionable at one time to speculate about what would happen to whatever Government was in office if the Prime Minister of the day should walk into the path of a bus. It is improbable that such a fate will overtake Mr Marlowe, because he has rarely been seen to walk anywhere; but if that, or some similar calamity should befall, where lies the succession to his uneasy throne?

"Normally, it would go to the Chancellor or to the Foreign

124

Secretary. The holders of these offices are usually regarded as a Prime Minister's chief and closest aides, and therefore as his most likely heirs. But does that position hold in the present Government? Many people at Westminster think they see a third possible heir emerging. Certainly, at this moment, the status of Mrs Helen Chadwick, both at Westminster and in the country, is far beyond that achieved by any recent holder of her office.

"She is the woman of the hour."

THE woman of the hour had a problem of which *The Times* political correspondent was unaware.

Keith Shalton.

Since Bernard's departure from the flat, he had been there a couple of times. In his case, there was no need for concealment. They were ministers in the same Government. On some matters, their responsibilities converged. What more natural than for him to drop in for a drink and a discussion of mutual problems. They rode together in Helen's official black Princess car, with the detective sitting in front with the driver.

Keith was disgruntled. He saw himself as the secret architect of the Government. But for his intervention, Marlowe would have done his deal with Bainbridge. He, Keith Shalton, had saved the soul of the Tory Party, had saved the party from the disintegration that would have followed a poor coalition. But his rôle had been secret, and must remain so; for to disclose it would fatally weaken Marlowe's authority. No one knew that Keith Shalton had saved the Tory Party; and his reward for doing so was minuscule.

Marlowe, the wily Marlowe, had unerringly assessed the situation. He knew that Keith could make no public protest;

for if Keith's rôle were disclosed, some might see it not as saving the party but rather as being disloyal to the Party leader in a time of crisis; and they might regard Keith as an irresponsible and ambitious leader of a small faction. Keith knew he had been swindled, and that the trivial post he had been given was a sign of Marlowe's utter contempt for him. And he found no consolation in Helen's meteoric elevation.

As they drove to the flat for the third time, he pointed to the detective in front, and asked: "This gallant protector of yours. If need be, he lays down his life for you. Am I included in the package?"

"While you are with me, I'm sure he'd stretch a point."

In the flat, she said: "Pour me a Scotch."

"I'm not your bloody butler."

"I gather you're not happy in your work."

"I save Marlowe from making an historic fool of himself. And what do I get for it? This piddling job at the Commonwealth office."

"What did you expect?"

"I didn't expect to be treated with contempt."

"I don't see that Marlowe could have done much more. You weren't exactly anybody's blue-eyed boy at that time. He'd have had some explaining to do if he'd shoved you up far too soon."

"This, of course, is the senior minister explaining the facts of life to the impetuous beginner."

"Must we fight?"

"Why should you worry? You've done all right."

"I'll see you get full recognition when I write my memoirs for the Sunday papers."

"I was hoping for some rather earlier recognition."

He put an arm round her. She did not push him away, but did not make any positive response. "Is it my imagination," he asked, "or are we lacking some of the old spirit?"

"Possibly."

"Overwork, no doubt. Burdens of office. Cares of state."

"Possibly."

"Musn't let things get you down."

"I don't."

"I'd hoped that when the dust settled, we might resume our

former happy association."

"Was that part of the contract?"

"No contract. A gentlemen's agreement."

"Women are not bound by gentlemen's agreements. Not that one existed, so far as I can recall."

"I thought there was a certain implied understanding."

"Was it part of the Lords plot?"

"One does not discuss ladies in the Long Room. However, I thought . . ."

"You thought you'd bought something, and now you've come to collect it."

"You have a crude streak," he said.

She was furious. "My God!" she said, "Why didn't I see it before. It's the new variation of the casting couch. Why don't you set yourself up as the Downing Street employment agency? Well, let me tell you this: I'm not a political chorus girl. And I'm not up for grabs. Not that way."

"Don't talk bloody nonsense."

"Tell me, in what way have I misjudged the situation?"

"You've got it just about as wrong as it's possible to be."

"Convince me."

"Does this convince you? What I had in mind, and still have in mind, was to ask you whether, at some future date, when we are both free from our present commitments, you might be prepared to consider being my wife."

That stopped her. She lit a cigarette. "I see. I'm sorry."

He let the tension cool. "Well, how do you view this situation?"

"I have a marriage going."

"That's up the pole, isn't it? You could get a decree any day of the week. Irretrievable breakdown. That's the thing these days. No problem."

"Has my marriage broken down?"

"I thought that was obvious. But it now seems equally obvious that you are giving me the brush-off. Am I right?"

"I think, Keith, you probably are."

It was his turn to say: "I see."

"Forget what I said about the casting couch."

"I'll try."

"I've said I'm sorry. I really am sorry. Would you like me to *show* you I'm sorry?"

"Not as an act of charity."

"It woudn't be that."

But each knew that it was not as before. "That was kind of you," he said afterwards. "A good try, in the circumstances. Well, no doubt we shall be bumping into each other from time to time."

"I'd think so. Toilers in the same vineyard."

He was in the act of pouring out a Scotch. He stopped. "What made you say that?"

"Say what?"

"I didn't know you had a Biblical streak in you."

"Nor did I."

"But I know who has. And so do you. You've caught it off the black man."

"Henry . . ."

"Yes, Henry the Great. You've had the black man here."

"I see him sometimes . . ."

"I know damn well you see him . . . *sometimes*. Do you think I'm blind? You've had the black man here. That's true, isn't it. You've had the black man here."

"I have whom I like here."

"And you like black men. Or at least, one black man. Tell me, was he good? Quite a performer, I'd think. Always noted for his straight drive. By God, I bet he gave you a straight drive. I see now why my paltry efforts drove you to boredom."

"You can get out."

He did so, slamming the door.

IN the House she was no longer the "honourable lady". She was the "Right Honourable Lady". The title that is accorded to Privy Councillors, all members of the Cabinet being automatically members of the Council. She was not quite sure what was involved in this elevation. She understood vaguely that the Council might have certain constitutional functions in the event of the unexpected demise of the sovereign. It consisted, she read, of "eminent persons", and she was by no means displeased to be included in that company.

A week after the hanging bill had received Royal assent and become law, she was again in the headlines.

Marlowe told the House: "The date for the forthcoming State visit to Britain of President and Mrs Maloney has been fixed for May the fifth to May the tenth. The House will understand that there are many matters concerning this visit that require discussion between the two Governments at ministerial level, for instance, the question of security, and the programme for the President's visit. I have therefore suggested to the United States Government that a ministerial delegation should shortly visit Washington to discuss these matters. It is inevitable that the Secretary of State for Home Affairs will be heavily involved in the arrangements for the state visit, and I have therefore suggested to the President that she should represent Her Majesty's Government in these discussions, and I am glad to tell the House that this proposal is acceptable to the President."

It was, in fact, more than acceptable. It was eagerly snapped up. To the President, Helen was by far the most intriguing member of the British Cabinet. It would be interesting to discover what made this dame tick. It could be extremely interesting. And in order that any researches he might make in this matter should not be unexpectedly interrupted, the President sent for Andy Dewhurst. Among the squad of F.B.I. men assigned to safeguard the President, Andy was certainly not the top man, perhaps not even the number two or number three. In fact, it was difficult to place just what slot he filled in that secretive hierarchy. But one thing was for sure: he was the President's man, the President's own man. The President entrusted him with certain personal matters which he did not wish to put through channels. Five years ago, at a party con-

129

vention there had been a slight embarrassment over a busty, red-headed secretary who had not taken kindly to Senator Maloney's injunction to git her ass out of here damn quick when Mrs Maloney unexpectedly decided to attend the third day of the convention. The lady could have made trouble. The President placed the matter in the hands of Andy Dewhurst. There was no trouble. Shortly afterwards, the secretary quitted the party organisation. It was generally believed that she had gone back to Texas, where there was ample scope for her secretarial and other talents.

"Andy," said the President, "when this broad comes over here, I may have a little job for you."

"I understand, Mr President."

The President gave one of his crinkly grins. "I thought you would."

From Hansard:

Mr Grant: Will the Home Secretary state what sum it is proposed to spend from public funds on decorations and the erection of stands for the forthcoming visit of the President of the United States?

The Rt. Hon Mrs H. Chadwick: Provisionally, the sum of £250,000 has been set aside from the Home Office allotment for this purpose. It is hoped that this will prove sufficient, but it cannot be stated in advance exactly what expenditure will be involved. I am sure the House will agree that this is a reasonable sum, in view of the importance of the visit, and the great pleasure it will bring to the people of the capital.

Mr Grant: I don't see any pleasure in this thing for ordinary people. I see a lot of junketing for members of the Cabinet and their wives, and the whole traffic of London being halted on the day of the State procession. On what grounds does the Minister justify this expense?

Mrs Chadwick: I am sorry the honourable gentleman should take that view. I do not think the country as a whole will grudge a little expenditure on some pomp and pageantry, and I do not accept that this country is so poor that we cannot receive a visiting head of state in the appropriate fashion. Discussions are already taking place to reduce, so far as possible, the disruption of traffic.

Mr Catchpole: Is it really necessary to go through the antiquated rigmarole of a State visit in order to sweeten up the President as a preliminary to the discussions about the American loan?

Mrs Chadwick: The two matters are not connected (Cries of "Oh"). I regard the suggestion made by the honourable member as offensive to the head of a friendly nation who is soon to visit these shores.

Mr Catchpole: Will the Minister be making any claims on public funds for a dress allowance for her initial binge in Washington?

Mrs Chadwick: It will be a working trip, not a binge. In regard to the matter of dress allowance, I trust my wardrobe will prove adequate for the occasion. If it does not, I shall replenish it from my own funds.

A member: Lucky you.

Mr Grant: Has the Minister received any specific instructions on softening up the President on the subject of the loan, and if so, in what manner does she intend to perform that mission?

Mr Speaker: I fear we are straying from the subject of the original question. I think we should move on. Question Number Fourteen . . .

OUTWARDLY, Helen had displayed calm, almost bored detachment. Inwardly, she was seething. If Henry Wilberforce Grant felt that the State visit was a waste of public money, he was fully entitled to get up in the House and say so. But Helen knew there was more to it than that. The big black man was saying: Goodbye, stupid white bitch. Get lost. Get out of my life.

Obviously he blamed her for the fiasco at the flat. Of course, she should have realised that Bernard would be having the place watched, and that he would have kept a key, and so to that extent it was her fault. It was clear that Henry Wilberforce Grant, member of Parliament and former Test Match cricketer, deeply felt the indignity of being put in the French farce situation of being caught on an illicit mission by a husband. She wondered if he felt it even the more keenly because he was a black man caught by a white husband.

On one thing she had no doubt: her affair with Henry Wilberforce Grant was dead.

So it was goodbye to Henry. Goodbye to Keith. She was not entirely sorry. It was, after all, rather unbecoming for a member of the Cabinet, a member of the Queen's Most Excellent Privy Council, to have to resort to subterfuge in her private life.

Anyway, she had plenty on her plate. The visit to Washington.

They briefed her thoroughly. She attended meetings with one of the Foreign Office's permanent mandarins, with an exquisite young man from the Treasury (in case the loan came up), and with the somewhat less exquisite but hard-headed Commissioner of Police for London. Some meetings were attended by two Special Branch men who looked like keep-fit bank

132

managers; and at one meeting there were the colonels of the Brigade of Guards and the Household Cavalry, and the G.O.C. for the London area.

Among the many files and documents produced at these meetings, the most interesting one, she thought, was that marked: "President Maloney – personal".

This was full of fascinating minutiae. The President, she learned, was a touchy man in various ways. He liked his beef rare; his wife liked hers well done. His bladder made unpredictable demands; therefore he should never be pressed to a second glass of wine at public functions, and in private discussions one must be prepared for abrupt, unexplained adjournments. He liked strong, firm hand-shakes and those who failed this test seldom recovered the lost ground. He did not approve of low-cut dresses but did have an eye for outlines revealed by lower garments.

"Our ambassador," said Helen, "has been doing his homework."

"Not the ambassador," said the Foreign Office mandarin. "The other man."

"The other man?"

The Foreign Office man was clearly embarrassed. He had let something slip, something which he knew, and which he had assumed was known to her; but was not.

"An observer," he said, after a considerable pause.

"He must be a pretty close observer."

The Foreign Office man passed on to other business with pointed haste, and Helen did not pursue the matter.

The Treasury man filled her in on loftier subjects. It was almost inevitable, he said, that at some point the question of the loan would come up. Although she was not, of course, authorised to speak on behalf of the Government in this matter, it would be helpful if, when she came home, she could report on "the temperature of the water". The target, she was told, was two billion pounds, but one and three-quarter billion would just do. For that, the British Government were willing to grant the Americans development rights in the highly promising Burrell oil field in the North Sea; but it would not hurt, if the occasion came up, to let it be known tactfuly that the West

133

Germans and the Dutch were getting together to put in a joint bid.

There were to be four in the party: Helen; Ian Blair from her department; a senior Special Branch man named Naismith; and a Mr Wilkinson who belonged to some obscure branch of the Civil Service and had spent his entire career studying matters of protocol and procedure. Mr Wilkinson, it appeared, was invaluable when it came to seeing that everybody was seated in the right place when it came to such functions as a State dinner; apparently there had recently been a crisis with a Gulf oil state because the sheikh, who regarded himself as an absolute monarch, had been seated (in Mr Wilkinson's absence) below the Bolivian ambassador.

They went the proud way, flying the flag. They flew Concorde.

It was a busy four days, and the President received them in style. He sent Helen's opposite number, the Minister for the Interior, to meet them at the airport. Squads of experts were at hand to discuss everything from the wardrobe that the president's wife should take, to fields of fire for picked security marksmen who would be stationed along the processional route; from menus to handling the British Press. The Americans were thorough in every detail. Where, for instance, in Buckingham Palace was the nearest small room to the Queen's drawing room, where the President would be received by the Sovereign? In view of his inconvenient disability, it was a matter of the utmost importance; his quest for relief might suddenly become so urgent that he would not have time to go hunting down long corridors. Helen got the Embassy to cable for this information, and she was able to produce a plan, with arrows, at the next meeting of that committee.

The loan had not so far been mentioned, but everything else was going well. The high spot (publicly) was the formal dinner which the President gave at the White House in honour of his guests. It was a full-dress affair, with music by a red-coated Marine band, with the President making his entrance by descending the great marble staircase, preceded by a soldier carrying the American flag.

And on his arm, as the chief lady guest, was Helen Mary Chadwick, Her Majesty's Minister of State for Home Affairs.

This, she thought, is not bad going. In six months from boot-maker's daughter to Cabinet Minister and Privy Councillor; and now the most powerful man in the world takes my arm and leads me into dinner; and every woman in this opulent assembly is squirming with envy, and every man is wondering whether I'm a good lay. She had chosen a simple, almost severe gown, and was glad she had done so because it set her apart from most of the women in the room. It was in saffron, high-necked, as instructed, and discreetly form-fitting lower down. Her only jewellery was small earrings and a ring with a modest diamond.

The splendour of the State dining-room, with its chandeliers and gold damask draperies, was breath-taking. There were no speeches, but the President proposed a toast. "Ladies and gentlemen, I ask you to charge your glasses and drink the health of the Queen of England, and our guests." So they all stood up and drank to "the Queen of England and our guests". Blair, who had served in a battalion of the Argyll and Suther-land Highlanders which had fought its way up Italy, and who had twenty generations of undiluted Scottish blood in his veins, winced. Wilkinson, he felt, should have had a quiet word with someone to head that one off. But no one else noticed, and the ambassador, in his daily report to the Foreign Office, said: "The President and Mrs Chadwick seem to be on the most cordial terms."

On the last night, there was a very different kind of dinner. It was in the President's personal dining-room. There were just four people present: President Maloney, Helen, the Secretary of State, William Harcourt, and the Secretary to the U.S. Treasury, Lewis Goldsmith. Clearly, this was to be the crunch session. One woman against three men. At first, it was small talk, but at least it got them over the "Mr President" and "Mrs Chadwick" stage.

"I'm going to show you what a friendly lot we Yanks really are, and I'm going to call you Helen. And you, ma'am, can call me Patrick, if that is your desire."

"I'm honoured, Mr President."

"Patrick."

"I say, isn't that awfully decent," said Lewis Goldsmith in a

135

grotesque mimicry of a film Englishman.

"You bums can pipe down," said the President.

He was interested in the daily things of life in Britain. Football pools, for instance. How did they work? Could a computer get the answer?

"It would be an interesting exercise," said Harcourt.

Maloney turned to Goldsmith. "You've got computers. Battalions of them. Give it a go." Helen was not sure if he was serious.

He was also interested in the fact that she owned a boot factory. How much did shoes cost in Britain? They cost too damn much in America. He stretched out his foot. "What would that cost me if I got it in England?" (He had still apparently not heard of Scotland or Wales or Northern Ireland.) Helen examined the President's shoe. It was of reasonable quality leather and craftsmanship, but nothing exceptional. She noticed that the stitching was fractionally uneven. It was obviously a hand-made article; but the new stitching machines at Midland Footwear turned out mass-produced shoes in which the stitching was not uneven.

"My people would make you that for about eighteen pounds."

Goldsmith translated: "Just over thirty dollars."

"Jeez! That bastard in Boston ran me for seventy-five."

"We don't build space-ships, but British know-how does still count in some things."

It did not go down well. She suspected that these men did not like being told that anybody could do anything better than America. Well, she wasn't here to grovel.

The butler brought brandy and coffee, and the urbane Harcourt smoothed over the little crack.

"You've got us beat, not only in boots, but in butlers. Take Mr Parkinson here. Mrs Maloney wasn't happy about the home-grown article, so she went shopping in London for a butler and came back with Mr Parkinson. And I don't know anything about butlering, but I would think that Mr Parkinson here is at the top of the heap."

"Very kind of you to say so, sir," said Parkinson.

Once he had left, the tone changed abruptly.

136

Goldsmith, who, Helen decided, had the sharpest brain in the room, said: "Now let's forget about butlers and state visits and all that Royal crap. That's fine for putting in the shop window. What we want to know is what's inside the shop. This oil field, the Burrell field. How do we know it's going to come good?"

"Lewis," said Harcourt, "is always succinct, but sometimes a little less than elegant."

"His folks came over in the Mayflower," said Goldsmith. "Mine came in a cattle ship from Poland in 1923. That's why I don't talk so classy."

Helen said: "Strangely, we thought this topic might crop up. When the Royal crap had been disposed of. I think I have the information you require."

She had brought with her a slim document case containing a detailed assessment of the potentialities of the oil field. She left her seat to get it. Her back was towards them. For this informal occasion she had chosen a simple discreetly cut fawn dress. She was conscious of the fact that she was being scrutinised by the commander-in-chief of the most powerful nation in the world, the man who controlled its financial policy, and the man who supervised its foreign affairs. The thought disturbed her not at all.

She handed the document to Lewis Goldsmith. It consisted of eight typed pages. It took him barely two minutes to flick through it and pick out its salient points. The man had a mind like a steel trap.

"You might have something going here. That's if this is straight up."

The last observation needled her. "Are you suggesting that the British Government would issue a false prospectus?"

"Simmer down," said the President.

Goldsmith went through all the figures, all the estimates. He wanted a mass of additional information. Helen took notes, and promised that the answers would be in Washington in a week.

It was ten o'clock before his inquisition had finished. In a grudging way, he seemed satisfied; or at least, half-satisfied.

Then the President flicked his eyes towards his watch. The

137

signal was barely perceptible; but it registered instantly with Harcourt and Goldsmith.

"We've done all there is to do tonight," said Goldsmith. "It's been a real pleasure meeting with you, Mrs Chadwick." He pumped her hand vigorously. Harcourt did so in a more restrained manner.

Within a minute they were gone.

For the first time, Helen Chadwick was alone with the President of the United States.

So this was the man with his finger on the trigger. She had read somewhere that whenever the President left Washington, another man went too, a man apart from the security guards; a man who carried a little black box which, by some electronic means totally beyond her comprehension, could activate the long-range missiles to strike against the Soviets. The President had only to order the box to be opened, insert a key in a slot, and turn it, and the remorseless computers would do the rest. Did the man in the box follow him around the White House? Was he sitting outside in the corridor now? She had certainly noticed one little man in the corridor, keeping unobtrusively in the background, but had assumed he was some kind of security guard (she had come to recognise the type since her elevation to Cabinet status). Did the President have the key in his pocket now? She wondered how Maloney or any other man could live with that load on his shoulders every minute of every day and every night. What did it do to him, the awesome knowledge that by the simple act of turning a key in a slot he could write "finis" to fifty million lives? Did it put him off his stroke at golf? Or in bed? Supposing he went bonkers.

But he looked sane enough. A tall, craggy man. A man utterly unlike any of her colleagues in the Cabinet. A rugged man. A man who had made ten million dollars from scratch. Marlowe was a rich man, too; but he was rich because his ancestors had shrewdly bought up a considerable chunk of Belgravia. This man had done it himself. Marlowe had Greek and Latin and knew about the Third Crusade and about wine. This man probably had none of those accomplishments. He had gone to the top because he was basically a primitive man; a no-frills man who could see what needed to be done, and did it, while others

138

stood by. But was being a primitive man an ideal qualification for holding the key to the box? Would that key, perhaps, have been safer with Marlowe, with his Latin and Greek and wine?

The phone rang in the dining-room.

The thought occurred to her: "Supposing that's some Army or Air Force commander saying 'It's started'." It would be a nice thing for the history books: that when it happened, the President was alone with a woman. If there was anybody left to write the books.

In fact, it was the butler.

"Parkinson is asking if we'd like some brandy and coffee. I could manage a nightcap."

"I shall have to be getting back to the Embassy soon."

The President put his hand over the phone. "For Chrissakes why? The ambassador won't be getting worried about you, will he? You won't get locked out if you're not home before midnight?"

"He might report me to my master."

"You know something? I think ambassadors are a load of crap. American ambassadors, British ambassadors, Portuguese ambassadors. Specially Portuguese ambassadors. Deadbeats. Fancy-pants deadbeats. All of them."

The same thought had occurred to Helen.

The President spoke into the phone again. "Yeah. Not here. Bring it into the sitting room." To Helen he said: "We got some talking to do. It will be more comfortable there." He led the way. There *was* a little man in the corridor, who followed them at a deferential distance, but so far as she could see, he had no black box. Perhaps that one was lurking by a phone somewhere in the mansion. The President opened the sitting room door and said "Grab yourself a pew." At the door he waited for a moment for the little corridor man to catch up.

She heard the President say: "All O.K., Andy?"

"Sure, Mr President." Then the President shut the door.

"What a pleasant room," said Helen, and immediately cursed herself for saying the banal thing. Though it was true. It was a spacious, high-ceilinged room, furnished in what must be American Regency style, if there was such a thing: high-backed chairs, a divan with carved legs, leather-topped tables, a grandfather clock in a gleaming mahogany case. Everything blended into a solid and highly livable elegance.

"Martha did it," said the President. "My wife. She knows about furniture. Reads books. Goes to lectures. Me, I don't give a damn so long as I've got somewhere to park my butt."

"She's made a great job of it."

"She'd be right pleased to hear you say that."

Where was Martha, Helen wondered. The President anticipated her question. "She's sorry she's not here. She's addressing some ladies' literary society in Philadelphia. I told her to get out of it, but she's stood them up twice. These damn book clubs are big things in America, I don't think they read the books. They just buy them and yak about them. It keeps them happy."

There was a knock on the door. The President knew that with Andy Dewhurst outside, only one man would get within knocking distance.

"Come in."

The butler came in with a tray bearing silver coffee pot and jug, cups, brandy bottle and glasses.

"Leave it there. Then you can hit the sack."

"Goodnight, Mr President. Goodnight, madam."

"I gather," said Helen, "that he was also one of your wife's acquisitions."

"She's from Boston," said the President, as if that explained everything. She decided not to seek enlightenment on what might be a touchy subject.

He reached into his pocket and brought out a cigar case. Helen took her cigarette case from her handbag. He hadn't asked her. Why should she ask him? It was a tiny thing, but she was determined to let him see that she, Helen Chadwick, was not overawed by being in the presence of the President of the United States. That they were just a man and woman, with coffee and brandy in highly-civilised surroundings.

The President nursed his cigar until it glowed. He stretched out his long legs, and said: "Well, did they fill you in on the loan?"

"It was mentioned *en passant* before I left London."

"I bet it was."

"Of course, it's not my department."

"But they told you to tickle my ass and see what gives?"

"The young gentleman from the Treasury did not put it quite in those terms."

"Near enough?"

"Something was said about taking the temperature of the water."

"The water is damn chilly. I'm going to have a rough ride in Congress."

"It's a two-way deal."

"Lewis did not go along with all the figures in that oil report."

"He banged about a bit. I thought he was putting it on. Didn't you?"

"Lewis is a pretty shrewd guy."

"Precisely."

The poker game had begun.

"The way I figure it, if the oil is O.K., I might screw Congress up to a billion and a half."

Her cigarette had gone out. She took her time over re-lighting it.

"Not enough, Patrick."

"Say again."

"Not enough, Mr President."

"You're an impudent bitch."

"So I've been told."

"I am offering you one and a half billion of the American taxpayers' money, and you just sit there and say 'not enough'."

"Precisely."

"Don't keep damn well saying precisely."

"I shall choose what words I think are necessary for this rather important discussion."

"There ain't going to be any more discussion."

"Very well, Mr President. In that case I must tell you that the oil deal is not likely to go through."

She had absolutely no authority for saying that. Her explicit instructions had been that if the matter were raised, she was tentatively to test American reaction, to report back, and to say nothing that would commit the Government in any way what-

141

ever. Marlowe would have been horrified. The Cabinet would be appalled. Metcalfe, pompous Metcalfe, would be livid at having his authority usurped.

But the poker game was on. And it was she who was playing the hand.

The President ground out his cigar. "I thought you said your brief was just to test the temperature of the water."

"This water is much too cold to take a dip in."

"Let's get this straight. Are you saying that you have authority from Marlowe to call off the oil thing if the loan sticks at one and a half?"

"I have the authority to inform you of the view of the British Cabinet."

It was a downright lie. No such view existed, let alone had been confided to her for transference to the President. The President was pretty sure she was lying, with her damn preciselys. But Christ, what a howl if he missed out on the oil.

For Helen, there could be no turning back; only pressing on.

"I realise, Mr President, that this is an informal discussion. But if you would care to have it minuted, for the record, I am quite willing. Of course, in any case, there will be the Press problem. I shall have the Press people on my tail when I get home tomorrow. I shall have to tell them something. It might as well be the truth."

"Don't see why you've got to talk to the papers. Bit early for that."

Could it be that he was just a bit shaken?

"Of course, Mr President, this will make absolutely no difference to the plans for the State visit. The two things are quite separate. You will be assured of a most cordial welcome."

The President said "Horseshit," but he said it to himself.

Aloud: "Helen—"

"Yes, Mr President?"

"Patrick."

"Mr President, while we're discussing affairs of state."

"Then what the hell do I call you?"

"Actually, I'm a Right Honourable. But in conversation, one normally drops that."

"Does one, indeed? Well see here, Right Honourable bitch.

How long have you been in politics? Six months?"

"A bit longer than that."

"Well I've been around for the best part of thirty years. State senator. On the Hill. Three years here."

"You wear well."

"That's about the first civil thing you've said to me."

"Do you want the respect due to your age?"

My God, thought the President, I know what I'd like to do to you.

"Would you be prepared to accept a little advice and judgment from someone who's seen a bit more of it than you have?"

"I might."

"*Might?*"

"You see, Mr President, in Britain we have a great admiration for the technical and scientific things you do in America. Space ships, moon landings, automation, that sort of thing. But we have less respect when it comes to simple ordinary commonsense and judgment."

"Indeed?"

"We think that you, that is the Americans, have made some calamitous mistakes. For instance, you held out of the first war until it was too late, and Europe was falling apart. And that opened up the way for Communism and for Hitler's lot. You had a chance to put some of that right if you had joined the League of Nations, and made it a real thing. But you didn't. In the last war . . ."

The President could stand no more of this. "In the last war, the Brits sat on their butts and would still have been there if it hadn't been for Georgie Patton."

"That's not quite how we see it. But, of course, there are different points of view."

"Mighty handsome of you."

"But—"

"Before I get another goddam lecture about what's wrong with America, I suggest you take it easy on this oil thing. If you must talk to the papers, leave your options open. Don't slam any doors."

The scent of victory was growing. But keep him groggy. Keep him on the ropes.

"If we're stuck, we're stuck."

"Supposing, just supposing, that oil report comes good—"

"I cannot make any promises. I don't understand half the report myself. It's not my line. But what there is to know is there. And I think I should tell you that we have had other approaches."

"Try pulling the other one. If it's as big as you say it is, it's got to be us. Nobody else could handle it."

"Two nations sharing it could."

So the crafty Brits were setting up a double-cross. And, of course, they knew that despite all America's riches, the experts were saying there would be a fuel crisis by the end of the century.

"If it worked out right, I say, *if* it turns out to be absolutely solid, I might be able to lean on Congress."

"For how much?"

God. Did she never let up?

"A billion and threequarters."

"That is something I would be prepared to pass on to my Government. But I cannot hold out any great hope of acceptance."

"For Christ's sake, how much do you expect?"

"The figure we had in mind was two billion."

"That's out. Congress would crucify me."

From the finality of his tone, she sensed that he was speaking the truth. But one more try. "I cannot commit my Government. And I don't expect you to do so either. But suppose we could agree on a working figure, as a basis for discussion, of a billion plus eighty-five per cent of a billion.

The President sighed heavily, "I shall have to talk about it to Lewis."

"Of course."

It was then she knew she had won.

The President poured out more brandies. Large ones. She asked: "Are you trying to send me back to the Ambassador tipsy?"

His inconvenience struck him. He departed abruptly. When he returned, she was standing, looking at his murals, brandy glass in hand.

He said: "You're a hard bitch. But I like your style."

"I like yours, too, Patrick."

"That wasn't the impression I got."

"You've misjudged me. I'm just a poor defenceless woman. Clay in the potter's hands."

"Jesus!"

"I think we've had quite a successful meeting. Any other business?"

He was standing close to her. Very close.

"We shall be seeing quite a bit of each other when I come over. I think we ought to build up a relationship."

"Years ago," she said, "there was something between America and Britain called the special relationship."

"Maybe we ought to get it going again."

She put her arms round his neck and gave him a long, warm kiss. "That's just to say thank you. Thank you for the extra hundred and fifty million."

Now his arms were around her. They were strong arms, hard arms.

"I like people who say Thank You. Seems to be going out of fashion."

"We Brits still have our manners. Some of us, anyway. Someone does something nice for me. I want to do something nice in return."

Now that the invitation had been spelt out, beyond any misunderstanding, he accepted it eagerly. His hand probed her spine for the zip of her dress.

"I think, Mr President, you will find a small hook at the top that has to be undone first."

He found it. Her dress, with a little persuasion, descended to her ankles. She stepped out of it. Her Majesty's Secretary of State for Home Affairs stood in front of the President of the United States in her Marks and Spencer briefs. She always purchased those garments at Marks and Sparks. Why pay more?

Gently he disengaged her arms from around his neck, and prepared himself for the encounter. She, too, made final dispositions.

"Turn," he said.

145

"I beg your pardon?"

"Turn round. Rotate. Slowly."

She did so.

"H'mmm."

"What the hell does that mean?"

"You know, I've been watching you for quite a while, ever since you had that shindig at the factory."

"You're watching me now. I trust all is satisfactory."

"You're quite a broad."

"Not too broad, I hope."

The action, she presumed, would be on the long, low divan. She was right. For a man of his years and heavy responsibilities, the President performed creditably. It was she who had to tell him at the start: "You're not catching a train." Her own performance was accurately timed, like a fifteen hundred metre runner who is content with second place for the first three laps, but surges ahead in the final straight. The President was considerably impressed.

"Any more at home like you?"

Her first instinct was to say No. She thought of Miss Alderton, her room-mate when she first went to the Commons. She could hardly visualise Miss Alderton in her own present position. But who could tell what Miss Alderton got up to after a day's tramping over the Yorkshire moors in her tweeds and stout brown shoes?

"I think most of us can cope. British know-how."

"So that was how you built your Goddam empire. That was how you took over India and Africa. I used to believe all that crap about the white man's burden. Now I know it was the girls who really did the work."

"Mr President," she said, "one day you will go too far."

GILBERT PARKINSON cleared away the coffee and brandy tray. He took it into his pantry. He did not lock the door. That would have invited awkward questions from any stray callers. But he put a stool where it would prevent the door being flung open and anyone making a precipitate entrance.

He then took a screwdriver from a drawer, unscrewed the false bottom of the coffee pot, and extracted the minuscule tape which had recorded every word that had passed the previous evening in the President's sitting room.

Gilbert Parkinson was the Other Man, to whom inadvertent reference had been made by a Foreign Office official during Helen's briefing before she left London; he was the man who, for three years, had been providing the Foreign Office with information which was often far more illuminating about the President's secret thoughts and attitudes than the ponderous despatches which the Ambassador sent in the diplomatic bag.

The planting of Gilbert Parkinson on the President's wife when she had come to England looking for an English butler had been a brilliant stroke by British Intelligence. However, the boss of Gilbert's section had overlooked, or rather ignored, one thing. It was obvious enough. Indeed, Gilbert Parkinson himself had been complaining increasingly about it in recent months.

Gilbert Parkinson was intensely bored with his assignment. He wanted a change. Also, he considered he was grossly underpaid. The boss of the section had told Gilbert that he was irreplaceable in his present job, and that there could be no question of transfer. As for money, the boss had said he was putting it through channels. It had got stuck in the channels. The boss had never really understood how deeply Gilbert felt on these matters. Nor did he know that Gilbert had another motive for wishing to end his butlering days. Gilbert was getting deeply involved with a refugee Polish countess who lived in Washington.

Gilbert Parkinson wanted to get out. He had been biding his time. When he had played over this most recent tape, he decided that the time might not be far off. He would send the first part of the transcript to London. But not, he decided, the later section.

There might be a private customer for that. Someone who

would pay far more than his niggardly paymasters in Whitehall. It would serve the bastards right.

The President had indeed gone too far. So had Helen Chadwick.

WHEN Helen flew back to London, there were reporters and photographers at Heathrow, and inevitably her picture appeared on the front pages, with her non-committal comments, which she confined to the preparations for the State visit. But the main headlines were on an entirely different subject.

They concerned one Stephen Barr.

Stephen Barr was a nineteen-year-old coloured youth; a misfit, a drop-out, a product of a broken home and of truancy; a minor criminal who had lately taken to mugging women in parks and snatching their handbags.

His latest victim was a seventy-three-year-old pensioner.

Two things made this episode totally different from the countless muggings which take place every week and go unreported. The first was that Stephen Barr had failed to notice the near-presence of a burly but nimble-footed man who turned out to be an off-duty policeman. Stephen Barr was pinned to the ground by this strong man within thirty seconds of his crime.

The second was that the old lady had died in the ambulance.

Thus, when Stephen Barr had appeared before the magistrates' court, he became the first man, since the passing of the Capital Punishment (Reinstatement) Bill, to be charged with Category A murder, for which he could, if convicted, achieve an unsought niche in British legal history; he could become the first man to be executed in Britain for fifteen years.

At the magistrates' court, his solicitor had argued that

Stephen Barr's deed was essentially the act of a petty criminal that had had unforeseen and unintended consequences; that the accused's background and limited education made it extremely unlikely that he had fully comprehended the significance of the new Act; and that the charge should therefore be reduced to one of manslaughter. But the Crown had contended that the crime of Stephen Barr was precisely covered by the terms of the Act. That he had inflicted death on a defenceless elderly woman for monetary gain; and the facts that the woman's handbag had contained only 53p, and that this had been in Barr's possession for only half a minute did not alter the nature of the offence.

The magistrates had, in effect, passed the buck to the higher court. They had refused to reduce the charge. They had committed Stephen Barr to stand trial for his life at the Old Bailey on the capital charge of Category A murder.

The newspapers, and their readers, were eagerly awaiting this event. At last there was going to be a real old-fashioned murder trial, with a life at stake at the end of it.

Helen read the reports of this case with some concern. For if justice took its ultimate course, she would have a highly personal rôle to play in this drama. As Home Secretary, she would have the duty of advising the Sovereign whether or not to grant a reprieve. It would be her decision, and her decision alone; not a Cabinet decision. That was the position that had exisited for many years when capital punishment had been previously enforced; that was the position that had been restored by her Act.

She had realised, of course, when she pushed the Bill through, that sooner or later this responsibility would devolve on her and her successors; but she had not thought about it perhaps quite as deeply as she should have done; and she had not expected to be faced with it in this exact form.

Her conscience would have been untroubled if Stephen Barr had been a completely adult criminal who had taken a gun on a raid, ready to use it to achieve his ends or make his escape. But this case was hardly like that; a coloured boy, out of work, from a deprived background, armed not with a gun but with a garage wrench. Even so, a heavy wrench was a lethal weapon. As she understood her own Bill, and she knew its provisions backwards, this was murder for monetary gain. Category A murder. Looked at any way, it was hardly an ideal test case for the new law, and she hoped that the judge would absolve her of her responsibility by reducing the charge to manslaughter. She tried to put it out of her mind during the next few days. In any case, there was nothing she could do about it for the present, and she had other things that needed attention.

Unknown to her, the Other Man's report of her session with the President – the first half of the tape only – had reached Marlowe, and he had shown it to Metcalfe. Marlowe was mildy amused; but Metcalfe was furious.

"Dear God! Do you realise that this woman has been playing games with the whole future of this country?"

"I thought she played them pretty well."

"Without an ounce of authority from the Cabinet, or from you, or from *me*." That was the thing that hurt. "Can you tell me, Prime Minister, how I'm supposed to run my Department if every *arriviste* in the Cabinet is to go around usurping the authority of the Treasury?"

"I think this was a rather special case."

"There are no special cases."

"My dear Charles, do you think you could have done better?"

"That's not the point."

"I think, in view of the state of this country, it is very much to the point."

"Do you intend to have it out with her?"

"It would mean telling her about the Other Man. I would sooner keep that to as few people as possible."

"You're probably right. She'd blab it all round the place."

"I think not."

Metcalfe was left fuming. But he made his point obliquely, though plainly enough, at the first Cabinet meeting after Helen's return. She reported the basis of the tentative agreement with the President, and there were some murmurs of approval and surprise. But Metcalfe cut in icily: "Some of us who have had rather more experience in Government than others will wish to wait and see what transpires. Meanwhile, Prime Minister, I am sure you will agree that ministers should be wary of venturing out of their own departments into territory where they do not have any experience, and where they do not have responsibility for ultimate decisions. This is a cardinal rule of Cabinet procedure, and I foresee all manner of difficulties if some members choose to ignore it."

Marlowe, who these days was beginning to feel very weary, was in no mood to cope with tantrums in the Cabinet. He had had a long day. He said mildly: "I think most of us would go along with that." And Helen let it ride. She knew she had brought off a triumph, and that nothing Metcalfe could say or do could alter that.

Metcalfe's mood was not improved when the talks between the Treasury and Washington reached the point at which a "declaration of intent" to proceed with the loan on the lines agreed by Helen and the President was announced simultaneously in Washington and London. It was a big story. The pound instantly picked up five cents. The Stock Market had its best day for six months. The financial commentators, reaching for their cliché books, began to talk about Britain beginning to "find a way out of the woods", and of seeing "light at the end of the tunnel". All of which should have delighted Metcalfe. It did not. And his displeasure was deepened further when one of the more astute commentators, the man who wrote the Wednesday column in the *Post*, pointed out that the agreement had been reached much more quickly than had been generally expected and asked why.

Could it be, he inquired, that matters other than those connected with the State visit had been discussed during the recent visit of Mrs Helen Chadwick to Washington? Could it be, he asked (much nearer to the truth than he could possibly know) that the Home Secretary had used her feminine charms on the President? And was the bonus for Britain the result, not of anything done by the Chancellor or the faceless men at the Treasury, but the consequence of plain, direct talking by a woman of commonsense?

The theme was taken up elsewhere. At Westminster, Helen's prestige rose daily. And it began to seep through to the ordinary people, the readers of newspapers and the watchers of television, that one member of Marlowe's Cabinet seemed to be outshining all others.

151

Not that outshining the others was all that of an achievement. It was, with few exceptions, a rather elderly and mediocre Cabinet, not exactly scintillating with talents. And, of course, she had the most photogenic and memorable face and figure. The *Post's* commentator put it accurately, if unkindly, when he wrote that if the Cabinet, *en masse*, were to take a walk along Brighton Pier, only one or two faces would dispel the belief that a midland Rotary club had gone to the Sussex coast for its annual outing.

HENRY WILBERFORCE GRANT sought an audience with the Home Secretary. They had not exchanged a personal word since he had slammed out of the flat. Now he came on official business, representing one of his constituents. That constituent was Stephen Barr.

He demanded: "Are you going to let them hang him?"

"He's not been found guilty of murder yet."

"Don't let's play around. He will be."

That was her own reluctant assessment. But she said: "I cannot express an opinion on a case which is still before the courts."

"The great Madam Minister is getting pretty good at the high and mighty talk."

"For God's sake ..."

"For God's sake, this kid is nineteen. He hasn't seen his father for ten years. His mother's got a fancy man and spends all her time with him. When the kid came home from school there wasn't a crust of bread in the place, and if he wanted to eat, he had to go and cadge from other kids or nick something from a shop. What chance has the kid had? You can't tell me that you're going to use your fancy new law on a kid like *that*?"

152

"I don't know."

"When will you know?"

"After the case. If he's found guilty. How soon after the case I don't know. I shall have to look at all the papers. See what the judge says. Medical reports. Psychiatric reports. You seem to know about him. Get it down on paper, and I promise you I'll consider it with the other papers."

"Papers. What do you want with papers? The kid's only nineteen."

"That makes him an adult."

"If he was a white kid, it wouldn't take you long to make up your mind. You wouldn't hang a white kid, not for that. But hanging a coloured kid, that will go down pretty well with your mob, won't it. Shows what a big strong white woman you are."

"I wish to God he was white. It would make it simpler."

"You want a big laugh? You tell that to them in my parish. But you won't be laughing if this boy gets the rope. You won't be laughing at all. You'll have big trouble, ma'am. I promise you that."

"Threatening me isn't going to change anything."

"Not threatening. Just telling you. Telling you plain simple facts."

"There's nothing I can do about it at the moment. But if he is sentenced, let me know what you know about this boy. But it's got to be on paper."

"You don't want any paper from me. You'll have plenty of paper. White man's paper. And I can tell you what it will say. It will say: Hang the little black bastard."

"I shall make up my own mind."

"You do that."

She tried to end the meeting on a less sour note. "White bitch will remember what black bastard has said."

It was a mistake. "Don't you ever call me that again. Not ever."

He stalked out.

While Stephen Barr awaited trial at the Old Bailey, others, great and small, went about their business.

In Washington, the President's wife presented him with the bill for the clothes she had bought for the State visit, and the

President took one look at it and said: "Suffering catfish!"

Lists were drawn up of who would fly to London with the President in his personal plane. One alteration was made at a fairly late stage.

"Mr President," said Gilbert Parkinson, "I gather that you will not be requiring my services during the visit to London."

"That's right. The Embassy is laying everything on. Take yourself a vacation."

"I was wondering if I might ask a small favour."

"Such as?"

"I would like to use the vacation to visit my mother in Bournemouth. That is a resort on the south coast of England. Very pleasant, particularly in the early summer. I was wondering if there would be a spare seat on the airplane."

Why not? The poor bum had a pretty drab life for most of the year. The President made a note on his pad, and said: "I'll see what can be done." Which was why the President's Number Three Press aide found himself inexplicably removed from the list of those who would fly with the President.

In London, Christopher Marlowe studied the programme for the State visit with increasing distaste. In the four months he had been Prime Minister, he had begun to feel inexpressibly weary. And now he was beginning to develop a nagging pain in his left side. Perhaps he ought to see a doctor, but to get a thorough going over would take at least a morning, and he just did not have a morning to spare. Recently, he had rarely been to bed before two a.m. There were always piles of documents to take up to the flat in the upper regions of Number Ten which was supposed to be the Prime Minister's home and refuge. Marlowe, a widower, had not found it much of a refuge. His ministers knew he was there, knew that he had no family diversions, and did not hesitate to make late-night calls, sometimes on the way home from a theatre. The latest batch of papers covered everything from the price of tomatoes in the European community to the appointment of the next bishop of Wilminster. Nothing could be skimped; least of all the appointment of the new bishop. Marlowe took his churchmanship seriously. The present bench of bishops, like the Cabinet, were a pretty mediocre lot. New blood was needed on the bishops' bench. He thought Cartwright might be the man. But would that stir up the Anglos?

And on top of all these day-to-day chores, there was looming the State visit. It would be a time-wasting business, but there was no getting out of it. And afterwards? The economy had picked up a bit on the news of the loan. But would that last? Marlowe doubted it. Ahead lay four, bleak, wearisome years of office. Marlowe wondered whether he could stand it that long; perhaps he would bow out half-way through, particularly if there happened to be an Oxford chancellorship going at about that time.

He made a decision. He would let his doctor give him a going-over; after the State visit.

THE Judge: "Stephen Barr, your case has been considered with great patience by twelve of your fellow citizens, and their unanimous verdict, with which I entirely concur, is that you are guilty of murder for gain, that is Category A murder as defined under the new Act.

"I have listened with great attention to the submissions made on your behalf by your able learned counsel, but I cannot accept – and the jury do not accept – that you were unaware of or incapable of understanding the law recently enacted. It is therefore my heavy duty to pronounce sentence under that law. I order that you be taken back to the place from which you came to this court, and thence to a place of execution, and that you be hanged by the neck until you are dead. And may the Lord have mercy on your soul."

Perhaps she would have reprieved him. If it had not been for the Clapham Common affair; and for Keith Shalton; and Bernard.

155

On Clapham Common, there was a gang fight. Knives were used. Two twenty-year-old youths lay in hospital critically wounded; no arrests had yet been made.

As *The Times* put it: "The passing of the Capital Punishment Act does not, in itself, seem to have reduced the incidence of crimes that may lead to loss of life. Possibly its enforcement will achieve this end. One can only speculate whether this affray would have taken the serious form it did if the Act had been in force six months earlier, and there had been examples for all to see of the retribution which it provides for those who put life at peril."

Keith Shalton came to see her at the Home Office. To plead for Stephen Barr; but on grounds totally different from those put forward by Henry Grant.

"You can't let him be strung up by the neck."

"Why not?"

"Bad for the image."

"Whose image?"

"Our image. The image of the Tory Party, the natural rulers of this country, established under the patronage of one Christopher Marlowe, by kind permission of Mrs Helen Chadwick. White men keep black men in their places. I'm all in favour of that. But white men don't actually kill black men any more. It just isn't done. Didn't anyone tell you? It went out with the Wind of Change, and all that."

"It is not a question of white or black."

"It is, my girl, very much."

"Don't 'my girl' me. I have a specific case to consider on it's merits. I don't give a damn what's done."

"Then it's high time you did. You do realise there's a by-election coming up in Birmingham?"

"So?"

"It's our seat. We won it at the election. We should win it again. But it so happens there's four thousand coloured voters in that constituency. It's quite clear that nearly all of them came over to us the last time. Do you want to push them back on the other side of the fence?"

"I'm not interested which side of the fence they are on."

"Then you damn well should be. That's what politics is

156

about. Which side of the fence people are on."

"You are a totally unscrupulous opportunist."

"I am a realist."

Pressure on any issue had always tended to tip her the other way. Perhaps the final straw was a letter which came to her at the office, marked personal. It was from Bernard. He wrote: "I trust that even you are not going to besmirch the reputation of the department which I had the honour to serve for so long, until my recent abrupt and enforced departure."

It all added up. In the opposite way to that intended.

Ten days after the judge had given his sentence on Stephen Barr, she handed to the impassive Blair a statement in her own handwriting for transmission to the Press: "The Home Secretary has deeply considered every aspect of the case of Stephen Barr and has reluctantly decided that she cannot advise the Sovereign to interfere with the course of justice as prescribed by the court."

The demos started that night, and continued sporadically for the twenty days that Stephen Barr had left to live. Transport in London was halted when all the coloured staff on the buses, the trains and the underground staged a one-day strike to march in a massive demonstration along Whitehall. Henry Wilberforce Grant was arrested when he tried to break through a police cordon. He was fined £50 or seven days' imprisonment. He served the sentence.

But the mood in the country at large was: He killed the old girl; he was old enough to know what he was doing; let him hang. Three hastily organised public opinion polls all put basically the same question: Do you think the Home Secretary did the right thing? The "Yes" vote was large, and remarkably consistent: 76 per cent, 73 per cent, 79 per cent.

And the newspapers, in the main, were on Helen's side. The *Post's* centre-spread headline praised the courage of "the loneliest woman in Britain".

The demos reached their peak on the day that the forces of justice and gravity combined to despatch Stephen Barr to face his Maker. They hanged him at Pentonville. There was a huge uproar outside the prison, and another massive march in Whitehall.

THAT was the day on which President Maloney flew from Washington to Britain in his Presidential plane for the start of his State visit.

On a seat near the tail of the plane, far removed from the bar where the President drank Scotch with a few chosen Press representatives, was the free-rider, Gilbert Parkinson.

WHEN Marlowe left Downing Street in his black Rover to drive to Heathrow to meet the President, it took fifty policemen to clear a way through the mob in Whitehall. Marlowe sighed. He had voted against the hanging bill, and now that the bill was law he felt it should be applied sparingly, and that the Barr case was the worst possible test case. But he had meticulously observed the rule that the decision should be that of the Home Secretary alone, with no pressure from the Cabinet, irrespective of whether the political consequences turned out to be good or bad.

Perhaps they would turn out to be good. The opinion polls, thought Marlowe, were probably a better guide than all the noise and commotion. That, he suspected, was confined mainly to London. In Bournemouth and such places, the Chadwick woman would be the toast of the town. It was truly remarkable how she had projected herself into the nation's consciousness. He tried to recall some similar previous example, but couldn't.

Anyway, in his weariness, he was finding it difficult to concentrate. Even the things he had prepared to say to the President seemed to be slipping away from him. He tried to pull himself together, but felt vaguely that the different parts of him were staying apart. He slumped back in his seat. His driver and detective in front, both fanatical trout fishermen, were discussing the nuances of that art. Neither noticed that the distinguished passenger on the back seat was lolling a little sideways, his mouth open, his eyes glazed.

Not until the car pulled up at Heathrow, and the driver opened the back door, was the Prime Minister's condition realised. Her Majesty's First Minister of State would not be on the tarmac to greet the President of the United States. He had suffered a catastrophic stroke.

ALL the elaborate arrangements made to welcome the President when he first set foot on British soil were cancelled. Instead, he, his wife and a couple of senior aides were hustled into a V.I.P. lounge, and then driven to the United States Embassy. The President's wife thought of the three huge travelling cases containing her wardrobe for this five-day visit; she thought, in particular, of the incredibly expensive silken gown she had bought to wear just once, at the dinner at Buckingham Palace. "Does this mean the show's off?" she asked plaintively. The President could not tell her. At that moment, no one could.

Unnoticed, Gilbert Parkinson detached himself from the American party, took the airport bus to the centre of London, booked into a commercial hotel in Bloomsbury, and then made a phone call.

He had done his homework. "The Salisbury Club? I believe that Mr Chadwick is one of your members and is now staying at the club as a resident. Would it be possible . . . yes, I'll hold."

"He's a goner," said the ambulance man who lifted Christopher Marlowe's stretcher into the vehicle. He was right. There was not a flicker of life in the Prime Minister's body when the ambulance arrived at the Middlesex Hospital.

The news was brought to the Sovereign as she was watching the Horse of the Year show on the television set in her private drawing room. Her daughter was one of four riders who had had clear rounds over the monstrous course devised for the President's Cup. The jump-off was just about to begin.

The Queen knew that once again upon her would devolve the responsibility of "sending for" whoever emerged from Marlowe's colleagues as his successor. But that could not take place until after the inevitable in-fighting to determine the succession. It might take a day, or a couple of days. But there was nothing for her to do at the moment, except initial the sincere Royal expression of sorrow at the death of a statesman. This was brought to her by a secretary. She signed it, and sensibly returned to the television, just in time to see her daughter knock a pole off a fence, and lose four points. The next rider, a dashing Argentinian, completed his round unscathed, and went on to win the cup.

By the time the Argentinian had been presented with his trophy, the in-fighting had started. Metcalfe was the first off the mark. He had been watching television, but not the show-jumping. He had been tuned into the other channel, which was recording the arrival of the President at Heathrow. He started making phone calls as soon as the first alarming snippets of news from the airport started to flash on the screen, and by the time of the official announcement of Marlowe's death, at a quarter to ten, he had assembled around him at his Westminster flat three of his closest Cabinet cronies: Torrington, the Foreign Secretary; Davidson, the Lord Privy Seal; and Rigby-Cooke, the Social Services minister. All were survivors of the Tory administration that had been tipped out of office by Bainbridge five years previously. Their average age was sixty-three.

"Someone," said Metcalfe, "has got to take this situation by

160

the scruff of its neck and put it into shape. By this time tomorrow night."

He was making his bid. He was seeking their backing.

They agreed, with less enthusiasm than he had expected, that soundings should be made. One thing comforted him. Even if they were less than ecstatic, among that lot, at least, there was no possible rival. Only he had the kudos of having been Chancellor, of presenting Budgets, of having been the right-hand man.

Helen was one of the last of the Cabinet to hear. She was alone in the flat. She had not had the television on. She was indulging herself in her end-of-the-day pleasure, *The Times* crossword puzzle. It was a sticky one, with far too much Greek mythology, which was not her strong point. Then the phone went. It was Willis, the Defence Minister, who had supported her over the hanging bill. He was calling from his home in Hampstead, and told her what had happened. "There are one or two people here talking things over," he said. "We think you should come along."

The secret conclaves in Westminster and Hampstead went on until two o'clock in the morning. But, in fact, the issue was being decided elsewhere. In Fleet Street.

NEWSPAPER editors like to think they influence events as well as report them. It seldom happens that way. It did on this night, Fleet Street's busiest for a decade.

For every newspaper, sedate or bumptious, the big angle of the story was not so much Marlowe's death, although that received massive coverage, but: *Who comes next?*

Working entirely independently of each other, they all came to the same answer.

161

The brash, mass-sale *Post* told its readers (nine million of them, more than two to each of the four million copies sold daily): "In this undistinguished Cabinet, this assembly consisting largely of tired, spent men, there is only one name and one face which make any significant impact on the public outside the confines of Westminster. The name and the face are those of Mrs Helen Chadwick." The *Post's big black* headline said: "IT MUST BE HELEN".

The Times was rather more restrained, but the message was the same: "In this crisis, the country needs inspiration. Whence is it to come? Among the late Mr Marlowe's senior colleagues are some who have given long and loyal service to their party and to the country. All honour to them. But the need of the moment is for firm and vigorous leadership; and that leadership must come from someone who has some rapport with the people at large. There is only one member of the Cabinet who has that rapport to any high degree; astonishingly, a member whose Parliamentary career is barely a year old . . ." The headline on *The Times* leader was: "A time for boldness".

Every single national newspaper, all seven of them – right wing, left wing, uncommitted, tabloid, broadsheet – put over the same message. Even those that normally gave unqualified support to the Tory Party, on this occasion proclaimed that the national interest overrode any normal succession along strict party lines.

Next morning, when Metcalfe saw this phalanx of opinion, he commented bitterly to Torrington: "I suppose they're getting rid of their sex repressions. Must be all that night work."

While Helen was reading the papers, Willis phoned. "Would you not agree," he said, "that our newspapers, like our policemen, are wonderful?" They discussed certain matters of strategy, and Helen put the phone down well satisfied.

It should have surprised her, or perhaps frightened her to think that barely a year after being rejected by a Tory selection committee, she was on the brink of becoming the successor to Pitt, Peel, Palmerston, Gladstone, Disraeli, Asquith, Lloyd George, Churchill and some lesser ones. In fact, the prospect did not surprise or alarm her at all. Everything had happened incredibly quickly, but in a kind of pre-ordained sequence. She had no qualms about her capacity to do the job. Or that before the day was out, it would be hers.

In that last assumption, she was wrong, but only by one day.

At ten a.m. the Cabinet met. Metcalfe presided. He made the inevitable oration about the loss of our "esteemed and wise leader". Then he said: "The Government of the country must go on."

Helen said nothing. It was Willis who took the initiative. It had all been worked out at one o'clock in the morning at Hampstead. He said: "If this were an administration based purely on the Conservative Party, the next step would be clear. There would be a poll of the party's M.P.s and peers, soundings would be made in the constituencies, and the person elected from within the Party would become both leader of the Party and Prime Minister. His name would be submitted to the Sovereign, and that would be that.

"But this is a two-party Government, holding power because two parties whose views differ on some things have pooled their talents and resources. Therefore, the procedures of any one party cannot apply. The entire talent of the administration is available. For myself, and not only for myself, because I know I am speaking for some others around this table, I believe the most suitable person to fill this vacancy was not one who was elected as a member of the Conservative Party at the last election. Though I am a member of the Conservative Party, and my record is such that I do not think anyone can challenge my loyalty to the party, I am firmly convinced that the most suitable person to fill this vacancy is Mrs Chadwick. I believe she is the obvious choice. It is quite clear that this view is held very strongly in the country. This morning's newspapers give it unqualified endorsement."

Phillips and Matheson backed him up. So did Hewett (Leader of the House) and Stevenson (Commonwealth Secretary). Davidson and Rigby-Cooke spoke for Metcalfe.

Metcalfe was certainly not prepared to let it go without a fight.

"In this Parliament," he said, "there are around three hundred Conservative members. Are you suggesting that we, in this room, should assign the Premiership to some one outside

163

the Party, to some one who, in fact, caused the party very considerable embarrassment at a by-election, without consulting the Parliamentary Party? The party would never stand for it."

It was his last card. And Willis had a trump for it.

"The Sovereign, I am told," he said, "is an astute reader of the newspapers, and has other sources of advice and information. Let us consider a position in which the Tory Party reverts to its normal succession procedure. We then submit a name to the Sovereign. But in this unique situation, she is not obliged to accept that name. She has an alternative choice. It would be within her perogative to reject the name we submitted to her. I foresee a situation in which the Conservative Party might find itself in conflict with the Crown, and would suffer a humiliating rebuff. That would be a position utterly without precedent. It would be a catastrophic thing for the party. But it could happen. It not only could happen. It very probably would happen."

Metcalfe insisted: "You cannot ignore three hundred members."

"Then let us not ignore them. Let the Chief Whip take soundings and find out whether the members at large wish to embark on a course which could put this party into a head-on collision with the Crown. The Chief Whip should make the implications clear, though I don't imagine that will be necessary in many cases. Above all, let us remember that the Queen does read the newspapers. And that her prerogative is a real thing, should she choose to exercise it."

That was something which Metcalfe could not dodge. The meeting ended after only twenty minutes. Helen had not spoken a word.

The Chief Whip did his duty. The Tory members, some grumbling, accepted the inevitable. The sounding procedure took a day.

When the Cabinet re-assembled at ten the following morning, Metcalfe acknowledged defeat.

"Outside this room," he said, "there is a gentleman from the Palace. He is waiting to hear whether we have any advice for the Sovereign on the question of the appointment of a Prime

Minister. It is clear that in this room, and in the country, there is a strong feeling that we should recommend to the Sovereign that she should invite Mrs Chadwick to fill the vacancy. Mrs Chadwick, with whom I had a short discussion before this meeting started, is willing to undertake this onerous task. We have to submit a name to the Palace. Is it your wish that that name should be Mrs Chadwick?"

The vote was unanimous, or at least nem. con. Metcalfe did not indicate his own opinion.

"Thank you, gentlemen," said Helen. They were the only words she had spoken during the two crisis Cabinet meetings.

That afternoon, a summons reached her at the Home Office. She drove from there to Buckingham Palace. The return journey was slightly different. It ended at Number Ten Downing Street.

All newspapers keep in reserve extra large type which, since the D-Day invasion of 1944, has been known as "invasion type". These huge letters are seldom used, because the news seldom justifies doing so. But on that afternoon the evening newspapers did get the invasion type out of the rack. The headline said: THE QUEEN SENDS FOR MRS CHADWICK.

THE President's wife said: "Shit." She had just heard that in view of Marlowe's death, the programme for the State visit would be "modified".

"What the hell does it matter who's Prime Minister of this dead-beat outfit?" she demanded. "We had a contract, didn't we. Now they've got us here, you're not going to let them stand us up, are you?"

The President could not immediately give her an answer. But in the event, the two items most important to the President's wife went ahead. There was the state drive, with the Household Cavalry, from the Palace to the Guildhall, with the President, in frock coat, sitting at the side of the Queen, and the President's lady at the side of the Queen's husband; and there was the State dinner at the Palace, at which Martha Maloney, in her costly dress, was indeed a sensation. But the crowds on the route and outside the Palace were thinner than had been expected. The nation, it seemed, had other things on its mind.

Helen's participation was required for both these events; and on these, her first public appearance as Prime Minister, she displayed a cool assurance which was just about right for the muted festivities. But her mind, too, was on other things.

Principally on the composition of her Cabinet.

There would have to be changes. Some of Marlowe's choices had appalled her. But she decided not to rush things. The one immediate problem was to fill the vacancy created by her own elevation.

Keith Shalton wanted the Home Office job. Badly. He came to see her at Number Ten, and practically demanded it, as of right.

"Prime Minister," he said, with false subservience, "I think the time has come for me to emerge from the shadows. Not only the time. But also the opportunity."

"It's time I paid my bills?"

"I wouldn't put it in those terms."

"Then I must have misunderstood you."

"I think we understand each other pretty well."

"Of course," said Helen, "I'm new in this job. But aren't we rather departing from protocol. I thought the drill was that when a Cabinet vacancy arose, the Prime Minister sent for someone. I seem to recall tales of people sitting by telephones."

"If it will make you happy I will go and sit by a telephone. But perhaps you might deign to let me know roughly when I can expect the call."

"Keith, I think we should get this straight. There isn't going to be a call. Not for you."

Very slowly, he reached into his pocket for his cigarette case, extracted a cigarette, and lit it.

"I see."

"I'm sorry."

"Might I inquire your reasons? I would have thought, in the circumstances, that what I had in mind was reasonable enough."

There was no point in dodging it. He'd asked for it. She gave it him.

"One reason."

"Which is?"

"In my view, you are not Cabinet material."

His venom was almost frightening.

"You have the impertinence to lecture *me* about Cabinet material? How the hell do you think you got into the Cabinet in the first place? I put you there. I did it from the word go. I put you up for Midhampton, and with your incredible stupidity and arrogance you cocked that up, and damn near wrecked my career in the process. But I got you into Parliament. You don't think that bunch of gorillas at Midhampton would have dreamed of giving you a run if I hadn't pointed you in that direction in the first place? And I got you into the Cabinet. Once again I put my career at risk, and got you into the Cabinet, and don't you ever forget it. You hardly knew how to put your cross on a ballot paper, and I made a Cabinet minister out of you."

"Don't tell me you organised Marlowe's stroke too."

"Would you enlighten me, from your vast Cabinet and Prime Ministerial experience, in what way I fall short of your exacting standards?

"I think you're too damn clever."

"It's my cleverness, as you disparagingly call it, that has got you into this room."

"You set me on the way. I acknowledge that."

"And my reward, I presume, will be an O.B.E. along with the hall porters and charwomen. I gave you a piece of advice a few days ago, and you chose to ignore it. I told you it does matter which side of the fence people are on. You may find that is more true than you had thought. Good morning, *Prime Minister*."

"Hi, Helen." The President, accompanied by a Downing Street detective had gone up in the Number Ten lift to the Prime Minister's flat on the second floor. It was the last day but one of his visit. He would be flying back to the States on the following afternoon. They had met on no fewer than four formal and public occasions, but this was the first time he and Helen had been alone since he had arrived at Heathrow.

Helen wished the place was in better shape. It provided a somewhat meagre comparison with the President's sumptuous quarters in the White House. Marlowe's personal things, his paintings and his books and one or two personal pieces of furniture, had been removed. The Ministry of Works' temporary replacements, though adequate, were not exactly inspiring. Helen had not yet had time to impose her personality on the place.

"I am afraid," she said, "that this is rather less grand than the White House."

"But more cosy."

"It will be, when I've finished with it."

At least there were some drinks in the cupboard. She poured out Scotches. Large ones.

"My," said the President.

"On the taxpayers," said Helen. "I get a hospitality allowance. For entertaining visiting statesmen. Friendly ones, of course.

"To the taxpayers, God bless 'em."

"God help them."

She wondered how this session would end. Had he been getting it with his wife? She guessed that Martha might be quite a performer, if she was in the mood.

"I hope you've enjoyed your visit."

"Sure. Fine."

"And Mrs Maloney?"

"She'd take Buckingham Palace home with her, if she could. And some of those Household Cavalry dudes to go with it."

The President sipped his drink. "You've been having a

168

helluva time lately. That business with the darkie. Jeez, I'd never have dared to do what you did. Then the Marlowe business. I'd love to know what went on downstairs when that blew up."

Helen said: "I wonder what Bert Cooper thinks about it?"

"Who the hell's Bert Cooper?"

"In a way, he's the man who started it all. He was the man who started that strike at my factory. After that, one thing just followed another. I don't think I've done anything very remarkable, except put through a Capital Punishment Bill, and that was not exactly an original idea. Four out of five people wanted it, but nobody had got around to getting it down on paper and making it law. Well, I did. And now here I am, in Downing Street, talking to the President of the United States. And as I say, it was Bert Cooper who started it all."

"Then here's to Bert Cooper."

"I suppose we ought to be discussing affairs of state. Matters of common interest to our two great countries."

"Sometimes I get fed up to the back teeth with my great country. I guess that will finally happen to you too. Give it time."

"I'm sure it will."

"I've got another eighteen months to do. Then I'm getting out. You've got what – another four years, or something like that? Four years in the fish bowl. You on the inside, everybody else looking in."

She was pretty sure he was dangling a bait. She took it.

"No one's looking in here."

The President put down his glass and moved a little closer to her. "Your boys got this place buttoned-up?"

"Buttoned-up tight."

The President, it seemed, was not quite ready to press on. "What were those affairs of state we were supposed to be talking about?"

"My mind's gone blank."

"Of course, we could resume our discussion about what's wrong with the United States. What bums we are, and how only the fancy-pants English really know what's what, old boy, when it comes to diplomacy or statesmanship."

169

"I would not dream of being so discourteous to a guest."

"Then," said the President, "it seems to me that we have the choice of two things."

"Which are?"

"We can see off this bottle of Scotch between us. I reckon you and I could manage that. Then there's the other thing . . ."

"Let's do both."

"Why not?"

"Which first? Must get the priorities right."

"I would say the other thing. But I'm open to argument."

"Be my guest," she said.

The mission was accomplished as before.

Afterwards, she said: "I trust all was satisfactory?"

"It was kind of you, very kind."

"You're welcome."

"That's what American girls say."

"In these circumstances?"

"How would I know?"

"Perhaps some of the younger men around the White House could keep you up to date."

He was about to take reprisals when the phone rang. The number was, of course, ex-directory, and known only to a limited circle of people, such as ministers, senior civil servants and a few other special contacts. Her first inclination was to let it ring. Then she decided she had better answer it. It could probably be heard outside the room. The detective might start wondering, and draw some conclusions. The right ones.

"Yes? . . . why . . . I don't know." Long pause. Then: "All right. Tomorrow. Here. Nine o'clock."

"You want to change that number," said the President. "You'll find too many people know it. All Marlowe's hangers-on. What was it all about, anyway. Got to send a gun-boat somewhere?"

"It wasn't that."

"Not the newspapers. *They* haven't got the number, have they?"

"It was my husband."

THERE had, of course, been speculation in the newspapers about her position in relation to Bernard. His total non-involvement in her political activities had been noted, but this had been put down to his meticulous observance of the rule which bars Civil Servants from politics. His move from the Home Office had also been reported, but this had also been in accordance with the code of public service. Neither from her, nor from Bernard, had one word leaked about the deeper, personal implications of that business. And her arrival at 10 Downing Street had been so precipitous, with so many other matters calling for headlines, that the newspapers had not yet picked up the fact that only she, and not Bernard, had taken up residence there.

That revelation, of course, could not be long delayed. Perhaps, she thought, the newspapers had been hounding Bernard about it; that could well be the reason for his urgent demand that he must see her to discuss "our personal affairs."

She had not seen him since the night he had found her with Henry Wilberforce Grant at the flat. That was six weeks ago. As he was shown into her private office on the ground floor she noticed, or thought she noticed, a change in him. He came in briskly, like a man with a job to do, and determined to get it done quickly.

As soon as the door had closed behind him, he said: "Is it in order for one of my humble position to be seated in the presence of the mighty?" Without waiting for an answer, he took a chair. This was indeed a different Bernard.

"I congratulate you," he said, "on your meteoric progress." But there was no gentleness. No affection. The tone was sardonic, the manner glacial.

"How are things with you?"

"The Stationery Office? A new, exciting world. Did you know that the various departments of your Government need no fewer than around five thousand three hundred forms of different kinds to conduct their business, and that the number is increasing by twenty a week? Fascinating work. For clerks with two O levels."

171

"Perhaps we could do something about that. Now that I'm no longer at the Home Office."

"And have the newspapers and everybody in the Service saying you'd fixed it for me. No *thank* you."

"You said something about personal affairs."

"I've had the newspapers on to me."

So that *was* it.

"One impertinent fellow wanted to know if and when I was moving into Downing Street, and if not, why not."

"What did you tell him?"

"I put the phone down."

"I suppose," she said, "we ought to draw up an agreed statement. Perhaps get it lawyered."

"You can issue what statement you like. I shall issue my own."

"And what exactly will it say?"

"It will say I am seeking a divorce."

"I see."

The timing of the thing was cruel. He could have done it at almost any other time over the last dozen years or so. To wait until this moment to deliver the blow was spiteful, vengeful. But of course, she conceded, he had some grounds for revenge. It was the job thing, the career, that had wounded him most. She was sure of that.

He said: "I don't think you do see. Yet. I have stood your outrageous behaviour for the best part of fifteen years. I have let you have your amusements without complaint. You get yourself mixed up with a bunch of Fascists or near Fascists, and I say nothing because, for the moment, you find it amusing. Though I did try, in an unobtrusive way, to steer you off this political nonsense."

"You did what?"

"I placed certain information in the hands of a member of the selection committee at Midhampton."

"*You* did that? *You?*"

"With your best interests at heart."

"God! I should have known. But I never knew you hated me that much."

"I don't hate you. At least, I didn't then. I wanted you. For myself."

"And supposing you'd had me. For yourself. What could you have done?"

It was a vicious thing to say. But he, too, had been vicious.

"I am, I think, a fairly mild sort of person, but recently there have been three things which cannot by any stretch of the imagination be put in the category of amusements, and which I find unforgivable."

"Only three?"

"There is a fourth. But here are the three: You drove me out of a job which I loved, and which I did rather well. Then, by your handling of that reprieve business, you brought shame on the place which I still regard as my office. And thirdly you slept with a black man."

If only, if only, Bernard had had the guts to speak his mind like this years ago.

Helen said: "I admit the first. I've told you I'm sorry, and I mean that. If you will let me repair the damage, I will do so. The second thing is purely a matter of opinion. And the third thing just isn't true. I never, repeat, never slept with Henry Grant. And in any case, what does his colour matter anyway? I thought you belonged to the all-men-are-equal brigade. I find this very odd. I mustn't hang a black man. But I mustn't sleep with one either. Even if I did, which I didn't. There's something there that doesn't add up. No doubt you, with your impeccable logic, can explain it to me."

"I do not propose to explain anything. I have enough circumstantial evidence of your association with the black man to convince any court that there were sexual relations. And I am quite prepared to use it."

"I shall deny it."

"Of course."

"You don't want a divorce. You don't give a damn about the divorce. You just want your revenge for the job thing. You want to ruin me."

"Many politicians are divorced without being destroyed," said Bernard. "It's quite the normal thing these days. And according to your way of thinking, as I understand it, the colour of the people involved is quite irrelevant. That *is* what you were saying, isn't it?"

"You bastard."

"Mind you, should there be any doubt about the evidence relating to the adultery with the black man, I have other evidence, irrefutable evidence, of adultery with a white man."

"You'd drag Keith Shalton into this and destroy him too? You've been putting your spies onto Keith again?"

"Now I find that interesting. A very interesting admission. But in fact he is not the person I have in mind."

"*Not* Keith?"

"Not Mr Shalton. A political person though. But one rather more exalted than Mr Shalton. Indeed, far more exalted."

"I haven't—"

"You have. Indeed you have. I think you should spare a moment or two to look at this."

He took a typewritten document from his briefcase and put it on her table. She had only to look at half a dozen words to know what it was.

"*I think, Mr President, that you will find a small hook at the top that has to be undone first.*"

"It appears," said the *Evening Mail* the next day, "that Mrs Chadwick and President Maloney have established an exceptionally cordial personal relationship. There was fresh evidence of this rapport today, when the President paid a brief flying and unscheduled visit to Downing Street just before noon for a final, personal session with the Prime Minister before flying back to Washington later in the day. This augurs well for the future relations between Great Britain and the United States."

In fact, this hurried meeting between the Prime Minister and the President was far from cordial.

"Jesus on the mountain," said the President when Helen showed him the transcript of the tape which Bernard had received from the Other Man.

She told him the whole story; how Bernard's complaisance had suddenly turned to bitterness because of the disruption of his career; how Bernard, despite his façade of liberality and goodwill to all men, had reacted to her association with a black

174

man; how Bernard had said he would use his evidence against Wilberforce Grant, which she would deny; and how Bernard had threatened to use the transcript, too, if it should be necessary.

The President said: "Where does this leave me when the shit hits the fan? Think what the newspapers will do to me. *And* there's Martha."

She was angry at his concentration on his personal predicament, without a thought for hers. "Wherever it leaves you, I shall be there, too."

"You never told me you were shacked up with a darkie. That I was sharing you with a darkie."

"I was not shacked up with anyone."

He did not believe her; and he was in no way mollified when she pointed out that it was his security arrangements, not hers, which had broken down.

"I suggest, Mr President," she said icily, "that you mend your fences."

"I'll do that."

He did so within fifteen minutes of arriving back at the White House. He sent for Andy Dewhurst, the man to whom he had entrusted the privacy of his personal life, and said: "You screwed it up." The President showed Andy Dewhurst the typescript (Bernard had left two copies in Helen's office). Averaging one expletive every four words, the President inquired how Andy Dewhurst visualised the reaction of the American public, not to mention the reactions of the President's wife, when it became known that he, the President of the United States had seduced, or been seduced by, the Prime Minister of the United Kingdom; and what did Andy Dewhurst think it would do to his position as the most powerful man in the Western world when people in bars and at bus stops learned that he had shared the affections of his mistress with a goddamned black-assed bus driver?

Every word was a lacerating wound for Andy Dewhurst. He had a special relationship with the President; the President, from his own pocket, had helped Andy's son through medical school. Andy's loyalty to the President was total.

Andy Dewhurst did not know how it had happened. He

175

knew only that in the one matter which, above all others, the President trusted him, there had been a catastrophic failure; and that he had landed the President in the mire, right up to the eyeballs.

Andy finished his day's routine at the White House in a stupor. Then he went to Alf's bar for a stiffener, to pull his shattered soul together. After the third stiffener, a thought began to form in his head.

He had betrayed his master. The consequences of that betrayal were not yet public. He did not know when that would happen, but since it looked like a court matter, he guessed it might be some days, perhaps weeks. It might just be possible to avert the explosion. He, Andy Dewhurst, might yet be able to save the Presidential ship from the rocks. If other people perished on the rocks, that was just too damn bad. One thing, and one thing only, mattered. That the President should be saved and that he, Andy Dewhurst, would be able to look him in the eye again, and have that arm put round his shoulder again.

He had a fourth stiffener, but his brain was ice-cold. He began to work out the details. There were quite a few of them. It would be tough on the Chadwick guy, and tough on the Chadwick woman if anything went wrong. He felt no remorse, no pity. Only one person mattered. The President.

That night, he packed a weekend bag, and phoned his immediate superior to say he had an urgent job to do, and would not be around for a couple of days. He was not challenged. It was known that Andy sometimes received urgent instructions from the highest level. Next day, he flew to London. He arrived at five o'clock, and phoned a certain number.

Just as British Intelligence had Gilbert Parkinson in the White House, American Intelligence had their Other Man in the British secret service. He was a product of Charterhouse and the Brigade of Guards, and his name was Rodney Browne. He received a salary of £11,000 a year from the British Government for his services to the nation, but unknown to his official employers, he received twice that, tax free, delivered by special arrangement, from his American paymasters for keeping certain people in Washington informed about various matters not known to more than half a dozen people in London. Rodney

176

Browne's life-style (he hunted with the Pytchley) was based on that money. Everyone thought he had inherited wealth.

Andy Dewhurst met Rodney Browne in a cocktail bar in Regent Street that evening, and put a proposition to him. Rodney Browne was horrified; and alarmed. "Not on, old boy. Definitely not on."

Andy Dewhurst did not waste time. He went straight into blackmail. If Rodney Browne's dual role became known to his British masters, there would be no public scandal; neither nation could afford that. But Rodney Browne's way of life would be torpedoed for ever.

Rodney had second thoughts.

"How high does this come from?"

"The top," lied Andy Dewhurst. "And I mean the top. You'll be in the clear. All you've got to do is to talk to the guy I'll send over. But it's got to be a Britisher that talks to him. Not an American. Just in case anything goes wrong. Then there can be no feedback."

"No feedback for you," said Rodney Browne.

"Nor for you. You'll only see the guy for ten minutes. He won't know who you are. Won't have a clue."

"And what do you want me to tell this feller?"

Andy Dewhurst spelt out what Rodney Browne was to tell the feller.

"And you're sure this comes from the top?"

"Right from the top."

That made sense to Rodney Browne, after a fashion. He knew of Andy Dewhurst's special position in relation to the President. If this very odd job was to be done at all, that was the way it would be done. It was not something that could be put on the file, even the most secret file.

Finally he said: "All right. Send him over."

"Shall I tell him to call you?"

"For Christ's sake, no. I'll ring him. Give me the number where he'll be."

Andy went to the bar's phone box, looked up the address of a boarding-house hotel in Kensington, and came back with the number. He had one more request for Rodney. He wanted a certain London telephone number. Rodney said: "Do you want

177

to get me shot?"

Next day Andy flew back to Washington feeling a little easier in his mind, but there was a devil of a lot still to do.

The man he had in mind for the mission was Tony Baroni. In the Chicago City Police, where Andy had served for twelve years before taking up his White House assignment, there was a file two inches thick on Tony Baroni. He was a hit man. He was known to have done three jobs, possibly five. But never had there been a shred of evidence which would stand up in court. He was one of the best, a professional of a dying breed. A quick, clean operator. An in-and-out man, with no messing. But Andy Dewhurst could not deal directly with Tony Baroni. That could compromise the White House. The chain of command, so far as Tony Baroni was concerned, had to be entirely British.

Just in case of accidents.

No problem. Another unofficial recipient of the American taxpayers' money, for small and sometimes quaint services rendered, was the New York sales manager of British Chemicals Ltd. This gentleman, though completly mystified, carried out his instructions. He flew to Chicago, phoned Tony Baroni, and met him in a bar. He handed over 5,000 dollars which, in fact, had come from Andy Dewhurst's personal account (Andy was sure the money could be sorted out when it was all over) and promised another 25,000 dollars when the job was done. The President had a personal contingency fund, and his gratitude, thought Andy, would sure run to that. Mr Baroni was told that his presence was urgently required in Britain.

Tony Baroni flew to London knowing there was a job to be done, but not what it was. He did not take a gun with him. That would have been asking for trouble; but being a professional, he knew where he could pick up one in London. He did this, booked in at the Talbot Residential Hotel, and waited for the phone to ring; which it did.

A very English voice gave him precise directions to a public house just off Leicester Square. He knew neither the name of the man who had contacted him in Chicago, nor the name of the caller in London. But it seemed a pretty efficient set-up.

He was curious about the job, just as Andy Dewhurst had

expected he would be. "Who is this guy?" he asked the portly Englishman who had bought him a large gin. At first, the Englishman stalled. Better all round if you didn't know, old boy. High level stuff. But Tony Baroni said: "If I'm going to hit him, then for Chrissake I want to know who he is."

The Englishman said: "All right. His name's Chadwick."

"Was that the guy who was in that dope racket in Hong Kong or some place?"

"I think not. He's in a different line of business."

"What's he done? Rubbed someone the wrong way?"

"You could say that."

"Is he a big guy?"

"He's not.'

"Then why's he got to be rubbed out?"

"He wants a divorce."

"So what? Everybody wants a divorce. I want a divorce."

"Do you read the newspaper?"

"Not much."

"It's his wife. *She's* important."

"How important?"

"She happens to be Prime Minister of this country."

"Jeez! That broad the President's been talking to?"

"That's the one."

"And she don't want Mr Chadwick around no more?"

"That is exactly the position."

"What's biting her about this divorce? Lots of people get divorced."

"It's a rather special case. She *is* Prime Minister, that's like your President. And there's something else."

"Yeah?"

"She has been indiscreet . . . with a black gentleman. A black member of Parliament. Like your congressmen."

"She got laid?"

"She did."

"And Mr Chadwick, he don't like it?"

"Not with the black man. He's going to blow it all over the newspapers."

"And this dame, she don't want that?"

"She definitely does not."

179

"And that's where I come in. To keep everything nice and tidy."

"Exactly. To see everything stays nice and tidy."

"And that's worth twenty-five grand to her?"

"I told you. She *is* Prime Minister."

Rodney Browne had fed the tale exactly as Andy Dewhurst had directed. Then he got down to specifics. He produced a photograph and a street plan.

"You can do it?" he asked.

"Sure I can do it. For twenty-five grand."

"It mustn't go wrong."

"I'll see it don't go wrong."

"When? It's got to be quick. Or it may be too late."

"This guy goes to this club at half-past six? Every night?"

"That's his normal thing."

"I'll be around. Six thirty tomorrow."

Before they parted, Rodney Browne performed one final duty. He took an envelope from his pocket and handed it to Tony Baroni. It contained a hundred pounds in fivers. The envelope had arrived from Andy Dewhurst, in another sealed envelope, that morning, with instructions to pass it on to Tony Baroni.

"Just in case you need a bit of ready cash," said Rodney.

"This come off the fee?"

"No, it's on top of it."

Tony Baroni thought these la-di-dah Englishmen were good people to work for.

LIFE goes on; especially life for Prime Ministers. It was on May the tenth, the last day of the President's visit, that Bernard had come to see her at Downing Street. By a week later he had still made no public move. Could it be that he was having second thoughts? Or consulting his lawyers? In everything she did — and there was plenty to do, including attendance at

180

Marlowe's funeral – it was difficult to concentrate fully, knowing that any moment she might be plunged into a scandal that would make headlines across the world. But she did her best, and it was a pretty good best, for instance at an acrimonious Cabinet meeting when Metcalfe and Willis were in bitter conflict over Metcalfe's proposed cuts in Willis's defence budget, with Metcalfe accusing all the Services of thinking there was a bottomless purse to finance their wildest fantasies. She got them both to go away and think again. She did not normally like putting things off, but she just did not feel equal to handling a major conflict.

At one o'clock, she had to switch on the charm. She was guest-speaker at a Press Gallery lunch at the Commons. The journalists were hospitable. The chairman, in his speech of welcome, recalled that the invitation, issued some weeks previously, had been sent to Helen in her then capacity as Home Secretary. "Whatever our personal politics," he said, "and whatever the politics of the papers we represent, I am sure all of us join in congratulating Mrs Chadwick on her recent elevation, and in believing that she will bring charm and distinction to her present high office of state."

Helen wondered what the journalists would do if they had even the merest hint of the time bomb that was ticking away under her. She guessed that they would abandon the meal, and that there would be a scramble for telephones.

By three fifteen, she was in the House answering questions. Was the Prime Minister satisfied that the recently-produced cost-of-living index accurately reflected the changes of prices of goods in the shops, and was not the index a cover-up operation to make the Government's anti-inflation measures seem more successful than they actually were? Had the Prime Minister any statement to make on the decision to refuse entry into this country of a Left-wing Dutch trade union leader? And was this not a diabolical interference, on trumped-up security grounds, in the right of working men of all nations to confer together on matters of mutual interest?

She dealt with these matters in a calm and competent manner. The questioners did not get much change out of her.

At five o'clock the House began a debate on an educational

bill aimed at restoring to the grammar schools the status they had lost under the comprehensive school system established by previous governments. Helen's minister of education, Wilfred Chivers, was a bit of a lightweight, and she had decided to put her own authority behind the bill. It was 6.15 when she rose to speak.

"I must declare an interest," she told the House. "I am myself a product of the grammar-school system, and I have, at various times, conspired with others of like mind to ensure that the excellent school which I attended should retain its character and independence."

It was quite a short speech, but not without impact. She sat down just after half-past six.

IT was just about at that time that Tony Baroni did the deed.

He had acquired, without the formalities of purchase, an Aston Martin which had quite astonishing powers of acceleration. He parked it close to the kerb, and adjusted the driving mirror so that he could watch people walking towards him from behind along the pavement. On the passenger seat was his gun, equipped with silencer.

His man was five minutes late, but when he did appear, Tony Baroni had no doubt that this was the one. He made a quick check with the photograph that had been supplied to him. This was the guy, all right.

Tony Baroni checked the getaway situation. If there were any problems, he wouldn't do it; not tonight. They'd have to wait. He was in the hot seat, and he was not going to get his ass scorched. Not for any Brit. Not even for twenty-five grand.

But it was working out O.K. There had been a bit of a hold-up fifty yards ahead, but that was clearing now, and would be over by the time he needed the road. He wound down the near-side window, and started the engine. The guy came level with the car. Tony Baroni let him go on for another ten yards.

Now. Tony Baroni set the car in motion, slid over to the passenger seat, steering with his right hand. His left arm, with the gun in hand, was out of the window. He fired four shots, and had accelerated past the target even before the guy had hit the pavement.

It was a quick, clean, professional job. At least, it would have been, but for Mrs Mavis Forbes-Barrington.

Mrs Forbes-Barrington, who had failed her driving test three times, was having her forty-seventh driving lesson from the Easidrive School of Motoring. Tony Baroni had seen her car approaching slowly from the opposite direction, on the other side of the road, but it had never occurred to him that this vehicle would in any way hinder his escape. However, just before Baroni's silenced gun sent Bernard lurching to the ground, the Easidrive instructor, George Briggs, had told Mrs Forbes-Barrington: "Take the next turn on the right."

She misunderstood him. He had meant her to turn at the traffic lights a hundred yards ahead. Instead, she aimed for a right turn immediately ahead, which was little more than an alleyway. Grimly concentrating on what she believed to be her instructor's order, and totally ignoring anything else that was going on, she swung the car across the road. She swung it right across Tony Baroni's escape route.

Tony Baroni saw this maniacal manoeuvre developing, but could do nothing about it. He flung all his driving skill, and the immense power of the Aston Martin into a frantic effort to get clear before the other car completed its turn.

Surely the jerk would break and let him through?

He did not know Mrs Forbes-Barrington. She had been told to turn right, and by God, she would turn right. She came on remorselessly.

Neither Baroni's expertise, nor the surge of the Aston Martin, were quite enough. Tony Baroni thought he had just made it when there was a mighty crunch as the driving school car hit the rear wheel of the Aston, causing the car to change direction violently. It now shot diagonally across to the other side of the road, where it mounted the pavement and embedded itself in a shop window.

George Briggs, though naturally mainly concerned with the suicidal behaviour of his pupil, had noticed other things in those three climactic seconds. Mrs Forbes-Barrington was evidently unscathed. She was fiercely protesting her innocence. "You said 'Turn right'. That's what you said, 'Turn Right' . . ." George Briggs did not stop to argue with her. He raced over to the other car, from which the driver had not yet extricated himself.

On the front seat was a gun. George Briggs had been with the Easidrive Motoring School only six months. For twenty years before that he had been in the Metropolitan Police. He was still very much a copper.

He knew that in this situation, he had a duty to do. He did it.

AT seven-thirty that evening Helen drove to Buckingham Palace. Once a week, when the Monarch is in London, she requires the presence of her First Minister for a discussion on the state of the nation; and every prime minister of the present reign has found that these sessions are both stimulating and exacting; for the monarch takes a lively and informed interest about what is going on in her realm. This was Helen's first discussion session. She had gone to the Palace well briefed on all aspects of the economy and foreign policy which were currently in the news. But how could she have foreseen that the Sovereign would want to know if it were true that lengths of curtain material, now that they were measured in centimetres, cost more than they did when they were measured in inches? She would have to get an answer on that one before she made

184

next week's visit. Of course, there probably wouldn't be a next-week's visit if, by then, Bernard had blown the roof off.

She had no means of knowing that while she was driving back to the Palace, her future as Prime Minister was already being put in jeopardy.

Tony Baroni had started to sing.

He had started to sing that early because of something that had been said in the police car taking him to West End Central Police Station.

Sergeant Freddie Potts, with his wrist handcuffed to Tony Baroni's, said: "Where are you from?"

Baroni said: "Chicago."

"American, eh? Well, Mr American, I got news for you. Know what we do to bastards like you in this country these days? We put a rope round your neck, you stand on a little trap door, then a bloke comes along and pulls a lever – and bingo! And know what? I reckon you're just about the right size for that."

This was something which Tony Baroni's British contacts, either by accident or by intent, had failed to mention. Baroni suddenly realised what he had got himself into. The evidence against him would be bomb-proof.

He began to slide out from under.

"I didn't even know the guy," he told Potts. "A couple of Brits put me up to it."

"Don't tell me," said Potts. "Tell it when we get there."

Baroni did that. He started to sing as soon as he got to West End Central. And the song he sang caused the senior officer on duty there to phone Scotland Yard. This potato was too hot for West End Central.

Within one hour, the Commissioner of Police for the Metropolis was at West End Central. One hour after that, he was back at his office at Scotland Yard. With him was the Director of Public Prosecutions.

The D.P.P. said: "I'm beginning to sweat already."

The Commissioner said: "I reckon we're all going to lose some sweat over this one."

"This tale. What do you think of it? It's just about the damn craziest thing I ever heard."

"It's the fact that it is so crazy that makes it worrying. I don't see how he could have invented it, off the top of his head. He's too dim for that. Remember he's got a couple of broken ribs. He may be shaken up a bit, and when he sorts himself out, he may go back on it."

"I sincerely hope so. But he signed it?"

"He signed it all right," said the Commissioner.

"Everything according to the book?"

"Absolutely."

"But there's the medical situation. Man in state of shock. All that. He'll have to do it again. With his own lawyer there. Even then, I'm not at all sure I dare use it. Because if this is produced in court, you realise what this means?"

"I damn well do."

"Then I'd keep it under wraps for the moment. Pretty tight wraps.

"I'll do that."

"Anything for the forensic people to work on?"

"There's the gun of course. He didn't have much on him. Just an envelope with about eighty quids' worth of fivers in it. He says he was given it by the man who briefed him over here. I shall be sending it to the lab, of course. But I doubt whether the notes are going to help much. They are not new ones, and not in sequence."

"Shouldn't think we shall need much from the lab boys," said the D.P.P. "The actual shooting is plain enough. It's the motivation we've got to think about. I don't see how the lab can help on that. But let them do their thing, anyway. You don't want me for anything else tonight? I'm going home, and I'm going to pour myself a large gin and brood over this. Good night."

On the Commissioner's instructions, the name of the man who had been shot in the West End was not released to the Press. And when Tony Baroni appeared at Bow Street the following morning, it was not on a charge of murder, but of taking a car without the owner's permission. No newspaper reporter linked Baroni's two-minute appearance in court with the happenings of the previous night. Baroni was remanded in custody for seven days. It didn't even get a mention in the papers.

The West End shooting of an unnamed man did. But it did not register with Helen. She had other things on her mind. She had come to a decision. She would appeal to Bernard. Not crawl to him, but appeal to him. She would not contest the divorce, and there would be no problem about that; for there were obvious general grounds for asserting that the marriage had broken down. But did Bernard really want to drag her through the mud? And put the President of the United States there, too? Was he determined to bring about a political crisis, a scandal of huge dimensions, involving not only her, but the President? Bernard, in his quiet way, was a patriot. She would appeal to him personally, and on patriotic grounds.

She 'phoned the Stationery Office to fix a date for a meeting. She received a puzzling reply: "Mr Chadwick has not been into the office this morning."

Two minutes after she had put the phone down, her secretary told her that there was a gentleman from Scotland Yard waiting to see her on the most urgent business.

The gentleman from Scotland Yard had been chosen personally by the Commissioner for this delicate mission. He was Detective Chief Superintendent Ronald Creighton. He was an untypical policeman. He was a graduate of Balliol, and held both an arts degree and a law degree. He had made his reputation in the Force not by chasing villains in the East End, but by dealing with a rather higher class of villain. He had spent most of his service in the Fraud Squad. Ronald Creighton could talk to a company chairman about golf and the state of the market, drink the chairman's Scotch and smoke his cigars, and put only the most mild and casual questions about the company's affairs; but within three months the chairman would find himself charged with illegal manipulation of the company's funds, and the charge would stick. Creighton, known in the Force as Slinky Creighton, had come back to the C.I.D. in order to obtain promotion; and as the Commissioner (who had come up the hard way) put it to the D.P.P.: "Since we've got this posh bugger, we might as well use him."

Slinky Creighton's brief was that, with a due display of sorrow and sympathy, he was to inform the Prime Minister that her husband had been shot dead; and that he was to

187

observe and report her reactions.

Slinky Creighton performed the mission as directed.

"Well," asked the Commissioner when Slinky reported back. "What gives?"

"Nothing."

"Was she shocked?"

"Yes, quite a bit. I would say that. But bewildered more than anything else. She kept asking Who? Why?"

"You told her who?"

"I told her there was an American suspect."

"How did that go?"

"What American? Why? That sort of thing."

"Was she putting it on?"

"Personally . . ."

"It's got to be personally. You were the only one there."

"Personally, I don't think so."

"Was she grief-stricken, as the newspapers say? As they undoubtedly will say?"

"That's not exactly the word I would use. More baffled. That was the impression I got. Just plain baffled."

The fact that the Prime Minister's husband had been shot dead in a London street could not be suppressed indefinitely. The Commissioner decided to release it that afternoon, but making no mention of Tony Baroni.

It caused a sensation in Britain. And elsewhere.

In the Commons, Metcalfe for the Government, and Bainbridge for the Opposition both made brief statements expressing sympathy and horror. "I know," said Bainbridge, "that I am speaking for all sides of the House when I say we share a deep revulsion over this unspeakable crime, and we unite in hoping that the perpetrator will be speedily brought to justice."

For the newspapers, the big angle was: Who would want to kill the Prime Minister's husband? And why?

The most far-fetched theories were put forward.

Was it the deed of some international terrorist movement, showing their strength before making demands for the release of terrorists held in jail?

Was it the work of some lunatic fringe of the I.R.A.?

Could it even be the work of the K.G.B.? Had Bernard's

posts at the Home Office and the Stationery Office been the cover for something more sensitive? Was he a man who knew too much?

The Press Officer at 10 Downing Street was under constant harassment from the newspapers to persuade Mrs Chadwick to make a personal statement. But she was not ready to do so.

After the first stunning surprise, her mind had been racing through the possibilities; and one thing stood out: the American connection.

Maloney had known that Bernard was on the brink of involving him in the scandal to end all scandals. Creighton had told her that the suspect was an American. Therefore he must be one of Maloney's hired thugs. The American way of fixing things. She thought of Bernard lying on the pavement with four bullets in his back, and hated Maloney. But perhaps not quite as much as she should have hated him.

She used the scrambler 'phone to the White House. She had been assured that the security of this person-to-person device was absolute. Even so, she was guarded in what she said.

Maloney was less so. Evidently he had more faith in the system.

"I tell you I don't know a damn thing except what's coming out over here in the papers and on the screen. Who the hell's this American? What American? He's not one of mine. I tell you, he's not one of mine. And you tell your police to squeeze him until he squeaks, and let me know what sort of squeak comes out. I'll be mighty interested."

It seemed to Helen that Maloney was absolutely genuine. But if it wasn't Maloney, if he actually wanted the man to be made to squeak, then who?

One member of the President's staff was following the newscasts with special interest. Andy Dewhurst was not greatly disturbed. So Tony Baroni had got himself a rap. That was Tony's problem. And perhaps the Chadwick dame's problem too. He felt no emotion over her at all. It was she who had inveigled his master into indiscreet activities; that was clear from the tape. And if she was in trouble, she could damn well inveigle herself out of it. Anyway, it was unlikely the Brits would give a rap to their own Prime Minister. But if that did

189

happen, it didn't matter, not to Andy Dewhurst. The main thing was that the President was safe, and that there would be no feedback; no feedback at all. Not a soul from the White House had spoken a word to Tony Baroni. The Brits had done it all. The Brits had told Tony Baroni what he, Andy Dewhurst, wanted Baroni to be told. If the London cops leaned on Baroni, and he told them what he had been told, so what? That was the safety net. That, and the money envelope, if the Brits were smart enough to spot what there was to be spotted. The thing was to make sure in advance that the net was O.K., that it would take the strain. Andy Dewhurst was sure that his net *would* take the strain.

In London, police went over the room that Bernard had used at his club, and over his belongings at the flat, looking for anything that might give them a lead to the reason for the killing.

They found nothing. The tape which Bernard had purchased from Gilbert Parkinson, and the only other copy of the transcript, were in a weighted bag on the bottom of the Thames. Bernard, as Helen had hoped, was a patriot. He had decided, after all, not to use the evidence involving the President. It would do too much damage, both to Britain and America. In fact, Bernard had been having second thoughts about the whole thing. He would have his divorce, but he would keep it low profile. He would not hurt Helen more than was necessary. The vengeance mood had burned itself out. He had told Mr Freemantle, his solicitor, about his suspicions concerning Henry Wilberforce Grant, but he had been thinking, as he walked to his club, just before the four bullets hit him in the back, that he would tell Freemantle to forget it; just make it a quick, no-fuss divorce. He had told Freemantle absolutely nothing about

190

the President.

Tony Baroni's journey to London had, in fact, been totally unnecessary.

In the Commissioner's office, high up in New Scotland Yard, the Director of Public Prosecutions gazed out of the window across the Thames and watched a tug moving up river with barges for the Battersea Power Station.

"There's a happy man," he said.

"Who?" asked the Commissioner.

"The skipper of that tug. Making more money than I do, I bet. Master, under God, of his ship. And not a care in the world. I'd just love to swap places with him at this moment."

He sighed, and then asked: "Did you get on to the American Embassy?"

The Commissioner said: "The Embassy sent their legal man to see Baroni yesterday."

"Has Baroni now got a solicitor?"

"The Embassy have got him Benny Sallis."

"He can't complain about that."

Benny Sallis was not the Commissioner's favourite solicitor; or the Director's. At least five major villains were at large in London, enjoying the gentle early summer sunshine, because of the activities of Benny Sallis. Benny never did anything which could be legally construed as against the interests of justice, or which could land him into trouble with the Law Society. But Benny knew just about all there was to know about the criminal law as it affected his dubious clients, about the regulations for identity parades, and the taking of statements and the admissibility of evidence. If there was one man in London who could keep a villain out of gaol, it was Benny Sallis.

191

The D.P.P. said: "Well, we've got to do it, and the way I want it done is this. First this man Baroni has to be examined by a police surgeon and by a doctor nominated either by the Embassy or by Benny Sallis. They are to examine Baroni thoroughly to see whether he shows any sign of injury or violence which could possible have arisen while he's been in custody, and which cannot be connected with the injuries he received when he piled up the car."

"There's been nothing like that."

"I'm not suggesting that there has. But we've got to cover ourselves."

"I'll have it done."

"Furthermore, it has to be established that Baroni is in a fit mental condition to make a statement. No after effects of the crash, no shock, or anything like that. If necessary, get in a psychiatrist. Tell Sallis or the Embassy they may bring in their own trick cyclist if they want to.

"Then we've got to disregard the statement he made when he was brought in. It was too early after the incident. He could have been temporarily round the bend. It could be vulnerable in court.

"Baroni has to make that statement again, in his own handwriting, that is assuming he can write. And Sallis and the Embassy man have got to be there when it's done. At least, they've got to be asked if they want to be present, because everything, so far as Madam Chadwick is concerned, depends on that statement."

"All right. I'll have it done that way."

And that was the way it was done. It was a laborious business, and took a long time, because Tony Baroni was not exactly an artist with words. But next day, the Commissioner handed the document to the D.P.P. and said: "Is that what you wanted?"

The Director scanned through it, and said: "It'll do."

The Commissioner said: "He sticks by every word of what he said before. It's virtually the same thing." He read from the statement: " 'The man I met in London told me that the Prime Minister of England, Mrs Shadwick' — that's the way he's spelt it both times, but it's near enough — 'that Mrs Shadwick wanted

192

her husband rubbed out because he had found that she was being laid by a black congressman and he was going to make a big case of it and that would stop her being Prime Minister'."

The D.P.P. said: "It so happens that there is only one black congressman, or member of Parliament, and that is that big fellow Grant. And I hope you won't think I've been playing at being a policeman, but I heard an odd remark yesterday. I was in my club and there was a member of Parliament there, in the bar, a junior minister of some kind, though I can't remember what. Fellow by the name of Shalton. And I heard this Shalton chap say: 'Well, I know someone who won't be going to the Chadwick funeral. And that's the black chap.' So it does seem there is a bit of chit-chat going around Westminster about madam and this Mr Grant."

"We can't go on chit-chat from your club."

"I think the ball is in your court."

It was another job for Slinky Creighton.

He reported: "Mr Grant freely admitted that he had had a personal relationship with Mrs Chadwick. This, he said, was because when she first became an M.P. he sponsored her when no one else was willing to do so. Though they are of different political parties, they became friendly and met on various social occasions. I asked him if Mr Chadwick knew about these meetings, and he said 'What do you think?' I asked him if he could suggest anyone who might wish to do harm to Mr Chadwick, and he said 'Don't look at me'. I pressed him about the nature of his relationship with Mrs Chadwick, and finally asked him if they had sexual relations. He became very angry and said: 'Do you want me to put your teeth through the back of your neck?' I asked him if he knew that Mr Chadwick was contemplating divorce proceedings, and he said 'That don't surprise me'. On your instructions, I did not directly mention his possible involvement in divorce proceedings."

The D.P.P. said: "Interesting. Highly interesting. But not conclusive."

The picture was changed appreciably as a result of routine police work by a young detective at West End Central. In the search for anyone who might have a grudge against Bernard Chadwick, this sergeant discovered that Bernard's legal affairs

193

had been handled by the old-established law firm of Freemantle and Baker, and went to see the senior partner, Mr Freemantle. If there was a blackmail situation, or another woman with an angry husband, Mr Freemantle might be able to give a lead.

Mr Freemandle had been expecting the visit, and pondering his course of action. The information he received from his client was, of course, confidential, but this client was now dead. His final duty to his client would be to assist the police in any way he could to identify the killer; and, of course, a solicitor has an overriding duty to uphold the law in all situations.

Not that he could do much to help. Nothing in Bernard's affairs seemed, to Mr Freemantle, to have any bearing on his death.

The sergeant put the expected questions. Any woman problems? Any financial dealings with shady characters? Then he asked: "When did you last have any contact with the deceased?'

"Quite recently. Ten days ago."

. "Could you tell me the reason for that consultation?"

Mr Freemantle hesitated. But the information would go no further. It could have no possible bearing on the murder inquiry. "He consulted me about starting divorce proceedings."

The sergeant thought he saw a gleam of light.

"Was there another man involved?"

"There was."

"Could you give me his name, please?"

"This man cannot possibly have any bearing on your inquiries."

"With respect, I must be the judge of that. Or my superiors. This is a police matter."

"He's quite a well-known man. A man in public life. He doesn't go around shooting people in the streets."

"I am sure you are right, sir. But I must still ask for his name. Or would you prefer to give it to one of my superior officers?"

"The man whose name was mentioned to me by Mr Chadwick was a Member of Parliament. His name is Mr Grant. Mr Henry Wilberforce Grant. Mr Chadwick told me he intended seeing his wife the next day, if that were possible, and that he was going to inform her of his intentions, and that he had certain information concerning her association with Mr Grant."

The sergeant was both intrigued and deflated. Freemantle had been absolutely right. The idea of Mr Grant, M.P., being mixed up in violent crime was preposterous. Still, it was a tit-bit of information to put in his report. The lady Prime Minister having it off with a black member of Parliament. The sergeant knew absolutely nothing of Tony Baroni's statement. That had been seen by a few privileged eyes only.

But, unknowingly, the sergeant had provided a vital piece of the jigsaw.

"So," said the D.P.P., "Chadwick *was* getting a divorce. And you've checked with Freemantle that he had told nobody?"

"Absolutely nobody. That's what he says."

"The time has come," said the D.P.P., "for a recap of what we have. First there is this man Baroni in Chicago. He is a man of low character and intelligence, a suspect of various crimes in New York and Chicago. He hardly ever reads a newspaper, and has hardly heard of Mrs Chadwick. In fact, he still spells her name incorrectly.

"This man suddenly comes to London and shoots down Bernard Chadwick, of whom, until recently, he had never heard Why? He says he was paid to do so, and that at least rings true.

"He says, further, that the person who briefed him in London gave a reason why Bernard Chadwick must be killed; the reason being that Chadwick was about to bring a stinking divorce action over his wife's association with a black member of Parliament, and that when that happened, her career would be ruined.

"Now he did not read about any goings-on between Mrs Chadwick and Grant in the newspapers – which he hardly reads, anyway – because although there may have been a bit of saloon-bar chat around Westminster, none of it, so far as I know, had appeared in public print. Least of all did he read about Bernard Chadwick's specific intention to divorce his wife, because that was restricted knowledge. Highly restricted knowledge. In fact, so far as we know, it was restricted to three people.

"Those people were: Chadwick himself, and he didn't set up his own murder. Then Freemantle. I think we can rule him out as a leak. And finally Mrs Chadwick. That puts the man Baroni right on the inside track, in relation to Mrs Chadwick's affairs. We have to consider very seriously the possibility that the man who briefed Baroni was her agent, someone whom she had taken into her confidence. It is difficult to see any other explanation for how Baroni came into possession of that highly secret knowledge.

"We must also bear in mind the fact that Mrs Chadwick did have a motive for wishing her husband to be put out of the way. Because if he had blown the lid off, that would have chopped her political career stone dead. She is, by all accounts, a pretty ruthless woman. And we do have the fact that whoever spoke to Baroni in London had been told by someone not merely a vague story about an affair between Mrs Chadwick and Grant, but had been told quite specifically that a divorce action was pending. Who could have told him that? Only three people knew. We have ruled out two of them. That leaves us with Mrs Chadwick. It leaves us with the truly incredible possibility that our lady prime minister has set up the murder of her own husband, and therefore, in law, is as guilty of murder as if she had done the actual deed herself."

The Commissioner said: "I agree with your analysis. But there is one fishy thing. One mighty fishy thing."

"I know what you are going to say. But say it."

The Commissioner said: "It makes sense, of a sort, that Mrs Chadwick should set this thing up, though she must be a damn cunning woman and had some kind of private secret service to organise getting Baroni over here. But the thing is this: Why did the man who spoke to Baroni in London bother to tell him about Grant and the divorce? Why not simply identify the target for him, and let him get on with it? Could it be that somebody *wanted* Baroni to tell that tale if things went wrong, and he got grabbed?"

The D.P.P. gazed across the sunlit river. "That thought had been with me all the time. But it poses two problems. First, the man who did the briefing still had the inside knowledge, and therefore, according to our previous reasoning, must be in direct touch with Mrs Chadwick. And the other problem is that if that was *not* the reason for the killing, then there must be another one. Now why – leaving aside his marital problems – should anyone want to kill this harmless little man? He's hardly the man with a hundred enemies. He had only one potential enemy. And that was his wife."

"What about Grant?" asked the Commissioner. "Could he have set it up? He couldn't have been looking forward to the divorce action."

"But Grant did not know there *was* to be a divorce action. And even if he suspected it might come to that, sooner or later, he'd hardly authorise his agent to disclose his own involvement."

The Commissioner said: "But if we take the other view, it seems that Mrs Chadwick agreed to *her* name being passed on to Baroni. Unless the agent was a total idiot and blabbed without her permission."

"That," said the D.P.P., "is one of the deeper mysteries of this affair."

With a touch of malice, the Commissioner said: "Well, I've done my job. I don't see that I can take it much further. The ball is in *your* court now."

Still gazing across the river, the D.P.P. said: "I accept that. There are two things I have to consider. The first is not whether the Chadwick woman was in a conspiracy to kill her husband, but whether there is a reasonable case to put before a jury to that effect.

"The second thing is the position if I decide *not* to charge Mrs Chadwick. The man Baroni has to be charged anyway, and will be free to say what he likes in court, and of course, the statement which we have taken so much care over will be used by him at his trial to establish a diminished responsibility position. This means that, in any case, the whole world is going to know of the accusation against the Chadwick woman.

"And when that happens, the whole world will want to know why she has not been charged, and whether there is one law for squalid little gunmen, and another one for Prime Ministers. Since I am a Government servant, there is going to be the smear that I funked taking action against the head of the Government.

197

"There is yet one further point. Since Mrs Chadwick is going to face public accusation anyway, it could be in her own interests that she should do so in a way that would enable her to obtain a complete and final acquittal. She would be able to do that if she was charged, but not with the same degree of effectiveness if she was merely a witness at the Baroni trial."

"That," said the Commissioner, "would put her at risk."

"It would indeed. It would put her at risk of her life under the law for which she herself is mainly responsible. For I am sure I do not need to instruct you on the law. The law is very clear. If two people conspire to take a life, and that life is taken, then the question of whose hand did the final deed is irrelevant. Both conspirators are equally guilty.

"If Mrs Chadwick is charged, then there can be only one charge. That charge will be murder. It can be nothing else."

The Commissioner lit his pipe. He took a long time over it, and finally became enveloped in clouds of smoke. The Director continued to gaze across the Thames.

Satisfied that his pipe was going, the Commissioner put the question which the Director knew must now come. "We've come to the sticking point. Is it a true bill?"

The director gave his verdict: "I don't think so. Too circumstantial. Not a single direct thing to link her with Baroni except Baroni's own statement, and I am not going to put the Prime Minister of this country in the dock at the Old Bailey on the word of that moron. I may be shot at for taking that view. I have no idea who gave Baroni that information. But as I see it, the Chadwick-Baroni link is too vague and too speculative."

The Commissioner said: "I am immensely relieved to hear you say that. I was not looking forward to the next phase, if we *had* gone ahead."

The 'phone rang. It irritated him, because he had given instructions that he was not to receive calls while the Director was with him. But he instantly grasped why his secretary had used her discretion and allowed this one call to come through.

It was the forensic lab. The Commissioner listened attentively, and took notes. "Give me that number again. Thank you."

The Director was about to leave. The Commissioner asked

198

him to stay, just for a moment. The Commissioner then 'phoned the room at Scotland Yard which can put names and addresses to telephone numbers. The inquiry took longer than the Commissioner had expected. He did not get the information he wanted until the head of the 'phone-checking staff had assured himself that it was the Commissioner making the inquiry.

The Commissioner put the 'phone down. He told the Director the gist of the information he had received in the course of the two calls.

"Dear God," said the Director of Public Prosecutions. "That changes things."

HELEN had arranged Bernard's funeral as she believed he would have wished: a private service in the little Bedfordshire village church where Bernard had once sung as a choirboy. The assembly numbered not more than twenty. He had few relatives, and few friends. His job had been his life.

On the drive back to Downing Street, she tried to put her thoughts about the events of the previous fortnight in some sort of order. Marlowe's death; the succession battle; her elevation to the Premiership; her Downing Street session with the President; then Bernard's threat to involve both her and the President in a monumental scandal. Well, at least that wouldn't happen now. She was immensely relieved about that. Was her relief, her escape from that threat, more important to her than the fact that a human being, a human being whom she had once loved, had that day been interred in a dank churchyard? She tried to face that question and did not know the answer.

Bafflement was still her main reaction. Why should a man come from America and shoot down Bernard Chadwick as he walked to his club? There *must* be an American connection.

199

But she had spoken to the President again, and the President had again said: "Squeeze him until he squeaks." She was sure he was genuine in that. But the President, like her, had noted the immediate consequences of Bernard's death: "The heat's gone off one thing."

Her mind was still on these matters when the car arrived at Downing Street. When she had been in her office a couple of minutes, her secretary 'phoned from the outer office: "The gentleman from Scotland Yard is here again."

"Send him in." Presumably there had been some new development.

There was indeed a new development.

"Mr Creighton – or should I call you chief superintendent..."

"Whichever you prefer, madam."

"Mr Creighton, I just cannot believe that you are serious about this."

But she knew, as she said it, that Creighton was no joker.

"The decision is not mine, madam. I have merely been instructed to put it into effect."

"But for God's sake, I was in the House of Commons when my husband was shot. There were five hundred people there."

"Quite so."

"Well, then . . ."

"It would be improper for me to discuss with you any matters relating to the inquiries. I am merely the message boy."

"And your message is that I am to go with you to West End Central Police Station to assist the police in their inquiries."

"That is so."

"I am always prepared to assist you in your inquiries. But I have work to do. I will assist them here."

"I am sorry, madam. My instructions are quite specific."

"Anyone would think I am going to be charged with something."

Creighton said nothing. An absurd, appalling suspicion, began to take shape. "Are you telling me that when we get to the police station, I shall be charged with some sort of offence?"

"I am not free to comment on that . . . but if you would be so kind . . ."

That night, the invasion type was again needed in Fleet Street. "MRS CHADWICK CHARGED WITH MURDER" . . . "HANG 'EM HELEN FACES MURDER RAP". The *Post's* story began: "Mrs Helen Chadwick, the woman who brought back capital punishment to Britain, today faces a charge of murdering her husband, and if found guilty, could go to the gallows. . . ."

The charge was that she did, on diverse dates, conspire with Antonio Baroni and other persons unknown to feloniously kill Bernard Davenport Chadwick.

When the D.P.P. saw it, he said: "I wish people wouldn't split their infinitives."

After they had charged her, they drove her, in an unmarked police car, with an escort consisting of Creighton and a woman police inspector, back to Downing Street. This was to enable her to pack a bag. Then back to West End Central.

The book says: no bail on a murder charge; and West End Central played it by the book. If the court wanted to bend the rule in the morning, that was up to the court. But no one was going to say that West End Central treated Prime Ministers, even a woman Prime Minister, differently from anybody else.

In fact, West End Central made one concession. They did not put their distinguished prisoner in a cell. They put her in a medical treatment room with a comfortable cot. The room had a telephone, and Helen was allowed to use it. One call she made was to Mr Harrison, the amiable, portly middle-aged solicitor who had handled various matters on her behalf. He arrived within the hour, and said: "Well, this is a rum do, if you like."

Next morning there were five hundred people milling around outside Bow Street court, and forty reporters scrambling for a press bench that could only comfortably accommodate ten; all for a formal hearing that lasted only five minutes.

In a daze, Helen, escorted by a burly woman police sergeant, was led along an underground passage and up some stairs. She was in the dock. The Queen's First Minister of State was in the dock which, over the years, had been occupied by a succession of drunks, prostitutes, pimps and petty criminals.

Tony Baroni was already there, with an escort of two police officers. It was a big dock, and he and Helen were able to stand

201

well apart. The clerk to the court read the charge, and the magistrate said: "The prisoners may be seated." For the first time, Helen was able to take a sideways look at the man accused with her, the man with whom she was supposed to have entered some incredible conspiracy to murder Bernard. Did they really think that she, Helen Chadwick, would enter into any sort of joint enterprise with *this* man? He had high cheekbones, and his face reminded her of those she had seen in the mock-up drawings of wanted men. He was the archetype of the wanted man. She could well believe that this man would be capable of killing. But in God's name, how could anybody believe it possible that *she* would get involved with this cretinous creature for any purpose whatever?

Baroni's solicitor was on his feet, saying he had no objection to his client being remanded in custody for a further seven days.

Then up spoke Mr Harrison. "I would like, even at this early state, to make it clear that my client totally denies the charge brought against her. I realise that this is not the time to elaborate on that denial, but I would seek the indulgence of the court in the matter of bail.

"I realise that on so serious a charge, bail is not normally granted. But the circumstances are exceptional. It cannot be seriously suggested that my client has any intention to abscond. She is willing to co-operate with the police in any surveillance procedures they may require. And the court will realise that she has the most urgent and important public duties to perform."

The magistrate turned to the solicitor appearing on behalf of the Director of Public Prosecutions. "What have you to say about this, Mr Williams?"

Mr Williams had been instructed to be generous. "I fully acknowledge the unique circumstances of this case, and therefore I do not oppose bail for the accused Helen Chadwick. Furthermore, I am instructed not to require any large sum in the matter of recognizances. Some quite small or token sum would be acceptable to the prosecution."

The magistrate said: "Helen Chadwick, I bind you over to appear at this court this day next week. I grant bail in the sum of fifty pounds."

The headlines said: FROM THE DOCK TO DOWNING STREET.

In fact, it was from the dock to a Cabinet meeting. They were waiting for her like the elders of some eighteenth-century kirk assembled to try a sinner on the penitent's stool. Metcalfe had obviously assumed the rôle of chief elder. When she entered, they made a token effort to rise from their seats. Was this because she was Prime Minister or because she was a woman? It didn't matter. She knew that having faced one court, she was about to face another. And that this second court might be less meticulous than the first.

They stared at her. She stared back. She took her seat under the picture of Walpole, and said: "When we met last, there was a difference of opinion over defence spending. Is there anything to report on that front?"

Willis was prepared to maintain a façade of normality. "My people have been at it with the Treasury. They're still working things out."

Metcalfe cut in. "I think," he said, "that before discussing routine business we should consider the . . . er . . . developments of last night and this morning."

She had, of course, expected it, and she had her reply ready. "I have been charged with an offence. I am sure I need hardly tell you that it is a ridiculous charge. I anticipate that it will be thrown out before it gets to trial. I imagine the magistrate will find that there is no case to answer. I cannot imagine what possible case there could be."

Metcalfe said: "It would be improper for us to discuss matters which are *sub judice*."

She thought: You slimy swine. She faced them all and said: "It is widely accepted in this country that a person who is accused of an offence is considered innocent until proved guilty. Is anyone here proposing to depart from that procedure?"

"I am sure," said Metcalfe, "that none of us would dream of doing that (*Oh no? she thought*). It is not a question of expressing any opinion whatsoever on the matter before the court. The issue is: What effect do these unique circumstances have on the authority of the Government, both at home and abroad?"

"I do not see why it should have any effect whatever." But

she knew, as soon as she had said it, that she had put herself in a false position. Of course, it *did* affect the authority of the Government.

Metcalfe was quick to capitalise. "Prime Minister, let us face facts."

"What facts?"

"The fact that the Director of Public Prosecutions, rightly or wrongly, considers that there is a case to answer. It is inconceivable that he would bring a charge against a person in your position if he thought it was going to be thrown out by the lower court. We are thus faced with a position in which the chief minister is involved in prolonged litigation. From which, we all hope, she will emerge with her reputation untarnished."

I bet, thought Helen.

She said: "You can leave me to worry about my position while you concentrate on your departmental duties."

Torrington had to have his say. "What we must consider is whether Mrs Chadwick, with this pre-occupation on her mind, will be able to give her ministerial duties the full attention they deserve."

Another slimy one.

Willis said: "Surely that is a question which only Mrs Chadwick can answer." Then Hewett started burbling about collective Cabinet responsibility.

Helen cut them all short. "It is clear to me that there is an opinion among some in this room that I should resign the office which I took up so recently. Well, I tell you this. I see no reason to resign because I have made a five-minute appearance in a police court. If the case goes to trial, that may be a different matter. But for the moment, I still sit in this chair. If any member of this administration is not happy about continuing to serve under me, I will accept his resignation. Now."

There were no takers. The uneasy assembly around the coffin-shaped table was not ready for a showdown. Not yet. But she knew she had overplayed her hand. The Metcalfe faction could afford to wait. By waiting, they would put a gloss of respectability and virtue on their actions. They would be exuding British fair play, while waiting for the prize to fall into their hands.

She reckoned that she could hold out for a week, until the next hearing at Bow Street. But she was realist enough to accept the fact that if she was committed for trial, with a wait of a month or more before the trial took place, then it would be utterly impossible to sustain her position. Apart from anything else she was due to go to Brussels in three weeks' time for an E.E.C. assembly. She could hardly face the statesmen of Europe on equal terms if they knew that within a week or two she would be in the dock on a capital charge.

It was the future of her position as Prime Minister which filled most of her thoughts, rather than the case itself. The idea that she might actually be found guilty on this monstrous charge, and stand in peril of the penalty which she herself had introduced, did not at first penetrate. It only began to do so when she had her first full conference with her legal advisers.

Mr Harrison, after his response to her fire-engine call, had thankfully retired from the scene. He was hopelessly out of depth, and willingly passed the case on to Messrs Powell and Davis, a law firm greatly experienced in criminal matters. They had briefed Sir Richard Carter, Q.C., a tall, elegant barrister with a great reputation at the criminal bar.

"You realise," Sir Richard told her, "that in this early stage I must assume the rôle of devil's advocate. I have to ask you questions which you may find offensive, in order that we can deal properly with these same questions if they are raised later by the other side. I am sure I need hardly tell you that you must be absolutely frank with me. That is the only basis on which I can prepare an adequate defence."

He questioned her insistently about her relationship with Bernard over the whole period of the marriage.

She told him the truth.

Then he asked her: "When your husband visited you at Downing Street, and threatened to expose your relationship with Mr Grant, was any other matter raised at that time?"

She lied.

There was absolutely no point in involving the President. He had no relevance to the case, and if her association with him was dragged in, it would not only brand her even more plainly as a scarlet woman; it would do immense damage to the relations between Britain and America. It might even mean that Maloney would have to quit; and if he did, his successor might renege on the loan. All without helping her own cause in any way. She was determined to keep Maloney's name out of it.

"Nothing," she said. "That was all. Bernard was mad about Grant. And about the job situation. Nothing else."

Sir Richard asked: "Did you tell anyone, I repeat, anyone, that your husband had made this threat to expose your connection with Mr Grant, and thereby possibly ruin your political career? Did you tell *anyone* that?"

For the same reason as before, Helen lied again. "No one."

Sir Richard said: "I think I must tell you we have a fight on our hands."

When she appeared at Bow Street after the seven-day remand, she was represented by Powell, the senior partner of the law firm. Apparently it was not the done thing for a barrister to appear in the lower court if his services might be required at a later trial.

The hearing lasted four hours. Because of the restrictions on reporting evidence at that stage, the madly curious public had no indication at all about how the battle lines were being drawn; but as the prosecution outlined their case, Helen listened with mounting bewilderment and anxiety, and realised with sickening certainy that there was indeed a case to answer.

That was the view the magistrate took.

He committed Helen Mary Chadwick and Antonio Baroni to stand trial at the Central Criminal Court, better known as the Old Bailey, jointly charged with the murder of Bernard Davenport Chadwick.

This time, despite the energetic appeal of Mr Powell, the magistrate refused bail. He felt that it would be wrong to give different treatment to two people jointly accused of the same offence.

Helen did not need anyone to tell her that no government could survive while its head was occupying a cell in Holloway Prison.

She wrote: "Your Majesty, You will be aware that circumstance have made it impossible for me to continue to perform the duties which you recently entrusted to me as your First Minister. I therefore humbly ask that I should be permitted to

206

relinquish my seal of office."

The Queen's Secretary replied: "I acknowledge receipt of your letter of today's date, and I am instructed to inform you that Her Majesty accedes to the request made therein."

This time, there was no succession battle. The next day, Metcalfe, in morning coat, drove to Buckingham Palace in a black Rover.

IT would be the trial of the century. All the newspapers were agreed on that. The greatest free show that the nation had ever had. The only trouble was that only a handful of people could be present in person. The court could only hold a couple of hundred, the legal profession had hogged fifty seats, and another fifty had been allocated to the reporters.

The queue for the remainder began to form outside the court thirty-six hours before the case was due to be called. Just like Wimbledon, commented the *Post*. Some in the queue had equipped themselves with sleeping bags, camp stools and stoves. There was a minor riot when half a dozen near the head of the queue, after waiting for twelve hours, wanted to have a break and have their places held for them by hired stand-ins. Those who had not thought of this stratagem protested vehemently, and it took a police inspector and three constables to sort things out. Finally, to the cheers of those further down the queue, the inspector ruled that anyone who left the queue would rejoin it at the tail.

Helen had waited for this day calmly enough. There was nothing she could do. She had put her fate in Sir Richard's hands. It was rather like stepping aboard an airliner. You put your trust in the pilot, and hope he knows what he's doing.

Her cell at Holloway was austere but not uncomfortable. Three wardresses shared a round-the-clock supervision, the one on duty always being in an adjacent room. One was a motherly type, and brought her roses from her garden. They played innumerable games of cribbage, and Helen won most of them. She had learned the game from her father at the age of seven, and he had taught her well. Fifteen-two, fifteen-four, fifteen-six, a pairs eight, a run of three . . .

"Anything you want, duckie, just let me know," said this kindly woman. At Helen's request, the wardress produced a dictionary, an atlas and a volume of Shakespeare's plays. She needed them for crosswords. She did four a day, starting with *The Times* puzzle. One day she thought she found a minor inaccuracy in a clue about Chinese art, and toyed with the idea of writing a short letter about it for *The Times* letter page. It might start a correspondence that would trickle on for months. All the oriental professors and museum curators would get in on the act. Then the grim thought occurred to her that the correspondence might continue after its originator had ceased to have an interest in Chinese art or anything else. And anyway, would *The Times* publish a letter signed "Helen Chadwick, Holloway, London N."?

She read the papers. She learned that Metcalfe was "restructuring" the government, moving people around. Willis had not been moved round. He had been moved out. Possibly at his own request, thought Helen.

The item of political news that intrigued her most was that Metcalfe had filled the post of Home Secretary, which had been vacant since her own elevation to the Premiership.

The new Home Secretary was Keith Shalton.

The day came.

THE thing that had been worying Helen almost as much as the uncertainty over the verdict was the prospect in sitting in the dock for hour after hour, possibly for several days, with the odious Baroni. She had not once spoken a word to him, and during the committal proceedings he had not even glanced at her. He seemed sunk in a sullen world of his own. She hoped it would be a big dock. It was.

As at Bow Street, she made her appearance on the stage by going up stairs into the dock, a policewoman on either side of her. Did they think she was going to leap out of the dock and assault the judge? Or perhaps they thought she might faint at vital moments. She had no intention of doing *that*.

The first thing she saw, directly facing her as she reached courtroom level, on the other side of the square room, was a hook-nosed, be-wigged figure in scarlet: Mr Justice Wellbeloved. It was an inappropriate name. He was beloved neither by barristers, who feared his sarcasm, nor by defendants, who feared his sentences. He was a "strong" judge; a known supporter of both capital and corporal punishment.

Then she saw the two long rows of wigged heads. Surely it was not possible that all these barristers could have their own rôles to play in her trial? In fact, only six had. The rest were there for the free show.

There was not an empty seat. In the public benches there was an astonishing number of women who seemed to be dressed as for a Buckingham Palace Garden Party. These ladies had clearly not stood in a queue for a day and a half. They had been wangled privilege tickets as the wives of barristers or others capable of pulling strings. Helen thought she recognised one angular face. It was that of Metcalfe's wife. So Metcalfe was present by proxy. No doubt every grisly detail would be reported and eagerly devoured.

The clerk to the court, sitting below the judge's throne, had started to intone: "Antonio Baroni, you are charged that you did on divers dates . . . How say you? Guilty or not guilty?"

In a flat voice, Baroni replied: "Not guilty."

Everyone knew that this, in his case, was a formality. The basic facts of the shooting could hardly be challenged. No doubt his barrister would try some variation of the diminished responsibility, very-sorry-won't-do-it-again theme. In fact, few people cared greatly what happened to Baroni. It was the other defendant on whom every eye was centred.

"Helen Mary Chadwick, you are charged that on divers dates . . . How say you? Guilty or not guilty?"

In a voice that carried to every corner of the court, she replied: "Not guilty."

"My lord, members of the jury . . ."

By common consent the portly Sir Percy Kibble, the Attorney-General, leading for the Crown, was not one of this century's most distinguished holders of his office. He had got the job because almost literally there was no one else. The Attorney-General has to be a member of Parliament on the Government's side of the House. The days when a talented barrister could combine law and politics in one glittering career had long since gone. All the barristers who were any good were making their pile in company litigation, leaving the second-raters to dabble in politics. Kibble had been Marlowe's choice because the legal talent available to him had been even thinner than in other recent administrations. His appointment had been the subject of much derision in El Vino's, the Wig and Pen Club, and other places where barristers refresh themselves after their labours.

But now Sir Percy was the man of the moment. He was, as it were, the Crown's centre-forward; a somewhat ponderous one, but nevertheless the centre-forward. The midfield players, the police and the D.P.P., had put the ball at his feet and retired. It was up to him.

"My lord, members of the jury. I appear for the Crown in this case, and the prisoners Helen Chadwick and Antonio Baroni have the advantage of being represented respectively by my learned friends Sir Richard Carter and Mr Simon Phillips. It is with a heavy heart, and only after deep cogitation, that I have undertaken this onerous duty . . ."

Helen wondered if there was just the suggestion of a muted groan emanating from the barristers' benches.

. . . "but before proceeding to the substance of the charges, I crave the indulgence of the court to permit me to deal with a matter which has caused me some personal anxiety. I am not anticipating anything which may be stated in evidence when I

210

say that one of the accused recently held high office of state. In fact, the highest office to which anyone in the political sphere can aspire . . ."

The Judge: "You mean she was Prime Minister. One would have to live in an enclosed monastery not to know that. I do not imagine that the jury are drawn exclusively from such institutions."

Sir Percy: "Quite so, my lord. I was about to say that by reason of my office, I was, during Mrs Chadwick's brief period of office as Home Secretary and Prime Minister, a ministerial and Governmental colleague of hers. The question has been raised in the Press as to whether, in these circumstances, I should personaly be involved in presenting the case against the accused, or whether the case for the Crown should be led by some distinguished member of the Bar who is unconnected with the Government. The question has been implied, if not directly asked, as to whether a law officer who is a member of the Government will rigorously present a case against a former Governmental colleague. I need hardly say that the traditions of my high office . . ."

The Judge: "The Attorney-General normally leads for the Crown in a case of exceptional public interest. That's what he get's paid for, isn't it?"

Sir Percy: "Quite so, my lord, but . . ."

The Judge: "Shall we get on?"

Sir Percy: "As your lordship pleases.

"Members of the jury, the charges against the two accused arise out of the death of Mr Bernard Chadwick, the husband of the accused Helen Mary Chadwick, a gentleman who had risen to a position of some seniority in the Civil Service.

"The marriage of Mr and Mrs Chadwick had, for various reasons, been in difficulties for some years, and by the beginning of May this year it was on the brink of breaking up.

"On May tenth, when Mrs Chadwick was Prime Minister, her husband called on her at 10 Downing Street. Since his position at that time in the Civil Service did not justify an audience with the Prime Minister on any official matter, it must be assumed that the purpose of the visit was to discuss personal matters. Indeed, there will be evidence to suggest that Mr

Chadwick went to Downing Street specifically to discuss the problems of the marriage.

"Seven days later, at approximately six thirty p.m. on May seventeenth, this quiet, law-abiding man – a man, one would have thought without an enemy in the world – was killed in the most brutal way. He was shot four times in the back as he walked along Belmont Street towards his club in the West End of London.

"The prosecution will contend that the hand that fired the gun was the hand of the accused Baroni. But it will contend, also, that the mind which conceived and organised this crime was the mind of Helen Chadwick; that it was she who, acting through other persons still untraced, hired a killer to shoot down her husband; and that therefore she is as guilty in law as if she had fired the gun herself.

"I am sure the question must be forming in your minds: What possible motive could Mrs Chadwick have for initiating such terrible action against her husband? The Crown will contend that there is, indeed, such a motive, and that it arose out of the visit paid by Mr Chadwick to 10 Downing Street on May tenth.

"The Crown will produce evidence to the effect that Mr Chadwick, who had been sorely tried over the years by his wife's attention to other men, went to Downing Street for the purpose of informing her that he finally intended to seek a divorce.

"Now members of the jury, you may think that a divorce to a person in the then position of Mrs Chadwick would be a cause of some embarrassment, but not an adequate motive for murder, or for using devious means to end a life. You will be aware that many persons distinguished in political or other public life have appeared in the divorce courts, and that their careers have seldom been damaged.

"It is, however, my painful duty to inform you that in the action which was to have been brought against Mrs Chadwick, there would have been a special circumstance which might easily have put Mrs Chadwick's brilliant career in peril.

"Her husband named a man whom he could be citing in the action. That man is also in politics. He is, in fact, a member of the House of Commons, but he does not adhere to the party

212

of Mrs Chadwick, or to the alliance which she finally headed.

"He is, in fact, a member of the Opposition. That, in itself, might well be enough, if it became public knowledge through the divorce courts, to end Mrs Chadwick's career as Prime Minister. What would the members of her Cabinet think about their leader sharing a bed with a member of the Opposition party? Would they not wonder if Mrs Chadwick's commitment to the policies of the alliance could remain total in those circumstances? And would they not feel fearful about the security of Cabinet secrets if they knew the Prime Minister was sleeping with a member of the Opposition?

"But there is another factor, which you will understand when I tell you the name of the member of Parliament. The gentleman named by the late Mr Chadwick is Mr Henry Wilberforce Grant, the member for the Carlington division of North London."

Some of those in court, lawyers and others on the inside track, had known what was coming, and had been waiting for it. But, because of the reporting restrictions on the proceedings in the lower court, this was the first time the name of Henry Grant had been mentioned in public in connection with the case. It was a total revelation to most of those in court, and it generated a subdued hum of excitement in the public seats.

The Attorney-General waited for it to subside, then continued:

"Members of the jury, most of you will be aware that the skin of Mr Grant is of a somewhat darker hue than that of most people in this court . . ."

The Judge: "You mean he's black."

The Attorney-General: "Now there is, of course, no reason in law why a white woman and a black man, if they are mutually attracted to each other, should not embark on an affair, just as if they were persons of the same colour. But you are men and women of the world and you will be aware that although racial discrimination is against the law of this land, racial prejudice still exists on a substantial scale. It is a fact of life, a sad fact, but it must be taken into account, particularly by those in high or public positions. There are a great many people who disapprove in the strongest terms of a white woman going to

213

bed with a black man. I am in no way supporting that view. I am merely saying that such an association can arouse the most widespread and intense oposition.

"We must, therefore, consider the position of Mrs Chadwick if her association with Mr Grant had been blazoned across the front pages of the newspapers, as would undoubtedly have happened if the divorce action had gone to trial.

"Her political career, though short, has shown her to be a fiercely ambitious woman. I do not criticise her for that in any way. But, because of the two factors I have mentioned – the fact of an intimate association with an M.P. on the other side of the House, and the fact that the gentleman was black – because of these two things, Mrs Chadwick's career would have been blasted into ruins, and her position as Prime Minister made completely untenable. There can be little doubt, indeed, that if the divorce had gone ahead, Mrs Chadwick would rapidly have ceased to be Prime Minister of this country.

"So Mrs Chadwick *did* have a motive, a strong motive, for silencing her husband. For ever.

"Let us now consider the events of May seventeenth. Bernard Chadwick was shot. Through the prompt action of a former member of the police, who happened to be nearby, an arrest was made. The man arrested was Antonio Baroni. That arrest was made within seconds of the shooting, and within one hour, Baroni made a statement. That statement, repeated later under the most stringent conditions to avert any suggestion of pressure or misunderstanding, was truly astonishing. You will hear that statement given in evidence by the officers who were present when it was made. For the moment, I will summarise it. The gist of what Baroni said was this: That in Chicago, he was approached by a man he had never seen before, a man who spoke with an English accent, and was told that there was a 'hit' job, that is a killing, to be done in London; that he was given money and an air ticket, and was told to go to a certain address in London where he would be contacted again. This, according to Baroni's alleged statement, worked out according to plan. The second contact – again Baroni is certain he was English – explained to Baroni why he had been brought to London. Baroni was handed a photograph – it was a picture of

Bernard Chadwick – and was told that this man was the intended victim; and that the victim, if he adhered to his normal practice, would be walking along Belmont Street at about six thirty the following evening.

"Understandably, Baroni was curious about who this man was, and said to his second contact in London something to the effect 'Who is this guy, anyway, and why has he got to be hit?' And Baroni alleges he was given a very remarkable reply.

"He alleges, members of the jury, that it was explained to him that the name of the victim was Chadwick, that Mr Chadwick was the husband of the Prime Minister, and that Mr Chadwick had to be silenced because he had discovered that his wife had had an affair with a black politician, and was about to 'blow it' by bringing a divorce action, with obviously disastrous consequences for Mrs Chadwick."

The Attorney-General paused to let that sink in while he made a pretence of wiping his spectacles, before delivering his punch line.

"That statement was made, in the first instance, at seven-thirty p.m. on the evening of the seventeenth. But who, at that time, knew that Mr Chadwick was specifically contemplating a divorce action against his wife, and involving Mr Grant in those proceedings? How could Baroni possibly have acquired that knowledge?

"Not one word to that effect had appeared in the newspapers in Britain or in America. It was a closely guarded secret, indeed, more closely guarded than a great many secrets of a political nature. So far as the Crown's inquiries have been able to establish, only three people in London knew, on May seventeenth, how things were developing in regard to this divorce action. They were Mr Chadwick, Mrs Chadwick, and Mr Chadwick's solicitor, Mr Freemantle, to whom Mr Chadwick had confided his intentions, on a professional basis. Mr Freemantle is adamant that he did not confide this matter to any other person.

"And yet, consider the strange behaviour of Baroni. He is living in Chicago. He is not a great student of public affairs. Indeed, his newspaper reading is normally confined to those pages of the American papers dealing with the potential per-

215

formances of racehorses. He has barely heard of Mrs Chadwick – indeed, in his statement, he spelt her name Shadwick – and has certainly never heard of Bernard Chadwick.

"Yet he abruptly leaves his native haunts. He comes to London, a city of around eight million people, and out of those eight million people he shoots down a man who happens to be Mr Chadwick. And then – you may think in understandable panic – he attempts to lessen his rôle, by saying that he was merely a tool, that he was hired to do a job, and he gives the reasons which have been given to *him* as to why the job had to be done. And in making that statement, he reveals knowledge which could only have emanated from Mr Chadwick, Mr Freemantle – or Mrs Chadwick.

"Mr Chadwick clearly did not set up his own killing. Mr Freemantle is a respected member of a respected profession. You will be able to judge his demeanour in the witness box. If, after seeing him and hearing him, you accept his assertion that he did not mention the matter of the divorce to a single soul, then, members of the jury, I suggest that logic and commonsense will drive you reluctantly but inexorably to consider the question of whether Mrs Chadwick, acting through agents, set up the killing of her husband in order to avert the scandal which was threatening to ruin her brilliant political career.

"Now if that were all I am sure that you would find the whole thing utterly mystifying, but probably just short of what would be required to convince you that Mrs Chadwick was, in fact, the instigator of this crime. I think you would say that too much depends on the word of the man Baroni, and that while we are deeply puzzled over how he came to be in possession of confidential information, we cannot convict a woman of murder if we have to rely wholly on this man's statement, and there is nothing else. I think you would say that there must be a more direct and personal link to tie Mrs Chadwick to this man, and to the enterprise he is alleged to have undertaken on her behalf.

"Members of the jury, I have to tell you that there *is* a personal and direct link between Mrs Chadwick and the accused Baroni.

"When Baroni was arrested, he was found to have in his possession an envelope containing sixteen five-pound notes. The envelope and the notes were submitted to forensic examination. The notes did not produce any information. The numbers were not in sequence, and although they bore many finger-prints, none seem to have any relevance to this inquiry.

"The envelope, however, produced some illuminating information. On it were three very clear finger-prints, and the impression of some written figures, caused, apparently, by someone writing those figures on a piece of paper which, at the time, was resting on the envelope, with the result that an indentation of what had been written carried through to the envelope, and although invisible to the naked eye, the numbers can be brought to life, as it were, by modern police methods.

"Those numbers are the numbers which form a London telephone number. It is an ex-directory number. It is known to a very small circle of people. It is the number of the telephone that Mrs Chadwick uses at 10 Downing Street for her most personal and confidential conversations."

Something like a long low whistle went round Number One Court at the Old Bailey. But Sir Percy had yet further disclosures to make.

"Mrs Chadwick, in fact, had two ex-directory telephone numbers. One is known to a fairly wide circle of people. For instance, a substantial number of governmental colleagues, senior civil servants and senior political journalists and so on. The other number is much more restricted than that. It is known to a very small number of people indeed, those who might be called the Prime Minister's inner circle. It is that specially restricted number which is indented on the envelope found in Baroni's possession.

"And now to the fingerprints. They were compared, in the first instance, to prints left by Mrs Chadwick on the metal of her car. They tallied exactly. Later, Mrs Chadwick was finger-printed by the normal method used in any police inquiry, and again, there was an exact match with the prints found on the envelope.

"How did those prints, and that indented phone number, come to be on an envelope found in the possession of the man

Baroni? The contention of the prosecution is that at some point in the setting up of this crime, Mrs Chadwick handed to her agent an envelope containing some ready-cash money for Baroni; and that she gave the agent her most secret personal phone number so that he could contact her should it be necessary to do so; and that the agent wrote down the number on a piece of paper which happened to be resting on the envelope, thus causing an indentation of the figures to carry through.

"I would stress that the experts who carried out the examination of the envelope had no idea what the figures represented, other than that they were fairly obviously a telephone number. They merely passed the number on to their superiors, who established that the number was that of Mrs Chadwick's most private line.

"Members of the jury, I said that you would probably need a direct and personal link between Mrs Chadwick and Baroni in order to be convinced that she did indeed instigate this crime; that though the hand that fired the gun was Baroni's, the organising brain was hers.

"I suggest that the evidence which will be given by the forensic staff of Scotland Yard will supply that link."

Helen had known that this damning evidence would be brought against her. It had been presented at the lower court, and had utterly stunned both her and her legal advisers. Desperately, they groped for possible explanations. Had she left an envelope like that one lying around, or thrown one into a waste-paper basket, from which it might have been extracted by some plotter? She could not specifically recall doing so, but that was the line taken by the defence in the lower court. It had not convinced the magistrate. Would it convince the jury? As for the telephone number, Sir Richard Carter had pleaded with her: *"Please* try to remember if you have given that number to anyone who had not known it before, and would need to write it down." She had not done so. They had gone through the list of people who had been given the number. There were only twenty-one of them. All vehemently denied passing the number on to any one else. All were people of honour. Unfortunately, and unknown to Helen, one of them had been at Charterhouse with Rodney Browne, and Rodney knew the rea-

218

son for his abrupt departure while in the lower sixth, which was not something Rodney's old schoolmate wanted to have put around the clubs. Thus Rodney Browne had obtained the number which Andy Dewhurst had asked for.

The evidence on the envelope was the creation of Andy Dewhurst. It was part of his cover plan to ensure that if Baroni got himself into trouble, and started to spin the tale which had been fed to him, there would be something to back it up.

The telephone number had been easy. Having acquired it from Rodney Browne, he firmly indented it on the envelope in exactly the manner described by the Attorney-General.

The fingerprint business was more complicated, and was only made possible by the fact that Jimmie Schumaker, who worked in the F.B.I. fingerprint department, was an old chum from many late-night poker sessions; and was willing, for a fee of five hundred dollars (which had come out of Andy's own bank account), to do a "little job" which took Jimmie only thirty seconds.

For Schumaker, prints were not only a job; they were a hobby. He collected prints of the famous like other people collect autographs. He had Churchill's, F.D.R.'s, J.F.K.'s, Marilyn Monroe's, Mr Khrushchev's . . . It was not difficult of course. There were always domestic staff in the White House and at other places where the mighty assemble who were willing, for five or ten bucks, to hand over some small item used by the distinguished visitor. It might be a cup, a spoon, an ashtray. Jimmie had devoted years to building up this collection, which he kept on shelves in one room of his bachelor apartment in Washington. All the items were labelled with the name of the distinguished "printer", and there was, in each case, a photograph of the print by the side of the article.

At a poker game at Jimmie's two days after Helen's visit to Washington, Andy had noted the latest addition and had said: "I see you got her." There, on the shelf, was a whisky glass labelled "Mrs Helen Chadwick".

"No problem," Jimmie had said. "Ten bucks for that Parkinson guy. It's his rate. We do a regular trade." Then he had astonished Andy by saying: "I'm going to scrap all this junk." But, he explained, that did not mean scrapping the prints. He

219

would still have the prints. How come? Well, there was a new thing out. A way of "lifting" prints. It was something like those transfer papers they used to have as kids. You put this special paper on the print, then when you lifted it off, the print came too, much clearer than any photograph could be. It was the actual print itself that was on the transfer paper. All nice and handy for filing and for producing in court. But Jimmie doubted whether it would ever be officially adopted. The lawyers didn't like it, and with good reason. Once the print was on the transfer, it could be put anywhere. A suspect could be given a glass of water in a police station, the print "lifted" from the glass, and slapped on a gun which had killed a policeman. And the guy would have a helluva job talking himself out of that.

Andy Dewhurst remembered all that when he was brooding over ways of making the Baroni story bomb-proof. When he asked Jimmie to put the Chadwick prints on the envelope, Jimmie was not at all keen. But it wasn't every day you can pick up five hundred bucks for half a minute's work. He handed the envelope back to Andy Dewhurst, holding its corner with a pair of tweezers. "They're on," he said. "I'll say they're on. Now you take that outa here and don't let me hear any more about it. I just don't wanna know."

FOR the British jury, the fingerprint is still the one foolproof thing. A witness can lie; a camera can be made to lie; so can a photo-copying machine. But a fingerprint cannot lie.

At the lunch interval, the verdict in the pubs and sandwich bars around the Old Bailey, the verdict among the barristers, was: "Old Perce is not doing badly, not badly at all."

"Call George Briggs . . ."

The ex-policeman driving instructor gave his evidence in a brisk, businesslike way, as he had been taught to do in the Force.

"At approximately eighteen thirty hours on May seventeenth last I was proceeding in a southerly direction down Belmont Street in motor vehicle registration number PHG 725 N etc etc etc . . . I apprehended the person in the Aston Martin vehicle and kept him under restraint until police officers arrived . . ."

To the great chagrin of Mrs Forbes-Barrington, that evidence was considered sufficient to cover the events in Belmont Street, and she was not required as a witness. She had been to Harrods to purchase an outfit specially for the occasion.

"*Call Frederick Potts . . .*"

Sergeant Potts, too, was short, sharp, and to the point. But in his case, Baroni's barrister, Mr Phillips, decided to have a go.

Mr Phillips: "Did you, in the police car on the way to the station, have any conversation with the accused Baroni?"

"There was a bit of talk."

"Did you say to him 'You know what we do to bastards like you? We string them up, and you're just about the right size for that?' "

"No sir," lied Potts virtuously. "That would be a most improper thing to say to a person in custody. I would never say a thing like that."

"I put it to you that you did speak those words, or something like that?"

"No, sir, I did not."

No one could understand precisely what Mr Phillips had hoped to extract from this exchange, except possibly to win a little sympathy for his client, and bring in the emotional stress thing in some form.

Sir Richard Carter, for Helen, saw no point whatever in examining either of these witnesses.

"*Call William Freemantle . . .*"

"You are a qualified solicitor and commissioner for oaths? How long have you been in practice? Did you know the late Bernard Chadwick? In what capacity? When did he last consult you in a professional capacity?"

After these necessary formalities, finally to the nub of the matter. There had been a few coughs and sneezes in the public benches, but now there was absolute silence.

"Mr Chadwick telephoned me on the morning of May seventh and I arranged for him to call at the office later that morning."

"What was the purpose of the consultation?"

"He told me he was contemplating divorce proceedings against his wife."

"Did he specify what grounds he had for taking such proceedings?"

"He told me he had had his wife kept under observation by a private detective, and that from the detective's report, and from his own observations and suspicions, he concluded that his wife was having an affair with Mr Grant."

"What did you say to that?"

"I told him that in view of Mr Grant's position as a public man, as a member of Parliament, one would need to be very sure of the facts before taking an allegation like that to court."

"What was his response?"

"He said he was pretty sure that the evidence he had would be sufficient."

"Did he elaborate on that?"

"No, this was a short, hurried meeting arranged at short notice, and I was late for another appointment. We arranged that Mr Chadwick should come back in a week's time, and we would go into details. But he told me that before the next meeting, he intended to go to Downing Street and have it out with Mrs Chadwick over the business about Mr Grant."

"Now, Mr Freemantle, this is very important. Was anything put on paper in your office about the substance of your conversation with Mr Chadwick?"

"Nothing. Absolutely nothing."

"Did you discuss this matter with any member of your staff, or indeed with any other person?"

"I most certainly did not."

"Could any member of your staff, or any other person, have had any inkling of the matters discussed by you and Mr Chadwick?"

"I do not see how anyone could know what is said in my

private office."

"Thank you, Mr Freemantle."

It was time for Sir Richard Carter to start earning his £3,000-a-day fee.

Sir Richard: "How long had Mr Chadwick been a client of yours?"

"About twelve years."

"On what matters did he consult you?"

"Mainly about some property he owned in Bedfordshire."

"During your association with Mr Chadwick, had he, previous to that consultation on May seventh, raised the question of his domestic difficulties?"

"They were mentioned."

"You keep a file on Mr Chadwick?"

"I do."

"Does that file contain any mention of Mr Chadwick's matrimonial difficulties? And if so, what does it say?"

Helen was listening intently. Was Keith Shalton's name about to be dragged into court. Why was Sir Richard taking that risk?

"The references relate to about eight or ten years ago. They concern a person who, I believe, was fairly well-known as a racing driver, and also a ski instructor."

"Anything else on those lines?"

"Nothing."

Helen prevented herself from giving any visible sign of relief.

Sir Richard was following up his point, which Helen was just beginning to grasp. What was the security on the filing system? How many secretaries and clerks were employed in the office? How many who might have seen the file had since left Mr Freemantle's employment?

It seemed that there might be five or six people, all highly responsible and trustworthy, insisted Mr Freemantle, who might have been aware that Mr Chadwick's marriage had, at various times, been in difficulties.

"Mr Freemantle," said Sir Richard, "am I right in thinking that your practice deals extensively in matrimonial cases; that you are what is sometimes called a divorce lawyer?"

"We do a lot of divorce business, certainly."

"So any member of your staff seeing Mr Chadwick arrive at your office, or indeed any other person, perhaps someone who had been deliberately following him, noting his visit to you, might reasonably assume that his business with you would be concerned with divorce litigation?"

"That would be a possible deduction. But we do a substantial amount of general business."

Sir Richard left it at that. He had not achieved much; but he had, perhaps, put just the tiniest dent in the prosecution's case. The prosecution had claimed that Bernard's personal affairs were a tightly-kept secret. Sir Richard had planted the thought in the jury's mind that the secret was not kept quite as well as the Crown had claimed.

Soon Sir Richard was to make another, slightly larger dent.

"Call Herbert Phipps . . ."

Herbert Phipps was a private detective and looked the part. He did not actually wear a dirty, belted raincoat, but one could well imagine him doing so. He was the man who, on Bernard's instructions, had tailed Helen and Henry Grant on their meetings; the man who had been playing the fiddle outside the Indian restaurant in Croydon. The man who had followed Grant to Helen's flat, and had informed Bernard in time for Bernard to return.

He gave his evidence fairly enough. Then Sir Richard rose to cross-examine.

"Mr Phipps, this was what you termed an observation exercise. Would you say it was a successful exercise?"

Phipps blundered into the trap. "I would say so, certainly."

"A *very* successful exercise?"

"I think so."

"Quite a coup, in fact. You, a private detective had acquired some highly delectable information about a lady who was a member of Parliament, who was later Home Secretary, and finally Prime Minister. You must have been bursting with pride."

"I did the job."

"And did it very well. Something to boast about, wasn't it?"

"It might have been. But all our work is confidential."

"Come, come, Mr Phipps. It must have been very difficult

224

for you to keep this titbit to yourself."

"I told you . . ."

"Mr Phipps, do you get talkative or boastful when you have had a few drinks?"

Everyone in court knew that this must be leading up to something. Only Sir Richard – and Phipps – knew exactly what was coming.

"I don't think so . . . not especially . . ."

"You were at one time in the Metropolitan police force?"

"Yes."

"Why did you leave?"

"There was an inquiry over a certain matter . . ."

Sir Richard pounced.

"And that certain matter was that a police operation which was on the brink of netting several quite important criminals was frustrated because you, who had been involved in the inquiry, were so proud of yourself, that you could not keep it secret. When you'd had a few pints in a pub you started boasting that there'd be some newspaper headlines next day that would make the villains sit up, and word got back to the criminals who cancelled their plans for a robbery, at which they would undoubtedly have been arrested. Thus an immense amount of police work was wasted, just because you could not keep your mouth shut. That was the certain matter which caused your sudden resignation from the force, was it not?"

Phipps whispered: "Yes."

The Attorney-General, in re-examination, tried to plug the hole. Remembering the utter solemnity of the oath, would Phipps say whether he had conveyed his special information about Mrs Chadwick and Mr Grant to any other person?

Phipps spoke up bravely and boldly. "I swear I did not mention it to anyone."

To some in court, it seemed he had the genuine air of a man who had been wrongly maligned. But Sir Richard had made a good point. A potentially unreliable man had known about Helen and Henry Grant, and might have spread it around. The prosecution case was that, leaving aside the respectable Mr Freemantle, only she could have passed the information on to Baroni. If Phipps *had* been talking, there might be others. But was that enough? Did that really break the chain, Helen wondered, which the prosecution had tried to stretch between her and this creature in the dock with her?

She was glad that no one had asked Phipps about other shadowing jobs. In fact, it wouldn't have mattered. Phipps had done this one job for Bernard, and knew nothing about Keith Shalton.

"Call Henry Wilberforce Grant . . ."

This was a moment for which the public in the court had been waiting since Grant's name had first been mentioned by the Attorney-General in his opening address. He strode purposefully towards the witness box, not giving a glance at the woman in the dock.

Yes, he had been Labour Member for Parliament for Carlington for the last ten years.

The Attorney-General: "How long have you known the accused, Mrs Chadwick?"

"Since she came into Parliament just over a year ago."

"You are a political opponent of Mrs Chadwick?"

"That's right."

"Yet you formed a personal attachment with her?"

"I did."

"Why was that?"

"Because I liked her style. Because she had some go in her. Not like most of the dead-beats on that side of the House."

The judge: "This is a court of law, not a political meeting."

The Attorney-General: "And you met Mrs Chadwick on various social occasions. You took her out to dinner. You went to her flat?"

"I did."

"Were you in love with her?"

"I wanted her."

Hum of pleasure in the public benches.

The Attorney-General laboriously thrust the point home: "You wanted her in a sexual sense?"

"I sure did."

"And did you – er – have her in that sense?"

"No."

"Why not?"

226

"Because there was only once when I could have done that, and that was at the flat, and then Mr Chadwick, he walked in."

"His unexpected arrival put you off your stroke, as it were?"

The Judge: "Sir Percy, I do not like vague colloquialisms."

The Attorney-General: "After the unexpected arrival of Mr Chadwick, your ardour abated?"

"Yeah, it abated all right."

"Are you saying that during the whole year of your association with Mrs Chadwick, you and she never once had sexual relations?"

"That is what I am saying."

"And you expect the jury to believe that?"

"They can believe what they like. I'm just telling what happened."

The Attorney-General had no more questions, and Sir Richard Carter decided to put no questions either. He had no desire to prolong this witness's stay in the box.

The Judge: "Thank you, Mr Grant. You may stand down."

The public, and the reporters, felt that somehow they had been cheated. The evidence of Henry Wilberforce Grant had lasted only five minutes.

"Call Ronald Creighton . . ."

The Attorney-General: "When you informed Mrs Chadwick that her husband had been killed, what was her reaction?"

"Surprise, more than anything else."

"Was there any sign of sorrow or shock over the death of her husband?"

"Surprise was the main thing. That is how I remember it."

Sir Richard Carter: "What was the reaction of Mrs Chadwick when she was charged with complicity in her husband's death?"

"So far as I could judge, one of complete disbelief."

"Call Henry Ryland . . ."

"I am a chief superintendent of police. I was present when the accused Antonio Baroni made a statement on May twenty-first. All regulations pertaining to the taking of statements were rigorously observed."

The Attorney-General: "Is this the statement?"

"It is."

"Would you please read it to the court?"

"The statement says: 'I, Antonio Baroni, am an American citizen and I live in a lodging house at 824A Becker Street, Chicago. Sometime round about the second week in May I received a telephone call at the lodging house. This man did not tell me what his name was. He did not speak like an American, but like one of those English actors on television. This man asked me to meet him in Luigi's spaghetti joint at eight o'clock that night. I went there and a man came up to me, I think it was the same man who had phoned, and asked me like how I was doing and how was I making out, and then he asked me if I would do a job in London. I said what sort of a job, is it a hit job and he said yes. I said I might do it if the money was right. He gave me five thousand dollars and said there would be another twenty thousand when the job was done. This man said I was to go to London and check in at a joint called the Talbot Hotel and he gave me an address. He said a friend of his would find me there.

" 'I flew to London on May fifteenth and went to the place the man had said, and when I had been there about two hours they told me there was a 'phone call for me, and the man who 'phoned said I was to go to a place called the Peacock Bar, and he told me how to get there. I went there and got myself a drink, and a man came up to me, he was English I guess, the same man who had 'phoned me soon after I got to London, and he bought me another drink and took me over to a table.

" 'This man showed me a photograph of a man, and I said is that the guy I am to hit? and he said yes, that's the man. We talked a bit more and the man showed me a street map and marked a place where I was told the guy I was to hit would be the following night or almost any night.

" 'I said who is this guy, he must have got up somebody's nose pretty bad, and the man said Yes, he's done that all right. He wants a divorce and he's going to make a big show of it if someone don't quieten him down. I said so what, everybody wants a divorce, is he a big guy. The man said no, he's not a big guy, not really, but his wife is a big noise. I said how big, and he said you heard of Mrs Shadwick and I said no, then I remembered there was something in the paper about a dame of that name and President Maloney and I said is that the one? The man said yes, that's the one. She's our Prime Minister, like your President, so it would be a bad thing for her if her husband got a divorce. I said is she the one who's putting up the bread, and the man said that's right. I said she must be nuts, why's she so steamed up about getting divorced and the man said it's a special divorce on account of Mrs Shadwick getting laid by one of your black congressmen and it would make a big smell and she'd lose her job. That was why she was having him hit and it had to be done quick or the guy would have it all over the papers.

" 'The man gave me an envelope with some British money and said it was on top of the twenty grand. I went to the place where the man had shown me on the map, but there were too many cars around and I couldn't do it. I went there the night after that and shot the man, then some crazy dame in a car piled into my car and I was caught. I am very sorry for what I did. I do not know Mr Shadwick. I only did it because it was two English guys who told me to do it and I thought if they wanted this guy hit there must be a good reason for it.' "

"Call Henry Rowlandson . . ."

"Yes, I am one of Her Majesty's Inspectors of Ordnance. Yes, I have examined the gun, Exhibit A, and the bullets, Exhibit B, and I am satisfied that those bullets were fired by that gun."

"Call Dennis Smythe . . ."

Here he comes, thought Helen. The man who's going to put a rope round my neck; one of them, anyway. She had heard him give evidence at the magistrate's court.

"I am employed at the forensic laboratory at Scotland Yard, and have worked there for twelve years. I have made a special study of fingerprints, and attended the six-months advanced course on this subject at the Hendon Police College, and qualified first in my group.

"On May twelfth, I was asked to examine a brown paper envelope, which is Exhibit C. There were two clear fingerprints on it, and one thumb print. A comparison was made between these prints and those held in the fingerprint records section at Scotland Yard, but no matching prints were found. On May thirteenth, I was handed a photograph of some fingerprints. I did not know whose they were. I found they exactly matched those on the envelope. The photograph is exhibit D; I had photographs taken of the prints on the envelope. I draw the court's attention to certain similarities which are apparent even at a first scrutiny. In my view, the conclusive points . . ."

Sir Richard Carter: "It may save the time of the court if I say that the defence do not challenge the integrity or efficiency of this witness, or the accuracy of the evidence he has given."

This time, definitely, a long low whistle round the court . . .

"*Call Richard Holmes . . .*"

Here comes the other one, thought Helen.

"I have worked in the forensic laboratory of Birmingham City Police for seven years, and have been at Scotland Yard for the last four years. I have made a special study of evidence relating to handwriting and typewriting and other matters concerning written or typed documents. One of the matters I have studied is indentation, that is the impression found on a piece of paper when someone has written something on another sheet, and the impression has carried through to a lower piece. These impressions are sometimes visible to the naked eye, but when this is not so, there are certain technical processes whereby an invisible impression can be illuminated, as it were, and then photographed. I applied these processes to a brown paper envelope which was handed to me on May thirteenth, and was able to activate the imprint, and photograph it. The photograph is Exhibit E. It shows the following series of figures: 88822262. It occurred to me that this was a telephone number, but I did not know whose . . ."

"*Call Mary Blenkinsop . . .*"

"I am employed by the Post Office. I am the registrar for the London area of ex-directory numbers for which special security or secrecy has been requested by Government departments or the Armed Services. The number 88822262 is one of the Prime Minister's personal phones at 10 Downing Street. It is in List A which means it must not be disclosed to anyone without the authority of the Prime Minister or certain other people, such as the Chief Commissioner of Police for London. The Prime Minister has another ex-directory number which is on List B, which means that though restricted, it is in a lower category than the other one. The number I have given to the court has now been taken out of service."

The Attorney-General: "That concludes the evidence for the Crown, my lord."

The Judge: "Mr Phillips?"

Mr Phillips: "I am not proposing to call any witnesses, my lord."

That answered one question which the barristers had been debating over their lunchtime beer. Phillips was not going to put his man into the box. Most of the wigged heads in court nodded sagely. Baroni made a bad enough impression on everybody just lounging there in the dock. He could only do himself harm in the witness box. Far better to leave it to his counsel to string a few silver words together. Not that even the most eloquent barrister could do much for a man in Baroni's position. But, in due course, Phillips would make a token effort.

The Judge: "Sir Richard?"

Sir Richard Carter: "I call my client."

In the evening newspaper offices, the headlines were already set in type: MRS CHADWICK IN THE BOX. Now relays of reporters, messengers and telephonists were poised to provide the copy to go under that headline.

Accompanied by one of her guards (did they think she would make a dash for freedom?) she walked with her head high from the dock to the witness box. An attendant who had been notified in advance of her intention to affirm, and not take the religious oath, handed her a card. She read the words in an unfaltering voice, and then gazed steadily into the eyes of the nine men and three women who had her life in their hands. It was something like that selection committee all over again. Was there a Harper bitch among this lot?

Sir Richard had decided to dispense with preliminaries, to get straight to the point, and to keep it short.

"Mrs Chadwick, did you have any part whatever in the death of your husband?"

"I did not."

"Did you at any time give anyone any instruction that could possibly have been interpreted to the effect that action was to be taken to kill or injure your husband?"

231

"I did not."

"You have heard the statement made by your co-defendant, Antonio Baroni. In that statement Baroni alleges that he was contacted by two agents who bribed him into shooting down your husband. Have you any idea who those two agents might be?"

"I have not the faintest idea."

"Did you wish your husband dead?"

"I did not."

"Even though he had the power to wreck your political career?"

"I would not have dreamed of causing him any physical harm."

"You have heard the evidence of Mr Grant. In your view, does that present a fair picture of your relationship with him?"

"It does."

"Did you commit adultery with Mr Grant?"

"I did not."

"Was your association with Mr Grant a complete secret?"

"No, I wouldn't say that."

"Who would know about it?"

"Mr Grant and I had drinks together fairly frequently in the various bars at the House of Commons. It was quite open. It would have been seen by a lot of people."

"And they might have assumed that your affair with Mr Grant had gone further than it actually did?"

"I suppose that is possible."

Sir Richard asked her what had actually been said between her and Bernard when he came to Number Ten. She gave a truthful account. Up to a point. She omitted Bernard's threat to involve the President.

Sir Richard: "Did you tell any other person whatever of what happened at that confrontation with your husband?"

"I did not."

"Can you think of how information about something said in your private office at Downing Street could possibly come to be in the possession of Antonio Baroni?"

"I cannot."

"Now about this envelope, concerning which evidence has

232

been given. I want you to examine it carefully." He handed it to her. She turned it over. It was a plain brown envelope, of rather stout paper, about five inches by two, a sort of short fool-scap envelope, with a flap at the end which had been slit open.

Sir Richard: "Have you, to your knowledge, ever had that envelope in your possession before?"

"Not to my knowledge."

"Is there any way in which it could have passed through your hands without the fact registering with you?"

"I receive a fair amount of personal or confidential mail, which I open myself. Quite often the confidential letter is placed in an inner envelope, and sealed in that, and then put in an outer envelope. I suppose it is just possible that this envelope was one of the inner envelopes, though I cannot recall seeing one of this shape and size recently. Of course, it depends how long ago. I suppose it could have come to me at the Home Office, and that would cover a period of several months."

"By what method do you open these confidential letters?"

"By slitting the top with a paper knife."

"So the manner in which this letter has been opened is consistent with the manner in which you open your mail?"

"That is so."

"What do you do with the envelopes after opening them?"

"I chuck them into the waste paper basket."

"So it might have been possible for someone to retrieve this envelope from your waste paper, and apply it to his own purposes?"

"If he could get access to it, but I would think that is unlikely. I don't know what happens to the stuff in my waste paper basket, but anything that is remotely confidential is destroyed by being put through something called a shredder."

"Did you often receive the mail of the type we have been talking about, that is, one envelope inside another, at home?"

"Just occasionally. Most of it went to the office."

"What happens to letters thrown away at home?"

"I put them in a waste bin; the charlady clears it when she does the flat."

"So it would not be all that difficult for someone who was prepared to bribe a refuse collector to obtain a considerable quantity of your waste paper, including opened envelopes?"

"I suppose it could be done."

It was not a very convincing try, but it was the best Sir Richard could do. The only other way would have been to challenge the honesty or the efficiency of the two scientific witnesses, and Sir Richard knew there would be no mileage in that. Indeed, he hadn't gone into the question of the imprint of the phone number at all, because there was no explanation for that whatsoever.

To get away from the technicalities, to end his examination of Helen on a broader, more human note, Sir Richard said: "I ask you once again. Did you in any way engineer the death of your husband?"

"I did not."

Sir Richard left it at that.

Ponderously, the Attorney-General rose to cross-examine, polishing his glasses as he did so, thus providing a carefully calculated pause before launching his attack. His first question was obviously intended to shatter the witness's composure.

"Were you in love with Mr Grant?"

Coolly, she answered: "I found him physically attractive."

"That does not answer my question. The question was: 'Were you, indeed are you, in love with Mr Grant?' "

"I don't think so."

"You don't *think* so?"

"It is difficult sometimes to distinguish between being in love with a person, and with finding him physically attractive. At least, that is my experience."

The composure-shattering tactic had failed, but the Attorney-General was quick to seize the chance she had given him.

"And you, I gather, have had some considerable experience in these matters. You have, at various times in your life, found quite a number of men physically attractive?"

"That is quite true."

"And your pursuit of these men inflicted great pain and humiliation on your husband?"

"I would not say I pursued people. It tended to be the other way round."

Titters from the public seats.

234

"But your association with these men, irrespective of how they were initiated, inflicted pain on your husband?"

"I suppose so."

"You *suppose* so?"

"Yes, it did."

"And you realised that when your long-suffering husband confronted you at Downing Street, he had finally reached breaking point?"

"He made that quite clear."

"And that meant that your political career was suddenly put in danger?"

"That was so."

"Are you an ambitious woman? Politically ambitious?"

"I think I am. One has to be ambitious to get anywhere."

"Quite so. And on that morning, you knew that all your ambitions were about to collapse in ruins, and you decided to take action, cruel action, drastic action, to prevent that happening?"

"I did nothing of the sort."

"Is it not a remarkable coincidence that within a very short time of that meeting with your husband at Downing Street, your husband had been silenced for ever?"

"It is."

The Attorney-General then turned to the envelope, the damning envelope.

"When you received these confidential letters, these letters enclosed in an inner envelope, was the inner envelope normally addressed to you as well as the outer one?"

"Usually, but not always. Sometimes the inner envelope was left plain, with no writing on it."

"Have you any explanation as to how this particular envelope could come to bear the imprint of your most secret, personal telephone number?"

"I am completely baffled by that."

"You have seen the photograph of the imprint. Are the figures in your handwriting?"

"They most definitely are not."

"Have you dictated your phone number recently to any person who might have to write it down to record it? Have you

235

done that to any person either in your presence, or over the telephone?"

"I have not. I have no explanation for how anyone would get that telephone number. I told you, I am completely mystified by that."

"So am I. And so, I imagine, are the jury. Unless they accept the hypothesis I put forward in my opening address."

The Attorney-General decided to finish with a flourish.

"You still say you had absolutely no connection with the crime committed in Belmont Street on May seventeenth?"

"Absolutely nothing."

"Can you suggest who, apart from yourself, could have any possible reason for harming your husband?"

"I cannot."

"Was he a man who had enemies?"

"He was a most gentle and mild person. I cannot imagine his having any enemies at all."

"Except one. Yourself."

"I had a considerable affection for my husband."

"Then, madam, I suggest you had a strange way of showing it."

Abruptly, the Attorney-General sat down.

It was just gone three o'clock.

As Helen walked back to the dock, head still high, Sir Richard rose and told the judge: "I have no further witnesses."

The Judge addressed the barristers: "Are you ready to proceed? It would be in the interests of all parties if this business could be settled tonight."

Sir Richard, remembering his £3,000-a-day fee, thought: You rotten old swine. But he said: "I fully agree."

The Attorney-General: "I am ready to proceed" (he was paid anyway).

Mr Phillips: "I shall not detain the court long."

The Attorney-General began his final speech for the Crown. He wasted few words on the obvious guilt of Baroni. Practically the whole of his speech was devoted to the case against Helen Chadwick. First he rammed home the prosecution claim that Baroni's knowledge of the imminent divorce action could only have come to him from Mrs Chadwick, via her agents. And if that knowledge came from that source, then by all standards of common sense, the instructions that Bernard Chadwick was to be killed came from that same source; which would make Mrs Chadwick as guilty as if she had pulled the trigger herself.

Sir Percy continued: "The defence has sought to implant in the minds of the jury the idea that the marital problems of Mr and Mrs Chadwick were widely known, for instance to members of Mr Freemantle's staff, and to members of Parliament who had observed the growing relationship between Mrs Chadwick and Mr Grant. And that therefore – I presume this is the contention of the defence – some person, sympathetic to Mrs Chadwick, or to the political cause which she embodied, anticipated the danger in which she was placing herself; and that without the knowledge or authority of Mrs Chadwick, this misguided person took it upon himself to deal with the problem in the most drastic way, by silencing Mr Chadwick.

"Members of the jury, once again it is a matter for simple commonsense. Even if every clerk in Mr Freemantle's office were a chatterbox – and I am sure this is not the case – and even if every member of Parliament who saw Mrs Chadwick and Mr Grant having a drink together were to initiate the most scurrilous gossip, what would be the sum total of information that would be disclosed to any eavesdropper?

"All that would have been revealed would have been that the Chadwick marriage was possibly going on the rocks, and that Mrs Chadwick was possibly forming a warm friendship with Mr Grant. But how could any picker-up of that kind of gossip have been in possession of the specific knowledge that Mr Chadwick was at that particular time on the brink of taking divorce proceedings against his wife? Yet it was that precise knowledge that came into the possession of Baroni.

"I ask you again – where did it come from, if not from Mrs Chadwick?

"There is, of course, the question of Mr Phipps, the inquiry agent, to which my learned friend has quite properly drawn attention. He would know, from the nature of his calling, that Mr Chadwick might be thinking of taking proceedings against his wife, and that Mr Grant would be involved. It is possible that in an unguarded moment, Mr Phipps did let something

237

of this slip, and that the information passed into other hands.

"But Mr Phipps could have known only in the most general terms of Mr Chadwick's intentions. He could not have known of Mr Chadwick's visit to Downing Street on May tenth, and what was said there. I draw your attention to the time scale. Mr Chadwick announces his intentions to his wife on May tenth. Within a very few days, Baroni is being briefed in America for his mission, which is to kill Bernard Chadwick. Can that really be coincidence? Again, it is a matter for normal commonsense.

"There are, of course, a number of baffling features about this case. For instance, the existence and activities of the two agents of whom Baroni has spoken in his statement; both, according to him, speaking English English rather than American English. You are entitled to ask: Who are these people, and how did Mrs Chadwick come so conveniently to have their services at short notice?

"I would draw your attention to the fact that Mrs Chadwick was until recently, for a period of some months, Home Secretary, and in that capacity she would have dealings with what is loosely called the Secret Service. I do not pretend to understand the ramifications of that Service, but it is well known that all nations' secret services have murky fringes, inhabited by people who are not established, salaried public servants, who are paid by devious means, who may be rather unsavoury characters, and who are called in when there is some particularly unsavoury job to be done.

"I think it is quite possible that as Home Secretary Mrs Chadwick would know of the existence of such persons, and possibly have had personal dealings either with them directly, or with some outwardly more respectable person who directed the activities of these shadowy figures. It would have been possible for Mrs Chadwick to issue an order: 'Fix it', and to leave the details to be worked out by others. You may think this is fanciful and bizarre; it is no more so than much else which has been revealed in this case.

"There is also another strange aspect of this case, which I am sure has not escaped your attention. That is that the man who dealt with Baroni in London revealed the identity of his

238

principal, and disclosed the reason for the action which Baroni was to take. You might think that that is the last thing that a person acting as an intermediary would do, and I would agree – if we were dealing with ordinary people. But what sort of people are likely to lend themselves to this sort of activity? They are likely to be people of low morals and low intelligence. And they could well be activated by the same emotions which my learned friend attributed to the inquiry agent Phipps: that is, they realised that they were in on a rather juicy situation, and were so full of themselves that they just had to show what important, high level operators they were. There is also the possibility that Baroni demanded to know what the killing was all about. It may be – indeed, it probably is so – that a hired killer is curious as to why he is being hired, and it could be that unless given some basic information, he would refuse to do the job. We shall not know about that, because the defendant Baroni has decided not to give evidence."

Sir Percy saved until near the end of his speech his observations about the envelope found on Toni Baroni. He did not speak at any great length on this matter. He did not need to. The facts spoke for themselves. The envelope *had* Mrs Chadwick's prints on it; it *had* the imprint of her secret, personal telephone number. The simple explanation, said Sir Percy, was that at an interview between Mrs Chadwick and one of her agents, the question of ready money for Baroni arose urgently, and that Mrs Chadwick provided it, putting it in a discarded envelope. She had then handed the envelope over, and the agent had said something to the effect 'How do I contact you if I need you in a hurry?' and Mrs Chadwick had told him the secret phone number, which the agent, in writing it down, had unknowingly imprinted on the envelope. What about the possibility of people probing Mrs Chadwick's waste paper, either at Downing Street or at her home? Sir Percy was content to let the jury form their own judgment on that proposition.

Sir Percy spoke for forty-five minutes. He ended: "I therefore submit that the hand that killed Bernard Chadwick was that of Antonio Baroni; but that the mind and will which set the enterprise in motion were those of Helen Mary Chadwick. If, using the normal standards of judgment and commonsense

239

which you apply to your own affairs, you reach the same conclusion, and do so without any reasonable doubt in your mind, then it is your duty to find both Antonio Baroni and Helen Mary Chadwick guilty as charged of the murder of Bernard Davenport Chadwick."

The verdict on the barristers' benches was: Not bad, Perce; not bad at all.

The Judge: "Mr Phillips."

Mr Phillips spoke for only three minutes. He said his client was a man of low intelligence, poor background, and scant education. He had grown up in a criminal background, where criminals accepted contracts for felonious deeds as naturally as normal people exchanged contracts for painting a house. He had not appreciated the enormity of the thing he agreed to do, and he had felt that since the briefing came exclusively from English agents, the victim must be some sort of public enemy in this land, someone whom people in authority wanted to be liquidated, and that they had come to him because for some reason a suitable British "hit man" was not available. "He is a stranger to these shores," said Mr Phillips. "He is unfamiliar with our code of law. He is deeply penitent for what he has done, and seeks the mercy of the court, and of those who might be called upon to review any sentence the court might pass."

There was not much else Phillips *could* say.

The Judge: "Sir Richard."

Sir Richard Carter slowly drew himself up to his full six feet two inches, clasped his hands under his gown behind his back, leaned forward slightly, and gazed straight into the eye of the juror who was third from the left in the front row. Sir Richard had found, in his long career as an advocate, that it was more effective to centre on the person of one juryman, than to address the jury as if they were a public meeting. Though, of course, he had to start: "Members of the jury . . ."

"Members of the jury, I greatly doubt whether any of you, eighteen months ago, had ever heard of Helen Mary Chadwick. Yet in that short time she has gained election to Parliament, she has risen to Cabinet rank, and more than that, she has won the highest political office this nation can offer, an office which even in these days of Britain's diminished importance, is still

240

probably only second to one other in the whole of the democratic world.

"She is, I am sure you will agree, a remarkable woman.

"Now she stands in the dock accused of a heinous crime. She does not complain over the fact that she has been charged with this crime, for she acknowledges that the law must apply equally to the high and the low; and that if it seems to those charged with investigating a crime that a *prima facie* case has been made out, then the case must come to the courts, irrespective of the status of the person involved.

"All Mrs Chadwick asks of you is justice; and that the high office which she so recently held should be a cause neither of prejudice nor of favour in determining her case."

After that rather high-flown introduction, Sir Richard got down to what he called "basic facts". The prosecution had claimed that only three people had known of the information which had been conveyed to Baroni; and that since it had obviously not come from Bernard Chadwick, and since Mr Freemantle was above suspicion, the agent who briefed Baroni must have received it from Mrs Chadwick.

"That," said Sir Richard, "is plainly an unsound proposition. First there is the proved unreliability of the man Phipps. In how many bars did he flaunt his piquant knowledge, acquired through his unsavoury activities? And how many ears were avidly listening? Then there is the situation at Westminster. The Palace of Westminster is probably the greatest scandal market in London. If a white woman and a black man are seen there constantly in each other's company, as Mrs Chadwick and Mr Grant were, do you really believe that every member of Parliament and every Parliamentary journalist would regard themselves as being under vows of secrecy and silence?

"You have been asked, several times by the Attorney-General, to use your commonsense in assessing the evidence which has been put before you. It is I who now ask you to apply your commonsense to that question.

"I do not wish to overstress the matter of Mr Freemantle's staff, but here again there is the real possibility that indiscreet use may have been made of the confidential information in that

241

office, possibly by someone who has since left Mr Freemantle's service.

"So, taking a realistic view, there were not just three people, but perhaps dozens of people who knew, or could have known, that the Chadwick marriage was in difficulties, and that Mrs Chadwick was forming an attachment for Mr Grant. And just as this situation is moving into its critical phase, Mrs Chadwick becomes Prime Minister.

"Now a head of state is at the centre of a huge apparatus of Government, and cannot possibly control all the tentacles. There is always the danger that some zealous but irresponsible person will take the law into his own hands and embark on a course of action which, if and when it is revealed, horrifies those in authority. For instance, some years ago, when two Russian statesmen were visiting this country, some obscure person took it upon himself to order a diver to pry into the underwater equipment of the Russian warship in Portsmouth Harbour. That was done completely without the authority of the then Prime Minister. It was a very grave incident.

"Then there was the case of the American airplane which was sent on an espionage mission over Russia without the knowledge or authority of the then American President.

"These things do happen. It is impossible to prevent them. I suggest that something like that happened in this case.

"The situation at the start of May was that the Prime Minister had got herself into a position that could not only bring ruin to her own career, but might well cause a Governmental upheaval which, in the delicate state of the nation, could have disastrous consequences.

"Some whiff of the danger, from one of the possible sources I have mentioned, reaches some self-appointed guardian of the national welfare in one of the more obscure regions of the secret service. This person may not have the specific information that divorce proceedings are to be initiated, but with gossip going around about Mrs Chadwick and a black man, he could well jump to the conclusion that a divorce action was both inevitable and imminent, indeed that Mr Chadwick would be practically forced into divorce proceedings. This person, this misguided patriot, therefore embarks on a course of action to retrieve the situation.

"You may think that this is far-fetched, but this whole fantastic case is far-fetched, and the suggestion I have made is no more improbable than those put forward by the prosecution in their efforts to associate Mrs Chadwick with this crime."

Sir Richard was nearer the truth than he could possibly know. When Andy Dewhurst read the report of the trial in the *Washington Post*, he gently perspired.

Sir Richard continued: "Can you believe that if Mrs Chadwick had master-minded this crime herself, it would have been botched in the way it was? Can you believe that this woman, whom no one thinks is a fool, would have confided to some "mystery man" the precise reasons as to why her husband should be killed? Would that not have been the height of folly? And do you think that she would employ someone so callow as to use her name in his discussions with Baroni? Does not the whole operation now begin to look as if it originated from some much lower and more stupid person?

"And do you really think that because a person has been Home Secretary for a few months, he or she has access to a network of sinister special agents, of the type seen on late-night television films, and that these persons will conform to the minister's personal, nefarious schemes?"

On the barristers' benches, the whisper was: "Good stuff, Dickie."

But Sir Richard now had to face some "basic facts" which were not helpful to his case; the most basic facts of all: the fingerprints and the imprinted telephone number on the letter. He argued that it would not have been difficult for a cunning and determined person to have come into possession of an envelope that had passed through Mrs Chadwick's hands. All that would be needed would be a five-pound note for one of the men on the dust-cart that called at Mrs Chadwick's flat.

Of the telephone number: "I have no theory as to how that came to be there. It could be that some person in Mrs Chadwick's entourage had occasion to write down that number, and that the envelope, after leaving Mrs Chadwick's possession, passed into that person's hands; a visitor to her office or home could have needed something to serve as a pad to write on,

243

and could have retrieved the envelope from a waste bin. It is a mystery. But there are many mysteries in this case. I do not think that you should single out one mystery and give it undue emphasis."

On the barristers' benches, the whisper was: "It won't wash, Dickie, it won't wash."

Sir Richard spoke for forty minutes, polishing points and tidying up. Finally: "You have seen Mrs Chadwick in the witness box. What impression did she make on you when she gave her evidence? Did her manner not strike you as frank and honest? Do you really believe that the woman you saw in the box has foully plotted to kill her husband? It may be that you do not approve of her way of life, or of her morals, but she is not being tried for her morals.

"And in any case, she has been severely punished for her departure from the accepted norms. The highest prize a political person can achieve in this country has been snatched away from her, never to be returned. But as I say, that issue is not your concern. Mrs Chadwick is being tried for murder, and on that charge, on the evidence which has been put before you, I submit she should leave this court a free woman."

It was twenty-past four. The judge's bladder was troubling him.

"I still hope and believe that we can finish this tonight. There will be an adjournment for twenty minutes. When we reassemble, I shall sum up."

In the robing rooms, the betting among the barristers was evens.

In a green-walled room below the dock, the elder of the two policewomen escorts said to Helen: "I could do with a cuppa. I bet you could too." She departed on this mission.

Helen was still feeling curiously detached, still in the airplane, leaving everything to the pilot; but the moment of touchdown could not be long delayed.

"You did all right," said the young policewoman. Then she shut up abruptly as her colleague returned. Presumably it was against regulations to comment on a prisoner's performance and prospects.

They drank their tea, then the elder one said: "I voted for your lot at the election. Benson, that was the name of the candidate. Didn't get in, but it was a near thing."

"I voted for the Patriot Party, too," said the young one. "So did my husband. He's a copper too. I reckon you got the police vote pretty solid. Must have been what you said about hanging. All the police . . ."

Then she froze, realising what she had said.

They drank their tea in silence until it was time to go up the stairs again.

Mr Justice Wellbeloved: "Members of the jury, I shall not address you at great length. It will not be necessary to do so, because no abstruse issue of law arises in this case. It is what one might call a commonsense case, and the judicial system of this country is based on the assumption that the combined commonsense of twelve ordinary citizens, wearing their ordinary clothes, is likely to be far superior to that of one man in the peculiar attire I am required to adopt.

"There is, however, just one point of law on which I must give you a firm direction. That is the law of joint responsibility. The law says that when two or more persons act jointly to take a life, and that life is taken, then both are equally guilty, irrespective of whose hand administered the fatal blow. The implications of that law in this case will, I am sure, be obvious to you.

"Now in regard to the accused Antonio Baroni, in view of the evidence, and in view of what his learned counsel has told you, I doubt if you will have great difficulty in agreeing on a verdict.

"But I imagine you will find the case of the other prisoner, Mrs Chadwick, rather more difficult.

"The first crucial thing, so far as Mrs Chadwick is concerned, is that the accused Baroni, immediately after his arrest, made a statement to the police indicating he had certain special information concerning Mrs Chadwick's marital affairs. You have to decide how he came by that information. That is the first big issue in this case. Learned counsel, both for the Crown and for the defence, have rightly put considerable emphasis on this point. If that information was put into the pipeline to Baroni by Mrs Chadwick, then you may think it a reasonable assumption that it was she who also put into the pipeline instructions that her husband should be killed. Wherever they came from, the instructions to kill and the information about Mrs Chadwick's pending divorce situation came from the same source. If you take the view, then, that the information came from Mrs Chadwick, then you will almost certainly also conclude that the instructions came from her; and if that is your view, then, because of the law of joint responsibility, it will be your duty to find Mrs Chadwick guilty of murder.

"However, if you take the view that the information could reasonably have reached Baroni from some other source, then you will probably assume that the instructions came from that other source, and it would then be your duty to acquit Mrs Chadwick.

"That is the first significant matter. The second one is this: What conclusions are to be drawn from the evidence found on the envelope which was in Baroni's possession at the time of his arrest? This indeed puts a very heavy burden on you. The accuracy of the expert witnesses' testimony in regard to that envelope has not been challenged by the defence. The defence accepts that the fingerprints are those of Mrs Chadwick. Therefore, at some point, the envelope must have been in her hands.

The question you have to decide is: Was it, as the Crown suggests, handed over by Mrs Chadwick to an agent with ready-cash money for Baroni? Or did it reach Baroni by some accidental – or at least accidental so far as Mrs Chadwick is concerned – and more complicated method?

"You must not rule that second possibility out. Used envelopes do get left lying around in offices, and picked up by people to whom they were not originally sent. And you must bear in mind the possibility raised by the defence that some-one concerned with the disposal of waste paper, either from Mrs Chadwick's office, or from her home, was bribed to provide specimens of it to some person who has no connection with Mrs Chadwick.

"Then, of course, there is the additional complication of the imprint of Mrs Chadwick's personal and private telephone num-ber on the envelope. How it got there is a matter for surmise. The Crown has put before you a specific set of circumstances explaining how this could have happened. The defence has been much less specific on this point. But that does not mean that you have to accept the Crown's suggestion. You are quite entitled to say: 'We just do not know how it got there'.

"Another matter which you must consider is the time sequence. Mr Chadwick had his interview with his wife at Downing Street early on the morning of May tenth. And according to Baroni's statement, a very short time after that, the plot to kill Mr Chadwick was being set in motion in America. Baroni was interviewed on the thirteenth; he was in London by the fifteenth, made his first reconnaissance of the murder scene the following day, and actually shot down Mr Chadwick the day after that. Just one week between Bernard Chadwick confronting his wife at Downing Street and his being left dying with four bullets in his back in the West End of London.

"That may strike you as a remarkable coincidence. You may think, given the first event, the visit of Mr Chadwick to Down-ing Street, the other events follow in natural sequence. But you may take an entirely different view. You may think this short time-span is in Mrs Chadwick's favour, in that there was just not time for someone on this side of the Atlantic, involved

247

incessantly in public duties, to organise this whole quite elaborate scheme, the first part of which was enacted in America. If she managed all that, then she is indeed a remarkable organiser. But, of course, the Crown suggest that she had someone who did the organising for her when he knew what was required.

"Then there is the feature which, I think I am fair in saying, has caused mutual puzzlement. That is, if Mrs Chadwick *was* initiating a murder conspiracy, why did she go into details of her marital problems when briefing her agents? Prudence would surely require her to say as little as possible, and to direct that her name should on no account be mentioned to the man who was actually to do the deed. But it could be that she was let down by boastful agents trying to impress this American visitor with their high place in their peculiar world. Drink could have been a factor. Baroni's statement mentions one drink. Possibly the briefing took some time, and there was more than one.

"A great many theories have been put up in this case to explain the inexplicable. It is for you to decide which theories best fit your judgment of the facts."

The judge spoke for another twenty-five minutes, recapping, polishing, warning. Finally: "Mrs Chadwick recently held the highest political office, and was the leading exponent of a particular political faction. Whatever your own politics, no matter how strongly you agree or disagree with Mrs Chadwick's political concepts, you will not let that issue rest in your mind for one second. You will reach your decision on what has been said in this court, and no other matter must be allowed to intrude.

"Members of the jury, you will retire to consider your verdict."

It was half-past five. The evening papers rushed out editions with the huge headlines: JURY OUT. Having done that, they instantly started on the next task. In each office, two sets of pages were prepared in advance of the verdict, so that whatever happened, printing could start the second the word came. The *Standard*'s "guilty" edition had the headline "Helen to Hang" and the story started: *Helen Chadwick, the woman who brought capital punishment back to Britain, was tonight herself found guilty of murder and sentenced to death. Only the intervention of the newly-appointed Home Secretary, Mr Keith Shalton, can save her from the hangman's rope . . .* The headline in the other version read: Helen Cleared. *Mrs Helen Chadwick was tonight found not guilty of murdering her husband, and walked from the Old Bailey dock a free woman . . .*

The type was set, the pages made up, the plates cast and put on the machines. All that would be needed would be for a machine-minder, on five pounds an hour overtime, to press a button.

The right button.

In the robing rooms at the Bailey, the betting was now five to four on a guilty verdict.

For the first time, Helen felt her hand shaking as she lifted the fresh cup of tea which the policewoman had given her in the room below the dock. She must conquer this. Whatever happened when she went back up those stairs, there must be no flicker of the turmoil inside her.

Oddly, her mind, as opposed to her thumping heart, was ice-cool. The young policewoman brought in the evening papers, full of the case as far as it had gone. She ignored the reports and turned at once to the crossword. She raced through it in ten minutes.

Six o'clock. The jury had been out half an hour.

The thought struck: this was the day, this was the hour when she would have been going to the Palace for her Prime Ministerial session with the Monarch. No doubt Metcalfe, beautifully groomed and powdered, was on his way to do some bowing and scraping.

He was there and she was here because of that crazy man Baroni, to whom she had still not spoken a single word. Of course, even without Baroni, it might have been Metcalfe going to the Palace, if Bernard had done what he had threatened to do. But would Bernard really have gone ahead with his threat? She doubted it. Bernard was not the spiteful sort, and he would just have hated the publicity resulting from a sensational divorce case. It was the job thing that had really stirred him up. She was sure of that. It had been selfish and unthinking of her not to remember Bernard's position when she had so eagerly snatched up the prize dangled in front of her by Marlowe. Too late for that now. Too late for everything. Supposing she was acquitted, what then? She was still a member of Parliament, and technically she could still hang on to that. But would she want to? Would she want to be a largely unemployed ex-prime minister?

At least she still had the factory. Nobody could take that away from her. Bert Cooper had tried, and she had beaten Bert Cooper. What was Bert Cooper doing at this moment? Probably stuck by his radio or television set, waiting for the verdict on the Fascist beast.

Supposing it went the other way. She, Helen Chadwick, to pay the penalty prescribed under Chadwick's Law, as one of

250

the newspapers had called it when the hanging bill went through.

An odd thought struck her. If it wasn't the end, if it wasn't total oblivion, somewhere in whatever lay beyond the trap door would be that coloured boy to whom she had refused a reprieve. Perhaps he'd say "Hello, white bitch, so they got you too . . ." if people talked to each other like that in the beyond.

Reprieve. Of course, Keith Shalton could do for her, if it came to it, what she had refused to do for the coloured boy. That was an odd turn-up. Keith, of all people. Keith, who had screwed her while the cricket commentary was on. Keith with whom she had been both hot and cold. Keith who had stage-managed her entry into the Cabinet. Keith, whom she had turned down for the Home Office job, telling him he was not up to it. Well, now he had the job. He had the whip hand over her. The rope hand.

If it came to it, would she *want* Keith to exercise his ministerial mercy? Could she face life imprisonment, fifteen years or more of it, fifteen years without a man? God, she'd be in the fifties before they let her out on parole. Wouldn't oblivion be better than that?

One damn thing she was sure of. No crawling. No crawling to Keith. She wouldn't do it herself, and she'd make damn sure that no one did it on her behalf.

Seven o'clock. The evening papers were normally shut down by five. The overtime was costing a fortune.

"We'll still get the West End sale," said the deputy editor.

"Another half-hour," said the general manager, "then call it a day. Let the mornings have it."

CLATTER of footsteps on the stairs.

"They're coming back."

The word was flashed to the newspapers. The solo schools broke up. The machine crews took up their stations, waiting for the word to press the button.

Which button?

IT was three minutes before the court was assembled. The judge was the last to enter, like a conductor who waits until everything is ready before he makes his entry at a concert.

This time Helen reached the dock before Baroni. She looked at him as they brought him up. She wondered if his heart was thumping as hers was. His face was still utterly expressionless. Of course, he knew, everybody knew, what the verdict would be in his case. Perhaps he was just plain bored by the whole thing.

She had read somewhere that in the old murder trials, when there was the death penalty before, that the accused could always guess the jury's verdict by noting where the jury were looking. If the jury looked straight at the prisoner, that meant not guilty; if they averted their eyes from him, that meant guilty. Were *this* jury looking at her? They seemed to be looking all over the place, some at her, some at the ceiling, some at the judge as he entered.

The judge took an unconscionable time to settle himself in his seat. She was standing at the front of the dock. No sitting down now, just because the judge had sat down. For this part of the play, she had to stand all the time. The two policewomen were very close behind her. Almost touching. Ready, perhaps, to catch her if she fainted. She wouldn't do that.

The clerk to the court, whose rôle throughout had been that

252

of an extra, now spoke his lines.

"Will the foreman of the jury please stand?"

A bulky man in a blue suit heaved himself to his feet. He looked like a retired police inspector turned publican. Probably he was.

"Have the jury reached their verdicts?"

"We have."

"How say you, do you find the prisoner Antonio Baroni guilty as charged, or not guilty?"

"*Guilty.*"

The buzz in the court was minimal. This was not what the vultures were waiting for.

"How say you, do you find the prisoner Helen Mary Chadwick guilty as charged, or not guilty?"

The foreman's resonant voice reached every corner of the court.

"*Guilty.*"

She had steeled herself for this moment to show nothing, whatever the verdict. She showed nothing. But around the court there was a great gasp as the tension burst. In the press section, there was a commotion as reporters and messengers began the great scramble for the phones.

The judge surveyed the scene with irritation. An usher called for order. Finally, there was total silence.

The Judge: "Antonio Baroni, I have few words to say to you. You are a citizen of another country. But that country's law, in relation to the crime you have committed, is little different from that of this country; indeed, the American criminal code is derived largely from British law. So I am in no way impressed by any suggestion that there was some element of ignorance on your part which must be taken into account. The only thing about which you may have been ignorant is the penalty now exacted in this country from those who take life.

"You were paid to kill, and you killed. You shot down a public servant, a man who had achieved some distinction in his chosen field. It was a squalid act, and for that act the law now prescribes one penalty. The sentence of the court is that you be taken from this court to a place of confinement; and thence to a place of execution, and that there you be hanged by the

253

neck until you are dead. And may the Lord have mercy on your soul.

"Take him down."

Baroni, still looking inexpressibly bored, turned and shuffled with his escorts to the back of the dock and down the stairs. Helen thought his jaw was moving. He was chewing gum.

The judge waited until there was utter silence again.

"Helen Mary Chadwick, you have been found guilty of initiating a sinister chain of events which led to the death of your husband. Your guilt is no whit less than that of the man whose hand struck your husband down. Indeed, some would say it is greater.

"You are a woman who has achieved great distinction in public life. But the law makes no distinction between the high and the humble; no distinction between those who shape the laws, and the nation at large.

"There is a tragic element of irony about your presence in the dock on this charge. You, above all people, must be aware of what the penalty in this country now is for those who wilfully take life. I have no choice but to impose that penalty.

"Helen Mary Chadwick, the sentence of the court is that you be taken to a place of confinement, and from there to a place of execution; and that you be hanged by the neck until you are dead. And may the Lord have mercy on your soul."

FIFTEEN-TWO, *fifteen-four, fifteen-six, run of three* . . .

Seventeen across, "priestly resources" . . . eleven letters . . . must be "investments" . . . that fits with seven down . . .

Cup of tea, dearie? Do you want anything? Don't be shy to ask.

Cup of tea, dearie? Do you want anything? Don't be shy to ask.

Fourteen across must be Waterloo. Nineteen down must be an anagram. Haven't got it yet. But I will. I'm not going to be beaten by the damn crossword. Not if I have to stay up all night to get it.

In the House: "Has the Home Secretary any statement to make in the case of Antonio Baroni and Mrs Helen Chadwick?"

The Home Secretary: "I have given long and deep thought to this distressing case, and have regretfully come to the conclusion that there are no grounds on which I could advise the Sovereign to intervene in the course of justice."

Not Cabinet material; that's what she had told him. Not Cabinet material.

LETTERS

From the President: "I am praying for you. I shall always remember you as a very lovely person."

From Henderson, the man who had pointed her towards Westminster, and unknowingly towards the Old Bailey and Holloway: "I shall always remember you as a person of great courage. How sad it should all end like this."

From Mrs Edith Higgins, of Dulwich: "My little séance circle meets regularly every Thursday evening at eight. My contact on the other side is a Red Indian, Thundercloud. Thunder-cloud will bring you to us next Thursday. Until then . . ."

THEY did the deed at Pentonville, taking her there in a black van on the night before. It was thought that an execution at Holloway might disturb some of the more emotionally unstable women prisoners.

She told the prison padre: "There's no need for you to get up early."

In the House:

Mr Raymond Remington (C., Tallingford): In view of the provisions made for pensions for former Prime Ministers, will the Prime Minister say what payment was made, if any, in the case of the late Mrs Chadwick?

The Prime Minister: Parliament has provided that former Prime Ministers should receive a pension of eight thousand pounds a year. Mrs Chadwick was in – er – retirement for two months. The amount due has been calculated on a pro-rata basis, and the sum of one thousand three hundred and thirty-three pounds and thirty-three pence has therefore been paid to the estate of the late Mrs Chadwick.